THE GAME OF TREACHERY

Recent Titles by Alan Savage from Severn House

THE FRENCH RESISTANCE SERIES
RESISTANCE
THE GAME OF TREACHERY

THE PARTISAN SERIES
PARTISAN
MURDER'S ART
BATTLEGROUND
THE KILLING GROUND

THE COMMANDO SERIES
COMMANDO
THE CAUSE
THE TIGER

THE SWORD SERIES
THE SWORD AND THE SCALPEL
THE SWORD AND THE JUNGLE
THE SWORD AND THE PRISON
STOP ROMMEL!
THE AFRIKA KORPS

THE GAME OF TREACHERY

Alan Savage

severn House

This first world edition published in Great Britain 2004 by
SEVERN HOUSE PUBLISHERS LTD of
9–15 High Street, Sutton, Surrey SM1 1DF.
This first world edition published in the USA 2004 by
SEVERN HOUSE PUBLISHERS INC of
595 Madison Avenue, New York, N.Y. 10022.

British Library Cataloguing in Publication Data

Savage, Alan
    The game of treachery
    1.   World War, 1939-1945 - Secret Service - Great Britain - Fiction
    2.   World War, 1939-1945 - Underground movements - France - Fiction
    3.   War stories
    I.   Title
    823.9'14 [F]

    ISBN 0-7278-6092-5

Typeset by Palimpsest Book Production Ltd.,
Polmont, Stirlingshire, Scotland.
Printed and bound in Great Britain by
MPG Books Ltd., Bodmin, Cornwall.

We for a certainty are not the first
Have sat in taverns while the tempest hurled
Their hopeful plans to emptiness, and cursed
Whatever brute and blackguard made the world.

A.E. Houseman

PART ONE

The Guerillas

Ho! Let the door be lock'd:
Treachery! Seek it out.

William Shakespeare

One

Pound

'There she blows,' Brune said. There was no moon, but the clear sky made the night bright, and James Barron could see the pale strip of beach only a mile in front of him. The Lysander seemed to drift as it left the water behind. Now James could see lights, away to the right. 'No blackout,' Brune commented. 'These characters hardly know there's a war on.'

'Haven't they got radar?'

'Not down here. Piece of cake. Ooops.' Even as he spoke a little white cloud appeared some distance to their left. 'Where'd that come from?'

'There.' James had seen the flash of an explosion.

'That's never happened before,' Brune complained, banking hard to his right. 'Let's get up a bit.' The aircraft soared higher. 'What the shit . . .' There was a tearing sound. Brune hastily looked over his shoulder. 'Christ Almighty!' James also looked over his shoulder, and saw the aircraft behind them. 'Messerschmitt,' Brune said. 'Going down. We're safer hedge-hopping.' Now that he had got over the initial shock, his voice was again calm.

James had also got his nerves under control, and looked up through the windscreen. The German aircraft, clearly much faster, had overshot them, and was now wheeling, trying to find them again against the darkness of the earth as Brune sank ever lower. 'That's not a Messerschmitt. It's not fast enough, and it turned too slowly. I reckon it's a trainer.'

'But it fires real bullets. Whoops!' Brune pulled back on the yoke as a church steeple suddenly appeared in front of them. They soared over it and looked down on the lights of another village. The enemy aircraft continued to wheel above them, seeking but not finding them, and then they were in open country, skimming the trees.

'Do you know where we are?' James asked.

'Oh, sure. The Gironde estuary is about fifty miles north of us. We'll be in Vichy in half an hour.'

'And you don't think the damage is serious?'

'One burst? She's flying all right. Mind you, if that stuff had got amongst the cargo . . . That character still about?'

'I don't see him.'

'Then let's get back up. There are hills ahead.'

Fifty miles from the Gironde, James thought. 'You ever drunk Gruchy wine?' he asked.

'Bit pricey for me.'

'Those women we're dealing with, they're Gruchys. Before the war their parents owned half the south bank of the river. Now they own their skins. Some of them.'

Brune glanced at him, but preferred not to comment. Now the hills were rising to either side. They flew just above them for another hour, then began the descent. Had he not made this journey before, James would have been apprehensive that they were certain to hit something as they dropped into the valleys. But after their brush with the German defences it hardly seemed relevant. Besides, he had faith in Brune's ability. Justifiably. 'There we are, Major,' the flying officer said. 'Spot on.'

James peered through the windshield and made out the twin row of guttering lights marking the landing field. Only a few more minutes now, and she would be in his arms. He felt almost embarrassed by the surging delight in his mind. Six feet two inches tall and built to match, a rugby player of some repute before the war, James Barron was not a man those who knew him best associated with either emotion or embarrassment. If he knew he was still

6

often astonished at finding himself seconded from his regiment to this extreme aspect of the secret intelligence service, known as special operations, he also knew that his superiors regarded him as a natural because of his apparently cold-blooded detachment as he went about his business. They knew the name Liane de Gruchy, of course: she was famous. But they did not know what she meant to him.

'Sit tight,' Brune said, watching both air speed and altimeter. Now he throttled back as trees came into view, rising to either side of the flickering lights marking the flight path. Then the machine touched, gave a little bounce, and settled, rapidly losing speed as it rolled across the uneven turf to come to a standstill.

Instantly it was surrounded by people. James made his way aft, between the various boxes that lined the interior of the plane, and opened the door. 'Major!' said the big man in the beret who was waiting for him.

James shook hands. 'Jules! Good to see you.' His French was just good enough for a brief conversation, and besides, this man was an old comrade-in-arms. As was the man beside him, thin and hatchet-faced. 'Etienne!' Another hand clasp.

'We did not expect you,' Jules said. 'We expected the plane, but—'

'I couldn't pass up the opportunity,' James said. It was necessary to conceal his real purpose from the rank and file. He jumped down and went towards a second group of people, waiting under the trees.

'James! We did not expect you.' This man spoke English.

James grasped Pierre de Gruchy's hand. 'Thank God you got out of Paris.' Pierre grinned. He was a handsome young man who wore rough clothes and a flat cap, although James principally remembered him in the uniform of a French officer. 'The Gestapo are not really very competent. You remember Henri Burstein.'

James shook hands with the small, dark, Jewish young

7

man. 'Of course I do. But you were reported missing, believed dead, after the retreat to Dunkirk.'

Henri smiled. 'So was Pierre, remember? He escaped to England, and went to work for you. I escaped into Vichy, and now I am also working for you, so they tell me.'

'You are working for France,' Pierre said, severely.

'We are all working for victory,' James reminded him, and drew a deep breath, almost afraid to ask the question. 'Your sisters are all right?'

'Oh, certainly. They are up at the camp. They will be delighted to see you. So will Moulin. You can stay?'

'For twenty-four hours. We must leave tomorrow night. This is Flying Officer Brune.' Brune also shook hands. 'Will you come up?'

As always, Brune shook his head. 'I'll stay with the old girl. We have a relationship. Besides, I need to check her out.'

'There is trouble?'

'We had a brush with a Jerry. I don't think it's serious. He wasn't a Messerschmitt, apparently.'

Pierre nodded. 'There is a training school close to Bordeaux. Well, if there is anything you need, let us know.'

James picked the four suitcases out of the luggage, gave one each to Pierre and Henri while carrying the other two himself, and the three men climbed the hill; the rest of the group stayed to unload the explosives, guns and ammunition that made up the cargo, and then to conceal the plane beneath leafy branches and painted sheets of canvas. 'What have we got here?' Pierre asked.

'Radios, and spare batteries.'

'You are bringing us radios? We are moving into the big time.'

'Could be.' James decided to change the subject; however critical the nature of his mission, he wanted to relax now that he was down and knew that Liane was waiting for him, even if she did not yet know it. 'Amalie must be over the

8

moon at having you back, safe and sound,' he suggested to Henri.

'She is,' Henri said.

James's memory drifted back to the day he had first met this family. It was not a date anyone was ever likely to forget: 9 May 1940, the day before France's world had collapsed. Just under a year ago. He had actually met the second of the sisters the previous Christmas, when on leave in Paris. As a recently promoted captain, with nothing but his service pay, he had been swept off his feet by the chic beauty and obvious wealth of Madeleine de Gruchy. Gauche and inexperienced, he had found it impossible to believe that she might find him equally attractive. He had not expected ever to meet her again, but then had come the invitation to her sister Amalie's wedding. As the western front had seemed utterly quiet, leave had been easily obtained, and he had travelled to Chartres, just south of Paris, and plunged into a world he had previously supposed only existed between the covers of *Tatler.*

Chartres had been only one of the de Gruchy's many houses. The vineyards from which they drew their wealth had been situated on the banks of the Gironde. But all the family and their friends had been assembled for the wedding of the youngest daughter – the first to marry – to her Jewish fiancé. He had gathered that not everyone had approved of it. But he had not been interested. Having supposed himself in love with Madeleine, he had then met the eldest of the sisters, Liane, and been swept off his feet all over again. For one glorious night he had lived on a scale to which he had never supposed he could aspire, treated as a friend and an equal by people who had so much wealth and prestige they seemed to be quite unaware of it. Twenty-four hours later their entire world had collapsed!

They had gone out with all the élan that was their nature. He remembered Liane carelessly getting into her father's Rolls Royce to drive her brother and her new friend up to their positions on the Belgian border, both unaware and

9

uncaring of the immense forces that were preparing to envelope her. When he thought of the weeks of imprisonment
and mistreatment she had suffered before France had surren-
dered he could feel his blood boil. Yet she had survived,
and taken her revenge, and was now the most wanted woman
in the country, just as Amalie had survived the trauma of a
marriage which had lasted no more than ten minutes before
her husband had gone off to war and her subsequent, near
fatal clash with the Gestapo. Then Pierre had survived to
reach England and return to France as a British agent,
controlled by the erstwhile wedding guest. Only one
member of the family had failed to fight, and endure. 'Is
there any news of Madeleine?' he asked.

'I imagine she is living it up in Berlin with her German
husband,' Pierre said. 'We do not speak of her anymore.'

'I am sure she had a reason for what she did.'

'No doubt. She claims it was out of gratitude because
Helsingen got Amalie out of the Gestapo cells. So she could
have slept with him. To *marry* a Boche . . . !'

James reflected how one year of war could change moral
perspectives. Last May the thought of his sister sleeping
with anyone out of wedlock would have had Pierre reaching
for a shotgun. But today it was preferable to marrying one
of the enemy. He wondered if Pierre knew anything about
Liane's private life. In which case his own position might
be dangerous. But Liane was, and always had been, a law
unto herself. For which he thanked God, even as it terrified him.

They had reached a small, tree-shrouded plateau, and men
were emerging. Two or three carried tommy-guns, but most
were armed with shotguns. 'Is it down?' one asked.

'It is being unloaded now,' Pierre said.

'One little plane,' said another man. 'What is it this time?
A couple of tommy-guns and a few sticks of gelignite?'

James looked at Pierre, who merely grinned. 'It takes all
sorts,' he said in English, then reverted to French. 'If you
want to find out what the plane brought, my friend, why

10

don't you go down and help unload it, instead of sitting on your ass up here.'

He led James past them, and through the last of the trees. 'His name is Monterre, and he is a Communist,' he remarked.

'Fighting with you? I thought the Communists were against this war?'

'They are, because Stalin tells them to be. But Monterre is wanted by the police, for forgery. So he came to us.'

'And you trust him?'

'No. But he is very useful. We have set him up with a workshop, and he produces identity cards, railway passes, anything we need.'

Beyond the trees, he escorted James to the cave which Jean Moulin used as his headquarters. Here several people waited, and one of them now ran forward, her yellow hair fluttering in the starlight. 'James! I had not expected to see you again.'

'Do you really think I could stay away?'

She kissed him almost savagely, but he had always suspected that was her true nature. Liane de Gruchy was thirty-one, four years older than himself. He had seen her first in all the glory of her family home, the exquisite perfection of an evening gown, her hair immaculately dressed as it lay past her shoulders in a glowing sheen, her perfect body shrouded in the compelling scent of her perfume; and he had fallen in love. Now he looked at baggy pants and a loose blouse, laced boots, and inhaled only her own scent, and still thought those fine-chiselled features, the perfect mouth, the wide blue eyes, the flowing hair, the most magnificent of sights. 'I am so glad to see you,' she whispered into his ear.

Then she was obliged to release him, because Amalie wanted to hug him as well. Amalie was taller than her sister, and extremely attractive without approaching Liane's beauty. 'Your coming always brings joy,' she said. She certainly looked happier than the last time he had seen her,

11

but he knew that had nothing to do with him; six months ago she had supposed her husband dead.

'James!' Jean Moulin clasped his hand. He too was hardly recognizable as the erstwhile prefect of Chartres, handsome and debonair, brilliantly efficient. James knew the story of how he had been arrested and savagely tortured by the Gestapo for refusing to cooperate with them, how in despair he had cut his own throat, how he had been found before he died and taken to the hospital to be stitched up, and how he had managed to escape, a bleeding wreck, to find his way into Vichy France and this haven in the lower slopes of the Massif Central. His throat had been so deeply cut that his larynx had been perforated, and he spoke in a hoarse croak, but his lively eyes, and the fact that these fellow outlaws acknowledged him as their leader even though he could no longer take the field, proved that his brain was as alert as ever. 'What have you brought us?'

'Radios,' Pierre said enthusiastically. 'Show us, James.'

'Not just now. There are matters that need discussing.'

'But you must be hungry. The inner man comes first.'

There was a fire inside the cave, and late as it was, past midnight, a meal was produced for the visitor; if the wine was rough, the cheese strong, the bread a trifle stale, none of it meant anything to James compared with the fact that he was sitting next to Liane, their thighs touching, and that afterwards . . . But he could not be sure of afterwards. One could never be sure with Liane.

'So how is the war going?' Moulin asked.

'Not brilliantly.'

'But you beat the hell out of the Italians in North Africa.'

'We did, last December. But the Germans got the wind up and sent troops to help a couple of panzer divisions, led by a character named Rommel.'

'Rommel,' Liane said softly. 'It was his troops that captured Joanna and me last May.' No one spoke, so she looked around their faces. 'He was very nice. He came to see us in hospital, and apologized for what had happened. And he hanged the men who raped us.' Again she looked around the carefully expressionless faces. 'Oh, what the hell. It happened. You cannot change what has happened. You can only remember, and profit from the memory. You were telling us about North Africa, James.'

'Well, briefly, Rommel's panzers have reclaimed all of Libya, except for the port of Tobruk, which is under siege. And now that we're committed in Greece, well, the whole thing is somewhat fraught. Which is one reason why I'm here.'

'Tell us,' Moulin said.

James looked around the anxious faces. 'I don't want anyone to take offence. What I am going to tell you are matters of fact. I hope I have said enough to convince you that we are at the present stretched very thin. It may appear as if the invasion of England has been shelved for the time being, but the defence of Britain remains paramount. Then there is the Middle East and Greece. Then there is the Far East, where we know the Japanese are putting pressure on the Vichy government to grant them military bases in Indo-China. Such bases can only be intended for use against Malaysia, the Dutch East Indies, and by projection, India. So you'll appreciate that every tommy-gun, every rifle, every bullet, in fact, has an anxious home waiting for it. So questions are constantly being asked about how to obtain the best value for our resources.'

'What you bring us here is a drain on Britain's resources?' Henri asked.

'There is an English saying, look after the pennies and the pounds will look after themselves. I hope no one here doubts that I am on your side. I set up the backing for the raid on the Paris–Bordeaux railway. But that was six months ago. During those six months we have kept up a steady supply of arms and ammunition. But nothing further has been attempted.'

'It was your command that we lie low for a while after that raid,' Moulin pointed out.

'I wasn't thinking of six months. Are they still searching for you?'

'I do not think so. They know we are in Vichy and they know we are in these mountains. We know that they have been applying pressure on the government. And we also know that the Vichy police know where we are. But they will not betray us as long as we do not make life difficult for them.'

'So you would like to spend the rest of the war hiding here and doing nothing.'

'No, no,' Moulin protested. 'But we must make sure that whatever is done cannot be related to us.' He watched the expression on James's face. 'But this will not satisfy you.'

'I'm afraid it will not satisfy my superiors. So what did you have in mind?'

'We are planning a campaign of assassination. One man acting on his own, moving into occupied France, far away from here, carrying out the murder of a German officer, the higher ranking the better.'

'The idea is ridiculous,' Liane said.

'You did it,' her brother snapped.

'Yes, I did it. But it happened in my Paris flat, where I had every advantage. In addition, Biedermann was a Gestapo officer on his way home from work. He had with him several signed but undated passes and travel permits, which I was able to use before anyone realized what had happened to him.' She spoke quietly and without emotion of what James had no doubt had been the most traumatic moment of her life. But that same act of unemotional coolness was the reason she had survived.

'So the situation was ideal for you,' Pierre said. 'For others it will be more risky. But as James has said, we must do something.'

Moulin had been studying the British officer. 'I think James has come here to tell us what he wants us to do,' he said.

James looked round the faces of the two women and the

14

three men. 'What I have to say must be absolutely confidential. Firstly, we are slowly putting our affairs back in order, both defensively and aggressively. I'm sure you appreciate that the events of last summer, the overrunning of Holland, Belgium and France by the enemy in a matter of days, overwhelmed our espionage and counter-espionage networks in those countries. These are being re-established, but it is obviously a lengthy and dangerous task where we are operating entirely in enemy-controlled territory. This makes your group, already established, the more valuable. Now we must operate with a system of passwords, known only to us.'

'Sterling,' Pierre said. 'That is our password.'

'It was. It has been changed to Pound. As of now, we are all Pounds. My superior is Pound. I am Pound One. My assistant is Pound Two. I control various other agents in the field who are Pounds Three to Ten. Then we come to you. Jean, you are Pound Eleven. Liane, you are Pound Twelve. Pierre, you are Pound Fourteen.'

'Who is Pound Thirteen? Pierre asked.

'We thought we'd omit that, as it's an unlucky number.'

Pierre grinned. 'I am not superstitious. I will take Thirteen.'

'If that's how you want it. Now, remember that you must use only these code names when communicating with me or anyone else. Anyone who seeks to contact you and does not identify himself, or herself, with a Pound number is a potential enemy and should be reported to me.'

'Don't I have a number?' Henri asked. 'And Amalie?'

'The code names are designated for commanders.' He smiled at the disappointed young man. 'Otherwise we'd have more Pounds than we'd know what to do with. But there is plenty for everyone to do. One of the tasks I am going to set you will require the involvement of your people here, but they are to be given no details until they are about to go into action. The other tasks must be kept to a minimum of people.

15

'I will deal with the second one first. We are now engaged in retaliating for the Blitz, as best we are able. Our aircraft are bombing Germany almost nightly, with some success. However, inevitably there are losses. In a large number of cases the aircrew survive, and sometimes manage to evade capture for some time. As a general rule they endeavour to make their way to the coast, and in this they are receiving considerable assistance, at great personal risk, from Dutch and Belgian patriots. Unfortunately, if they do reach the coast, it is too often a dead end. There are fishermen who are willing to help, but their activities are closely monitored by the Germans, and the success rate has been low.'

'You would like to bring them through France,' Moulin said. 'Through Vichy.'

'We are not sure that would be any safer than through the occupied territory. But we will take your advice on this. What we wish to set up is a regular and reliable escape route. This will involve the use of safe houses, where our people can lie concealed until the next stage of the journey can be arranged.'

Amalie clapped her hands. 'Just like *The Scarlet Pimpernel.*'

'But these men are not, I hope, to be snatched from the cells of the Gestapo,' Henri said.

'Under no circumstances. The essence of this operation, which will be dangerous enough anyway, is that there must be no clash with any authority. If there is the slightest risk of the Gestapo moving in, your people must move out and utterly disassociate themselves from the airman involved. You must be quite clear about this. The preservation of the escape route is of far more importance than the extraction of one man.'

'What about the one man?' Liane asked, quietly.

'Our men will be briefed on what they have to do in the first instance. Obviously it would be too risky for them to know the whole route, in case they were to be captured. From stage one they will be directed to stage two, and so on.'

16

'All the way down to Spain, and then Portugal,' Pierre said. 'That is how you got me in last year.'

'You wish us to organize the entire route?' Moulin asked.

'No. We have agents in Belgium and Holland who have already set up their end. Your people will take over once they are in France. Paris is the key. The evaders will necessarily pass through Paris. Not only will they be safer in a great metropolis than in a small town, where they will stick out like sore thumbs, but Paris is also the hub of the French rail network.' Another glance round the suddenly tense faces. 'You understand that these people you employ will have to be utterly committed, that any suggestion of treachery will have to be ruthlessly dealt with, and that they have to be talented, or have talented contacts; our people will need identity cards, travel documents, and some personal details.'

'I understand,' Pierre said. 'I will take care of it.'

'You?' cried both his sisters.

'Of course. I am the obvious choice. I have lived in Paris. I know the people—'

'And the people know you,' Amalie pointed out. 'There is a warrant out for your arrest. You would not last a week.'

'As for having lived there for a few months,' Liane said scornfully, 'I lived there for seven years. What is more, I know the sort of people we need to employ.'

'Do you?' Moulin asked.

The faintest hint of colour seeped into Liane's cheeks, and she gave James a quick glance. 'I lived – what shall I say? – a Bohemian existence there. I know the Left Bank cafes, the would-be artists and painters and actors and writers. And I also knew people outside the law.'

'And they accepted you in their society, Liane? You?'

'They accepted me because I was rich. I bought them drinks. And, well, I lived their kind of life.'

As earlier, there was total silence, and James realized that neither Pierre nor Amalie actually knew their older sister very well. But then, what of him? He did not know her at

17

all. If he had been almost unable to believe the way she had thrown herself into his arms within a few hours of meeting him, he had been inclined to think of irresistible chemistry rather than wanton desire. So did it make a difference? Never, to him. He would accept her on her own terms. But that meant . . . Pierre put it into words. 'It would be far too dangerous. You say there is a warrant out for me. My God, there is a *reward* out for you.'

'Do you really suppose anyone remembers what I look like? I left Paris last July. Anyway, I will be adequately disguised. I told you, amongst my friends were out-of-work actors. They told me all about the art of make-up. Monterre will make me a new identity card.' Now she gazed at James. 'Tell them that I am the obvious person for the task.'

'We'll talk about it. We also need staging posts set up in Orléans, Poitiers and Bordeaux.'

'Well, I can certainly handle that,' Pierre declared.

'It would be better if you found someone else. We need you for that second task, because this is a military matter. It will involve, as I have said, your entire force. There is a new unit being formed in England called the Commandos. These are elite, highly trained troops, to be used for inflicting quick raids across the Channel, hit the enemy hard, and then get out again. The intention is to keep the enemy in constant apprehension of where he'll be struck next, and force him to keep considerable forces along the French coast, and also to use these raids as rehearsals for our return to France as an army when the time is right.'

'Wheeee!' Amalie cried. 'When?'

'When the time is right. At this moment, we are talking about small raids. But they would be far more effective if they were to coincide with guerilla activity in the vicinity of the area being raided. Will your people take part?'

'Yes,' Henri said. 'Tell us where and when.'

James looked at Moulin. 'I think most of them would do so,' the prefect said. 'But unless you are speaking of the

18

Bordeaux area, which is a long way from England, we are a long way from the sea. Certainly the Channel.'

'You will be given ample time to move your people into position. You know the wavelength on which to listen, and you have your map references. Your call sign will be JJX. The messages will come through at three o'clock in the morning. The first will be "A nightingale sings". This will mean prepare to move. The second will be "Berkeley Square" and will be accompanied by a map reference. This will tell you where you should be four weeks to the day. Is that understood?'

The Frenchman nodded. 'And these new radios you have brought us?' Pierre asked. 'They are for this operation?'

'One is. One is for the Paris operator.' He glanced at Liane. 'The others are for your staging-post commanders. They are receivers only. I have a code system with me, which I will give you. You have handled a radio before, Pierre. You will instruct whoever is finally chosen, in both the assembly and the usage of these sets, and the use of the codes.' Pierre nodded. 'There is one thing more.' He glanced from face to face, and took a box from his pocket. 'There are forty capsules here. One must be issued to each of you people. It must be carried at all times, and kept in the mouth in time of danger. If captured, it must be bitten. Death is painless and instantaneous.' He did not dare look at Liane. 'Believe me, it is better than being tortured and betraying your associates.'

The Frenchmen exchanged glances, and Moulin took the box. 'I will issue them. Now, you must be very tired. I think we should all turn in.'

'But James and I have matters to discuss,' Liane said softly.

The night, already nearly over, was cool rather than cold. Liane picked two blankets and led James away from the cave and into the wood. 'Everyone will know what we're doing,' he said.

'Are you ashamed of that? Or are you ashamed of me, after what I said at supper?'

'The only emotion I ever feel when I think of you is pride. I am proud to have known you, been able to love you. I am proud of you, of everything you have ever done.'

She spread a blanket on the ground. 'If we take off our pants and roll them up, they will be our pillows.' He did as she wanted, took off his boots, as did she. Then she pulled the other blanket over them. 'You are proud of a murderess?'

'You did what you had to do.'

'I did what I wanted to do. In any normal society I would merely have called the police. But Biedermann *was* the police. And I did not kill him because he raped me; I killed him because he boasted of what they had done to Jean, to Amalie. Do you know what I did?'

'Ah . . .' He didn't really want to hear it, but he understood that she wanted to talk about it, and if she needed to share that experience with him, then he might at last be within touching distance of actually getting inside her mind, instead of only lapping at the physical periphery of her personality. 'You never told me.'

'After boasting of his exploits, he made me have sex with him. I could not prevent this, as he was so much bigger and stronger than I.' Her tone was entirely matter-of-fact. 'Then he wanted brandy, so I gave him some, but I dissolved several of my sleeping tablets in it. Do you know, he actually commented on the slightly different taste, and when I told him that it was our own brew, he asked me to order some for him. Then he fell asleep, so I went into the kitchen and got a carving knife, and cut his throat.' Her arms were tight on his body. 'That is what he boasted they had made Jean do. Only I made sure he was dead. Then I drew a hot bath. There was blood everywhere. Then I got dressed, took his pistol and his papers, and simply walked out of the flat.'

He kissed her. 'And became a legend.'

She made a moue. 'We have talked enough.' But as her

20

hands guided his to their goal, he realized that they had not talked at all about what was on his mind.

When James awoke it was broad daylight, and she was gone. But she returned a few minutes later with bread and a cup of wine. 'We do not have coffee,' she explained, kneeling beside him. 'You slept well. You snored.'

'But you stayed awake.'

'I have lots of time to sleep after you have gone.'

'You would have even more time to sleep if you came with me.'

She kissed him. 'You said that the last time you came here.'

'I am hoping that one day you will say yes.'

'When the war is over, perhaps.'

'That could be a long time.'

'Then we will have to be patient. You do not really wish me to desert my people? My friends? My family? That would make me very little better than Madeleine.'

'Do you hate her?'

Liane appeared to consider. 'Yes.'

'She would say she was trying to help.'

'And my mother and father are in a concentration camp.'

He sighed. 'Do you have news of them?'

'People in Dachau do not write letters.'

He put down his cup to hold her hands. 'Li, you know that I am in overall command of this operation. I can forbid you to go to Paris.'

'But you will not do so.'

'The thought of you having to bite one of those capsules . . .'

'Is death really instantaneous, and painless?'

'It's supposed to be pretty quick. As for being painless . . . No one who has taken one has ever got around to telling us.'

'Having one will be a great comfort. But you will not forbid me to go.'

21

He gazed at her for several moments. Then his shoulders sagged. 'No, I will not do that.'

'Good morning, sir. How did it go?' Sergeant Rachel Cartwright's tone was cold, as it usually was when James returned from a mission. This he knew was caused by several things. She could see no adequate reason why she was not allowed to undertake such missions herself. Certainly she regarded herself as better qualified than he, if only because she spoke fluent French whereas his was of the schoolboy variety. Then there was the business of the danger to which he was exposing himself. Rachel's affection for him was in many ways maternal. In many ways, but not all. For the principal reason she went into a sulk every time he went to France was that she knew he would be seeing Liane, and she also knew what would happen when he did that. He often wondered what would happen if the two women were ever to meet; he could not believe that there was a jealous bone in Liane's body.

Whereas Rachel . . . Tall and so slender as almost to be thin, and with delightfully long legs, with a wealth of black hair worn when on duty, as now, in a tight bun, with sharp features which were actually enhanced by her horn-rimmed spectacles, she was just as much of a blue blood as any de Gruchy, and whereas the de Gruchys had been pitched into the war and virtually told by fate to swim or sink, Rachel Cartwright had volunteered for the ATS, and then volunteered for special training, and then volunteered for special operations, simply because she had felt it necessary to do her bit to the maximum.

She could have wound up working for anyone in the SIS. But she had wound up working for him. Sharing so many secrets they could confide in no one else, experiencing the continual traumas of placing agents in the field to undergo the risks of arrest, torture and execution – or instant suicide – the fact that they had gravitated towards each other had been unavoidable however hard he had tried to resist temptation, and not only because of Liane: he had understood how incorrect it was for an officer to take an enlisted woman to bed. But it was what she had wanted, almost demanded, and she was a difficult young woman to refuse. At least he had never made any secret that he was in love elsewhere. She had said it didn't matter to her, presumably on the basis that she was *in situ* and Liane was a long way away. As a rule.

He sat behind his desk. 'I think it was very satisfactory. If a little hairy.'

'You had trouble?' Her voice was anxious.

'A German interceptor.'

'Oh, my God! But you're here!'

'We took evasive action.'

'But you had to come back.'

'True. But it was the next night, and there was cloud cover, and they weren't looking for us coming from inland. So there was really nothing to worry about in the air.'

'And on the ground? You read them their lecture?'

'Yes. They listened, and promised to do what we wished.'

'And I assume you saw Liane? Was that satisfactory?'

'Not entirely.'

'Oh?'

He grinned. 'Not in the sense you mean. She intends to take on the Paris set-up herself.'

'Won't that be frightfully dangerous? Don't the Gestapo have a reward out for her apprehension?'

'Yes.'

'But you're going to let her go ahead.'

'I can't stop her, Rachel. I can tell them what we want done, but how they do it, and who they employ, is their business. So tell me what's been happening here.'

'Pound has been on the line.'

James nodded. 'I'll make a full report.'

'It's not about the French. It's about your other lady love.'

James wagged a pencil at her. 'Joanna is not my lady love.'

23

'Are you going to tell me that you've never had her?'

'No, I have never had her. I don't even like the woman.'

'You don't like a seething sex bomb?'

'Certainly I do. I'm very fond of you.'

'Ha, ha, ha. Anyway, he said to be in touch the moment you got back.'

James sighed. 'Then you'd better get him on the line.'

'Pound,' the brigadier said.

'Pound One,' James acknowledged.

'Report.'

'I think it went very well. They understand what we require, and are prepared to cooperate.'

'I hope you are right. Questions are being asked, James, about the effectiveness of these people, about the value we're getting for supporting them. And now we have this de Gaulle fellow trying to muscle in. He feels that now that he is recognized as leader of the non-Vichy French – the "Free French," he's calling his people – he should have control over all French units opposing the Germans.'

'Is he recognized as leader of the non-Vichy French, sir?'

'Not everyone is happy with it. Between you and me, he's a damnably difficult fellow to get along with. But he has the ear of the PM. I don't suppose the old man likes him any more than the rest of us. But he reckons he's the best bet for rallying the anti-Vichy people, certainly at the moment.'

'And is he going to be allowed to take over our French agents?'

'I am arguing our case as strongly as I can, if only on security grounds. Once we let a bunch of Froggies into any of our secrets, who can tell where we'll wind up.'

'Absolutely, sir. I couldn't agree more.'

'The point at issue is, are these Resistance people our agents, or merely French patriots who we're sponsoring. Anyway, you can leave that with me. I want to talk about Pound Three. Where is she?'

'I expect she's in Berlin.'

'How can you operate an agent without knowing where she is?'

'Well, sir, possessing both American and Swedish passports she is free to travel as and when she chooses. That's her value, and after that stupendous piece of information that she gave us last year, I agreed to give her a roving role to see what else she could come up with.'

'When were you last in touch with her?'

'Just after Christmas.'

'Good God! Then she won't even know she's Pound Three.'

'I'm afraid not, sir. She will still be using Sterling when she contacts us. But we'll allow for that.'

'You are saying that for five months she has come up with precisely nothing.'

'We must give her time, sir. After all, we know her worth.'

'Do we? That "stupendous" information she gave us last year has turned out to be something of a damp squib.'

'With respect, sir, we don't know that.'

'We have to be realistic, James. Your girl told us as absolute fact that Hitler would invade Russia in mid-May. Well, that is only a week off now, and there is absolutely no sign of any split between the Soviets and the Nazis.'

'With respect, sir, we know there have been considerable German troop movements into the Balkans.'

'The Balkans are no launching pad for a war with Soviet Russia. And this is the point. Those troops are firstly to support the Italians in Greece and secondly to take care of the Yugoslavs. Whether he wanted this or not, Hitler has got himself fully committed down there. That's his programme for this year.'

'Yes, sir,' James said. He recollected that his superiors in Flanders in May 1940 had dismissed fairly obvious evidence of German troop movements saying that Hitler was fully committed to Norway and could not possibly consider another offensive until that was sorted out. But arguing with the brigadier was a waste of time.

'I can tell you,' the brigadier went on, 'that the old man is not happy about it. On the basis of Jonsson's information, which he accepted because we recommended her so highly, he communicated it to Marshal Stalin. Stalin did not even bother to reply. And now we, but more importantly the PM, are left with egg all over our faces.'

'We're still not into mid-May,' James said doggedly.

'I hope you're right. But now I am giving you an order. Find out where Jonsson is, and pull her out.'

'I can't do that, sir. I have no means of communicating with her.'

'Haven't we got other agents in Berlin?'

'Yes, sir, we do. But as you know, it is our policy never to let one agent know about another, except in the most extreme emergency.'

'Well, I would classify this as an extreme emergency, because if you don't get her home pretty damn soon heads will roll. Yours for a start.'

Two

The Spy

'The general will see you now, Colonel Kluck,' the secretary said. Hans Kluck stood up. A tall, thin man with a hatchet face and receding hair, he wore civilian clothes, and was doing his best to appear calm, but the woman, spick and span in her white blouse, black tie and skirt, black stockings and shoes, could tell that he was sweating. She opened the double doors and stood to attention. 'Colonel Kluck, Herr General.'

Kluck stepped into the room, stood to attention, throwing out his right arm. 'Heil Hitler.' Behind him he heard the doors close.

The office was high-ceilinged and spacious. There was a chandelier and deep, tall windows, presently open to let the May sunshine enter. A settee waited against one wall, and there were two comfortable chairs in front of a huge desk. On the opposite wall there was an inner doorway, slightly ajar, and behind the desk, between the windows, there was an immense colour photograph of the Führer. But Kluck had eyes only for the man who was now standing behind the desk. 'Heil Hitler!'

Reinhard Heydrich was actually younger than Kluck, and not as tall. But in his crisp black uniform, his wavy blonde hair, his coldly handsome features, the arrogance displayed in every movement, he epitomized the sinister glamour of the Nazi regime in a way his boss, Heinrich Himmler, or even Hitler himself, never did. Now he was smiling as he came round the desk to shake hands. 'It is good to see you, Hans. It has been a long time.'

Kluck grew more nervous yet. 'Three years, Herr General.'

'I hope you do not mind being summoned to Berlin?'

'I am flattered, Herr General. I prefer Berlin to Paris.'

'Absolutely. Sit down, man. Sit down. Cigarette?'

Cautiously Kluck lowered himself into one of the chairs before the desk. 'Thank you, no, Herr General. I do not smoke.'

'Of course. You have no vices.' Heydrich seated himself behind the desk, took a cigarette himself. 'I am interested in the progress of your investigation into the destruction of the Paris–Bordeaux railway line last October. I see that you have not yet made an arrest. In six months you have not made one single arrest. Why is this?'

'Well, Herr General . . .'

'You know who the ringleader of this gang of bandits was. Liane de Gruchy. A woman who was already wanted for the murder of one of your own colleagues, and was never arrested.'

'She escaped into Vichy.' ·

'And this brother of hers . . .' Heydrich glanced at the notes on his desk. 'Pierre de Gruchy. You say you are quite sure he was operating an illegal radio in Paris, sending messages to England. He has also slipped through your fingers. He is also in Vichy?'

'Yes, Herr General. If we were to be given permission to cross the border—'

Heydrich slapped his hand on the desk. 'The Führer does not wish to infringe Vichy sovereignty at this time. But Monsieur Laval is coming to Berlin in the near future and Herr Himmler intends to discuss the situation with him. However, I want these thugs apprehended the moment they again cross the border. What they did, and the fact that they are still at large, is an affront to the Reich. It must be possible to bring additional pressure to drag them into the open. Are there parents?'

'Yes, Herr General. Albert and Barbara de Gruchy. Albert de Gruchy was one of the leading wine growers in France.'

'Then arrest them. That will bring the children out.'

'I did that immediately after the outrage, Herr General, but it does not appear to have had any effect on the children.'

'They are conscienceless brutes. Where are the parents now?'

'They are in Dachau.'

'Hm. Any other brothers or sisters?'

'There were two other sisters. One of them, the youngest, Amalie, disappeared last summer. She was married to a Jew, you see, who was reported missing, presumed dead. This clearly upset her. Then when her parents-in-law were arrested she had a brush with the Gestapo. When she disappeared it was supposed she had committed suicide by throwing herself into the Gironde, which runs past her parents' home outside Paulliac, and the case was closed by the French police. But one of my assistants, Captain Roess, carried out his own investigation and is convinced that she staged her death. You know the sort of thing, clothes left on the river back, etc, and actually ran away.'

'So very probably she is also in Vichy. Probably linked up with her brother and sister. But you say she had a brush with the Gestapo?'

'She tried to stop her parents-in-law from being arrested, and struck one of my men on the head with a pewter vase. He had to be hospitalized.'

'And she was not executed?'

'Pressure was brought to bear by the local Wehrmacht commander, Major Hoeppner. He is a nephew of the panzer general.'

'I know Franz Hoeppner. He is a colonel now, and is in command of the Bordeaux district. What was his interest in this woman?'

'I don't believe he had an interest, Herr General. I believe he was acting on behalf of his friend Colonel von Helsingen.'

Heydrich snapped his fingers. 'Of course! Helsingen married the other daughter!'

'Who is living right here in Berlin. If I had permission—'

Heydrich waved his finger. 'Not at this moment. Helsingen's father is one of the Führer's oldest friends, and he gave his personal blessing to this wedding. Things may change in the course of time, but right now Frau von Helsingen must be considered inviolate. On the other hand . . . Has she never shown any concern about her parents, or her siblings?'

'I do not know, Herr General. She is out of my jurisdiction.'

'Yes,' Heydrich said thoughtfully. 'But it is difficult to accept that that whole family is so cold-blooded that it does not care whether its own parents live or die. I am going to issue an order releasing Albert and Barbara de Gruchy from Dachau, and allowing them to return to their home in Paulliac. You will inform Colonel Hoeppner of this, and request him to show them every courtesy.'

'But, Herr General—'

'Our objective, *your* objective, Kluck, is to lure the younger de Gruchys out of Vichy. Once they do that, it is up to you to arrest them.' Kluck took out his handkerchief to wipe his brow. 'You do not think you are capable of doing this?' Heydrich's voice remained deceptively quiet.

'Colonel Hoeppner will wish to know the reason for this volte-face.'

'You will tell him that arresting the old people was a mistake. That you now have evidence that they were not involved in their children's crimes, and that it is not the purpose of the Reich to lock up innocent people.' Kluck gulped. 'In fact,' Heydrich said, 'I think we will give the event maximum publicity. It will impress people. But you, Kluck, you will bring these wayward children to justice. I wish you to give that top priority.'

'I will do my best, Herr General.'

'I do not wish your best, Colonel. I wish you to succeed.

30

Your future depends upon it. Thank you for coming to see me. Heil Hitler!'

Heydrich waited for the door to close behind Kluck, then left his desk to open the inner door. 'Well?'

The man waiting there, like Kluck wearing a business suit, shrugged. 'You would have done better to sack him there and then. He has not the stomach for the job. He never did. That Roess he mentioned, his assistant, who worked out what must have happened to the Gruchy girl, is far better quality.' The Sicherheitsdienst officer was of medium height, heavy set, with lank black hair and penetrating dark eyes, often half closed. His features were also heavy.

'As you say, Oskar,' Heydrich agreed. 'But Kluck knows the country and the people. However, I do not intend to rely on him alone. It is the terrorists we want, and particularly the de Gruchys. I wish you to infiltrate one of your people into the group.' Oskar Weber stroked his chin. 'It must be a totally reliable man—'

'Or woman.'

'Or woman. He must have a foolproof cover story. He will make his way into Vichy and volunteer to join the terrorist group. I have no doubt they are recruiting. In fact we know that since we gave orders that half a million French workers are to be requisitioned for forced labour in Germany, quite a few people have just disappeared. Obviously most of them are cowering somewhere, but some will certainly have joined these people. Our man must do the same.'

'Or our woman.'

'Yes, yes, or our woman. He must also be very carefully briefed on what he has to do. There is no point in his informing us where they can be found as long as we cannot go in and get them. But surely they are going to be active again this summer. He must let us know where and when and how they mean to operate so that we can be waiting for them.'

'It will be very dangerous for him, or her.'

31

'Why do you keep interjecting "her" into this business, Oskar? This is man's work.'

'I am not sure of that, Reinhard. The information we require is not going to be easily obtained by a member of the rank and file. Our agent must be able to get into the inner council of these people, or at least become close to someone who is in that council. Now, we are fairly certain that this group is being led by Liane de Gruchy. If that is so, I think she would be more susceptible to making friends with a woman recruit than a man.'

'That is a very good point. You know of such a woman?'

'I think I do.'

'Excellent. You do understand the risk she will be taking? These people are killers.'

'I will make sure she understands that.'

'Very good. I will leave it in your hands. But there is something else I want done. I wish you to put a tail on Frau von Helsingen. This must be one of your best people, Oskar. Helsingen must never suspect it, which means that the lady must never suspect it either.'

'Are we looking for anything in particular?'

'I cannot say. I just find it difficult to believe that anyone could so completely turn her back on her own family, never make any attempt to do anything about her parents . . .'

'We don't know that. And it is very likely that it is not a case of her rejecting them than of them, and this includes her brother and sister, rejecting her for marrying a German.'

'These are things I would like to find out. This too I will leave in your hands, Oskar. I want the most detailed report on Madeleine von Helsingen's life. Everything she does, everyone she meets. But bringing this murderous creature Liane de Gruchy to justice is high on my list of priorities. Heil Hitler!'

'My darling!' Frederick von Helsingen said, opening the front door of his flat. 'I have the most tremendous news.' Of medium height, but well built, with dark hair and blue eyes and regular features, he was a handsome man, shown off to perfection by his uniform. Now he threw his cap on to a table and held out his arms.

Madeleine von Helsingen hurried out of the lounge for his embrace. For all the wealth and prestige of her husband's family, and him personally, which guaranteed her the respect of everyone she met, and invitations to every social event of consequence, she still felt very much a stranger in the heart of Berlin society, but it was not a situation of which she gave any external evidence. A few inches shorter than Helsingen, with her good body and loose dark brown hair, her green eyes and her splendid features, which were only inferior to those of her older sister, she made a striking figure, especially as she was always flawlessly groomed and dressed. 'Tell me that Britain has given up and made peace,' she said.

'Oh, they hang on and make noises. But they are being beaten everywhere. North Africa, Greece . . .'

'Hilda told me that a German battleship has been sunk.'

'Servants! How they do chatter. But this time I am afraid it is true. However, it is not the whole story. Yes, *Bismarck* has gone down. The Führer is very upset. But it took virtually the entire Royal Navy to do it, and before she sank she had herself sunk the biggest British ship, *Hood*, and severely damaged their newest, *Prince of Wales*. I think we can claim a tactical victory.'

Madeleine released him and led the way into the comfortably furnished lounge. 'That is good news?'

'That is entirely irrelevant news, from our point of view. Do you remember that I told you last year that the Führer had determined to settle with Russia, once and for all?'

Madeleine sat down. 'Yes. I remember.'

He frowned. 'You never told anybody, did you? That information was top secret.'

'Look at this dust,' Madeleine said, running her finger over the incidental table beside the settee. 'I sometimes wonder if Hilda is worth the money we pay her. Of course I did not tell anyone, Freddie. You told me not to.'

33

'Good girl. It is even more top secret now. Because it is going to happen.'

'You said it would happen this month.'

'We have been delayed by this business down in the Balkans. But we are at last ready. It will happen in June. The final orders have been given.'

'Oh, my God! You will not be involved?'

He poured two glasses of schnapps and sat beside her, giving her one. 'You know I have wanted a field command ever since the war with France. As soon as we had someone to fight.'

She put down her glass, untouched. 'Freddie! You can't! You're on the Führer's personal staff.'

'You mean I am a glorified office boy. My darling –' he held her hands – 'I have explained this to you before. Do you wish me to spend the rest of my life as a colonel, without any honours? I do not even have an Iron Cross. Yet. Advancement in armies only comes about quickly through war. Success in war. After this war is over, there will be no more wars, because we will rule all Europe. If I am going to make general under the age of forty it must be done now.'

'But the danger! The Russians! Don't they have millions of men under arms?'

'Well, we have a few million ourselves, you know. Our equipment is far superior. As for our command . . . Stalin shot all his best commanders back in 1937. I mean, even the Finns beat the hell out of them last year. Believe me, the Russian armies are just an accumulation of men waiting to be slaughtered.'

'Slaughtered!'

'Well, hopefully they will have the sense to surrender.'

'Oh, Freddie! I don't want you to go.'

'And I have explained that I must. But that is not all my news.' Her eyes became watchful. 'Your parents are to be released from prison.'

'I don't understand.'

'It is simply that that incompetent lout Kluck has realized

34

that there is absolutely no evidence against them, and that parents cannot be held responsible for the misdeeds of their children. I imagine Franz Hoeppner had something to do with it. He is a good fellow, Franz.' He frowned at her. 'Are you all right?'

'I . . . I am overwhelmed. Where are they to be sent? My parents.'

'Back to their home outside Paulliac.'

'Oh, thank God! They will be so happy.'

'I should think so. Would you like to see them?'

Madeleine stared at him. Throughout the six months since the bomb outrage and the arrest of her parents, she had begged to be allowed to see them, just as she had begged him to intervene. He had declined to allow either, explaining that it could be disastrous for his career, and that in view of the crimes committed by her siblings it was safest for her to keep a very low profile regarding them. She had accepted his advice, which had almost been an order, both because he was her husband and because she had been terrified. Now it was all a little too much to cope with. 'You mean . . . here?'

'Yes. They could come here before leaving for France.'

Madeleine looked left and right. Her mother and father had spent several months in a concentration camp. No one except the inner core of the party knew what really went on in such camps, and one was discouraged from believing the rumours of summary executions, of public floggings, of starvation, that occured there. But even if all those were terrible lies circulated by enemies of the regime, the camps were definitely prisons, where there were no servants, no comforts, no proper facilities, and above all, no privacy. What effect such conditions might have had on two elderly people who had lived their lives in the lap of wealth and luxury she could not imagine. And to have them here, to see the luxury in which *she* was living, and had lived in all the time they had been behind bars . . . 'I don't think that would be a good idea,' she said. 'Perhaps, when, well, they

35

have got used to the idea of being free . . . Perhaps I could go to Paulliac and visit them.'

'Perhaps. We'll talk about it,' he said, and she knew he would forbid it.

As usual, Frederick left the house early, and Madeleine breakfasted alone. But she only toyed with her toast, and drank several cups of coffee instead. She had hardly slept, although she had had to conceal that from her husband. But there were so many things to be concealed from her husband. At the lowest level there was the telephone call from Joanna, announcing that she was back in Berlin and intended to visit her that morning. Frederick did not like Joanna any more than Joanna liked Frederick; there had been no point in upsetting him.

But at the moment, her principal secret she did not wish to be a secret. The fact that she was pregnant should have them both jumping for joy. She had meant to greet him with the news, and instead had been overtaken by *his* news. Because of those other secrets. If she had always admired him, she had always hated his utter belief in the doctrines of his Führer. She could not blame him for the destruction of France, because he was a soldier who obeyed orders, but she could blame herself for having married him, an act of betrayal of everything she believed in, not to mention her country.

There had been no love then. If she had loved anyone, it had been that so appealingly gauche English officer, James Barron, who had so strangely entered her life, for so brief a period. Now she did not know if he was alive or dead. Of only one thing had she been certain: she would never see him again. His replacement by an entirely different, and, one would have to say, superior man, certainly in terms of sophistication and position, had been one factor in her willingness to accept Frederick's proposal. But there had also been the gratitude factor. Frederick had saved Amalie from the Gestapo. And Frederick had shown his willingness to help the entire de Gruchy family survive the war and continue to prosper. It was not his fault that Liane had turned into a wanted criminal, that Amalie had drowned herself, that Pierre had entirely disappeared. In fact, he was entitled to feel desperately betrayed at such behaviour from people he had only wanted to help. But apart from a single outburst when he had heard the news of the attack on the railway, he had uttered not a word of reproach.

Instead, she had betrayed that confidence he had shared with her last year, and betrayed him again by lying to him. She did not know if she had actually done any damage. She had reacted in a very immature way to the news of what Liane had done and was doing, had been overtaken by a surge of irresistible guilt, had lashed out blindly to the only person she still knew who could possibly help, who could use the information to upset Hitler's plans without in any way being able to harm the regime itself, or more especially, Frederick. And then Madeleine had sat back in horror at what she had done. But it did not appear as if she had done anything. Joanna was a journalist, who with her Swedish-American dual nationality and passports had free access to any country in Europe. That she apparently liked Germany, and more especially, Berlin, best, was not surprising. Right now, Berlin was the centre of the world, certainly as regards news and fun, and Joanna was a great one for having fun. But she did not appear to have used the information at all. Or more likely, her American editor had dismissed the idea of Hitler going to war with Stalin, after the hoo-ha and the success of the alliance signed in August 1939, as nonsense. Anyway, if Joanna was coming to see her this morning, having apparently just returned from a visit to her father in Stockholm, she would be able to ask her about it and beg her not to use it, at least for another month.

She finished her coffee, sat in the lounge with a magazine, without actually reading it. As always when expecting Joanna, she felt curiously breathless. It was not merely that Joanna would bring her news of the outside world which

37

would not be common knowledge in Germany; it was her outrageous personality that could embrace everyone in a room, and when there was only one other person in the room . . .

And then there was her beauty and her sexuality. It was not something to which she had succumbed personally, but she knew that was almost certainly because Joanna had never directed it at her. To Joanna, Madeleine had always been the little sister, just as Amalie had always been the baby. Joanna's special friend had been Liane, who was her own age. They had been at finishing school in Switzerland together, and had been expelled together – for being found in bed together! Such concepts, such aberrations, had been beyond the scope of Madeleine's imagination. She had been only twelve when it had happened, had not then known *what* had happened. It had been Liane herself who had told her, several years later. She had found it difficult to believe, even then. Because then she had been on a visit to her sister in Paris, staying in Liane's flat, unwillingly and yet fascinatingly drawn into her lifestyle, forced to accept that her glamorous sister was an utter hedonist, who accepted male or female lovers as it crossed her mind to do so. And protected as she had been by her parents' social prestige as much as by their wealth, she had known no check, had accepted no obstacle, in her quest for pleasure.

Madeleine had been left both shocked and envious. If she had known that she could never live like that, she still wished that she could. And being a practising Roman Catholic, she had always known that it had to end in disaster. It had never occurred to her that the disaster, when it came, would involve all of France, turn Liane, lovely, sophisticated, apparently delicate Liane, firstly into a victim, then into a murderess and now an outlaw.

So what did Joanna think of it all? Joanna, big, beautiful and boisterous. She had been with Liane when they were captured by the German deserters in that abandoned village

38

north of Paris, had suffered the same dreadful fate – Madeleine, who had only ever had sex with her husband, could not imagine what it must be like to be raped – and yet seemed to have shrugged it off, and resumed living her own careless life. But she certainly knew what had happened to Liane since then, because Madeleine had told her. And now she was here. Hilda stood in the doorway. 'Fräulein Jonsson, Frau von Helsingen.'

Joanna Jonsson was only an inch under six feet tall, and possessed a strong, voluptuous body which matched her equally strong, sensuous face. The whole was framed in long, straight golden hair, and emboldened by the glittering pale blue eyes. Her dress was dark blue and she wore three expensive rings as well as a gold bangle. 'Madeleine!' she said, embracing her. 'You're looking well.'

'As are you,' Madeleine said. 'Coffee?'

'I'd prefer a drink. Do you have any brandy?'

'Oh, yes. Cognac, believe it or not. How was Stockholm?'

'Still cold, I imagine. I've actually been in the States. Felt I had to see Mom.'

'You mean you crossed the Atlantic? Twice?'

'Don't remind me. I was scared shitless.' She took the glass from Hilda's tray and gave Madeleine a meaningful look.

'Thank you, Hilda,' Madeleine said.

Hilda, a small, dark woman, gave a brief bow and left, closing the door behind her. Joanna immediately got up and opened it again. Madeleine watched her with her mouth open. 'All servants listen at doors,' Joanna explained. 'Now come and sit beside me on the settee. That way we can keep our voices down. And stick to English.' She knew that Madeleine, like her sisters, educated at Benenden, spoke the language fluently.

Madeleine obeyed. 'What is this all about?'

'Lots of things. First, what is the news on Liane?'

'There is no news of Liane. No one has seen her or heard of her since the train outrage last year.'

'Shit! But if she was dead or been captured you'd know, wouldn't you?'

'If she'd been captured, yes. But if she's just died . . . I don't suppose the people she was with would publicize it.'

'Shit,' Joanna commented again. 'OK, now tell me about that bum steer you gave me last year.'

They were speaking in little more than whispers, but Madeleine cast an anxious glance at the open door. 'I don't know what you're talking about.'

'You told me that the invasion of Russia would start mid-May. That was yesterday.'

'Is that important?'

'You bet it is. My editor is hopping mad. Don't worry; I didn't let you down. I never told him my source, and I made him promise not to use it until just before the date. So he has his headline all set up to print, and nothing shows any sign of happening.'

'Oh, well, it *was* top secret. Let's forget about it.'

'Madeleine, darling,' Joanna said softly, 'you can't back off now. I want an update.'

'I said I don't want to talk about it anymore.'

'But I do. Have you any idea what Freddie would do if he found out you had given me classified information?'

'I thought you were my friend. Liane's friend. All of our friend.'

'Sure I am. And friends should stick together.'

'You are threatening me.'

'I need to know the situation regarding a war with Russia. Is it on, or is it off?'

Madeleine sighed. 'It was just put back a month, that's all, because of the business in Greece and Yugoslavia.'

'A month,' Joanna said thoughtfully. 'Great. Now tell me what else is new.'

'I am not going to tell you anything,' Madeleine said. 'I wish you'd leave. And I don't wish you to come back.'

'Who's getting all uptight? You can't get rid of me,

Madeleine. I'm your friend, remember? Now think. Freddie must still be telling you things.'

'The only thing Freddie has told me recently is that Mummy and Daddy are to be released from prison.'

Joanna frowned. 'He told you that? People don't get released from Dachau.'

'Well, they are going to be.'

'You should be over the moon. You don't look it.'

'Well, they've spent six months in there. I know that what some people say about concentration camps is quite untrue –' she shot Joanna a glance – 'but I don't know what they'll be like.'

'When are you going to see them?'

'Well . . . not for a while. Then I'll be visiting them.'

'Visiting them where?'

'At Paulliac, of course. That's where they're going. Home.'

'Your parents are being released from Dachau, and being sent home, just like that, with no strings attached?'

'Yes. Which just goes to show how wrong you are about the regime. They made a mistake about Mummy and Daddy's involvement in the destruction of that train, and they're honest enough to admit it.'

Joanna regarded her for several moments, then she said, 'Holy shitting cows!'

'What's the matter now?'

'It's a trap, don't you see? They, whoever is pulling the strings, are reckoning that if your parents go home, Liane will try to see them, or at least get in touch with them.'

'I don't believe that. You're just determined to prove that whatever the government does has to be evil.'

'Everything this government does *is* evil.'

'Look, please leave. And please don't come back. I don't want to see you again.'

Joanna stood up. 'You don't care what happens to your sister?'

Madeleine also stood. 'Nothing is going to happen to my

sister that hasn't already, except in your diseased imagination. Now get out.'

Joanna closed the door and went down the stairs. She wasn't angry with Madeleine, who was simply a poor mixed-up kid, but she was definitely agitated. She had spent the past six months thinking of Liane, brave, determined, resourceful Liane, out there on her own . . . James had seen her last October, and he had been with her on that tremendous raid on the railway line. He had said that she was fine, and surrounded by a band of loyal friends and followers, including Amalie. But that had been six months ago. Now . . .

The thought of Liane in the hands of the Gestapo made her skin crawl. While the success of that raid, and in avoiding capture afterwards, might just make her think she was invulnerable, and thus encourage her to walk into the Gestapo trap! Liane had always felt she was invulnerable.

Joanna reached the ground floor, nodded to the doorman, stepped on to the pavement, and checked. There was a man on the far side of the street, leaning against a shop wall, and reading a newspaper. Having been trained by British intelligence, Joanna knew immediately what he was, but she realized she would have known anyway; he had detective written all over him. For a moment she felt quite cold: however often she worried about Liane falling into the hands of the Gestapo, it had never really occurred to her that it could happen to her. Then she remembered that it *couldn't* happen to her. Not really. They could arrest her, but a simple telephone call to either the American or the Swedish ambassador would free her. And if there was a little rough stuff before then, well, that wouldn't be the first time in her life. The worst that could happen would be for her to be deported, which would mean the end of her career as a spy.

She felt almost tempted to cross the street and chat him up, let him know she was on to him. Then she suddenly realized that he need not be watching her at all. She had not been aware of being followed when she had left her hotel. And there was no reason for it. If the Germans had the least suspicion of who and what she really was, they would have arrested her at Hamburg, or prevented her entering the country at all. So he was actually watching the Helsingen's flat, or that of someone else in the building. But it seemed most likely that the Gestapo would be interested in the sister of a known terrorist, especially now that they were laying such an elaborate trap for that terrorist.

Should she go back up and warn her? She decided against it. Madeleine had made her own bed and seemed determined to lie on it, come hell or high water. She would have to take her chances with the people she now called friends.

Joanna hurried back to her hotel, avoiding the bomb craters which were starting to accumulate in Berlin despite Goering's erstwhile boast that it could never happen, went up to her room, and began telephoning. It took some time, as, like everything else, what she wanted required various permits, but in her case it was a matter of hours instead of days, and by late afternoon she had her seat on a train leaving Berlin for Lubeck the next morning, and a berth on a steamer for Stockholm the following night. Once she was there she could safely contact James and tell him to warn Liane of her danger.

She poured a hot bath and was about to get in when there was a knock on her door. She presumed it was the floor maid come to turn down the bed, and shouted, 'It's OK. Leave it.'

But a man replied. 'I have an urgent message for Fräulein Jonsson.'

Joanna considered for a moment. Gestapo? They would hardly be so polite. Someone from James? James had never made any attempt to contact her before; he left her to her own devices. But there was a simple way to find out. She pulled on her dressing gown, stood against the door. 'Sterling?'

There was a moment's hesitation, then the man said, 'Pound Seven.'

Joanna drew a deep breath, released the latch, opened the door and jerked it inwards, reaching though the aperture to grab the man by the lapels of his jacket and jerk him into

43

the room. Taken entirely by surprise he gasped, and before he could regain his balance Joanna had kicked the door shut, released him, and swung her right hand, slamming the edge with all of her twelve stones of weight into his right kidney. He went down with a faint shriek of agony, hitting the floor with a crash. Joanna crouched above him, placing her right knee on has back. 'Tell me when the pain starts to wear off and we'll have a chat.'

He continued to moan. 'You have injured me.'

'So be lucky. If I'd aimed that blow at your neck you'd be dead.' While she spoke she ran her hands over his jacket and then under it, but did not discover any concealed weapon. Satisfied, she got off him, rearranged her dressing gown, and went to the sideboard, where there was a bottle of cognac. She filled a glass. 'Come and get it.'

Slowly he pushed himself to his knees, remained there for several seconds while he got his breathing under control, staring at her. She took him in as well. He was a youngish man, only a few years older than herself, she estimated, not as tall as she was either, slightly built, and shabbily dressed. But he was quite good-looking in a mousy fashion. 'You'll live,' she assured him.

'I used the password.'

'You didn't reply to mine.'

'It has been changed.'

'Is that a fact. No one troubled to inform me.' The young man got to his feet and moved towards her, uncertainly. 'You wouldn't be thinking of trying anything stupid,' Joanna said. 'I could take you apart with one hand tied behind my back.'

'I have been told this.' He stood before her, and looked at the glass of cognac.

'Drink it. It'll put some colour in your cheeks.' He took the glass and gulped it. 'Have another,' Joanna invited. His hands were still shaking, and the neck of the bottle clattered against the glass. 'So the password is now Pound,' Joanna observed. 'Given to you by whom?'

This time he was able to sip the drink. 'By Pound One.'

44

'And you're not talking about Ezra.' Her intellectual witticism was obviously over his head, for he merely looked bewildered. 'You understand that you will have to identify yourself. What's all this number thing?'

'I know who you are. And the numbers are the new system. You are Pound Three.'

'Say, that must mean I'm senior to you. You said you had an urgent message.'

'London wants you back in England. Immediately.'

'Is that a fact.' She considered. 'OK. I'll go along with that. Are you in touch with them?'

'I can communicate. But it is dangerous.'

'Tell me about it. How long does it take you to get a message to London? You have a transmitter?'

'Yes. But I have orders not to use it except in circumstances of imminent catastrophe.'

Joanna considered, but she had to doubt if London would feel that the possibility of Liane being entrapped by the Gestapo a sufficient catastrophe to blow one of their so carefully planted agents. James, perhaps might think so, although she couldn't even be sure of that cold fish, but that stuffy brigadier who was his boss . . . 'So how *do* you communicate?'

'I have a courier who travels to Switzerland, where he can use a radio safely. Three days.'

'Um.' If everything went smoothly, she would be in Stockholm the day after tomorrow, when *she* would be able to use a radio safely. But there was always the chance of a hitch. 'Can he leave tomorrow?'

'I think it can be arranged.'

'Right. Have another drink.' She went to the table, used the pad of paper waiting there. *On my way. But best claret gone sour. Please abort all sales until I reach you.* She tore the sheet off and handed it to him.

'This is a code? I do not know it. And you have not used your signature.'

'It's a private communication between Pound One and

45

me. You can send it in clear. It's speed that matters.' He folded the paper and put it in his pocket. 'Now tell me how I can get in touch with you should I need you.'

'It would be very dangerous.'

'Don't start that again.' She indicated the pad. 'Write it down. I'll memorize it and then burn it. Promise.' He hesitated, then obeyed. Joanna read the address and wrinkled her nose; he apparently lived in about the least salubrious part of Berlin.

She raised her head and found him staring at her. 'You are a very beautiful woman.'

'What a charming thing to say.'

'Would you like me to stay for an hour? I cannot meet my courier until later tonight.'

'I'd love to, little man, but my bath water is getting cold. Besides, I might squash you.'

'One visitor all week?' Reinhard Heydrich leaned back in his chair.

'She seems to live a very quiet life,' Oskar Weber agreed. 'But the visitor was Joanna Jonsson.'

'I know this woman. I have met her at several party functions. She is an American journalist. I believe she is quite well known over there. She is also the daughter of an extremely wealthy American woman and a member of the Swedish government. The parents are divorced, so she spends some time travelling between their two countries. We have a file on her.'

'It does not appear to be very complete.'

Heydrich frowned. 'What do you mean? Her despatches are always submitted to the censors, and I am informed they are always pro-regime.'

'And her friendship with Frau von Helsingen?'

'I believe she knew the family before the war. There is nothing sinister in them visiting each other.'

'Did you know that she and Liane de Gruchy were at school together in Switzerland?'

Heydrich's frown returned. 'I did not know that. But surely that was some time ago?'

'1928.'

'And you think they are still friends?'

'Old schoolmates often remain friends for life. Did you know that Liane de Gruchy was raped by some German soldiers in the first days of the invasion, when she rather stupidly ventured north of Paris?'

'There was some such report. That does not excuse what she has done since.'

'Of course it does not. But do you know that she was not alone when she was assaulted? There was another woman with her, who also suffered rape. That woman was an American journalist who was a friend of the family. Joanna Jonsson.'

Slowly Heydrich sat up. 'Who knows about this?'

'The whole thing was hushed up as being bad for propaganda. The men were hanged for desertion, not for rape. But Kluck certainly knew about it. He was the senior Gestapo officer with Rommel's panzer brigade.'

'Who hushed it up?' Heydrich asked.

'Well, I have no doubt that he was acting on orders. And the matter was successfully brushed under the carpet. As far as I have been able to find out, Jonsson left France almost immediately and returned to America. It was apparently feared that she might publicize what happened, and cause us some embarrassment, but it seems that she either decided against it or was talked out of it. On the other hand, we know that she did not stay in America, but got her paper to give her an European assignment.'

'This is splendid detective work, Oskar. But it is all also very circumstantial. In fact, it makes it more reasonable for Jonsson to call on Frau von Helsingen, especially in view of such a shared experience.'

'It was not Madeleine von Helsingen who shared the experience.'

'All right. This woman was at school with Liane de Gruchy,

and shared an unfortunate experience with her. Have you any evidence to suggest that she is still in touch with her? Or wants to be? It is often the case that two people who share a common but distasteful experience become estranged.'

'I do not deal in psychology, Reinhard. I deal in facts, and the fact to which I would like to draw your attention is that this woman, who underwent a horrifying experience at the hands of German soldiers and left France in what we may assume was a distraught state, is back again, in Berlin, and has been back several times during the past six months, writing despatches extolling the virtues of Nazi Germany. I suggest you put that to one of your tame psychologists and obtain his opinion on the likelihood of any woman being that forgiving.'

'What are you suggesting?'

'I am suggesting that this woman is an enemy of the Reich. I am also suggesting that she has some means of being in contact with her old school chum and fellow rape victim Liane de Gruchy, and that she is acting as a go-between for the two sisters. Which must mean that she knows where Liane de Gruchy is, or at least how to get in touch with her.'

Heydrich drummed his fingers on his desk. 'Where is she living?'

'She uses the Albert Hotel when she is in Berlin. But she is not there now.'

'You said that she saw Madeleine von Helsingen only a couple of days ago.'

'That is correct. But she left Berlin again the following day, for Sweden. This, incidentally, after arriving *from* Sweden only two days before that. Which is in itself suspicious.'

'Do you expect her to come back again?'

'Well, she has been doing that fairly regularly since last autumn. Do you mean to arrest her?'

'How can I do that without causing a diplomatic row?'

'What about the Helsingen woman?'

'With her husband one of Hitler's blue-eyed boys? But there is a glimmer of light there. You know that Barbarossa is definitely on?'

'I know that we are forbidden to discuss it.'

Heydrich gave a cold smile. 'I issued that order. I also happen to know that Helsingen has volunteered, indeed he has insisted, on being given a field command. He dreams of military glory. So very shortly he will be leaving Berlin.'

'But he will be coming back.'

'Who can tell?'

'Is it not going to be a pushover?'

'Probably. But pushing over several million men, even if they aren't resisting very hard, still takes time and effort. And some of them will certainly resist. But whether he stops a bullet or not, I do not think victory will be secured much before the autumn. Even European Russia is a very big country. The moment Helsingen is gone from Berlin, I wish you to start putting pressure on his wife. Be subtle, but ruthless. She is not a very strong character. She will very rapidly panic.'

Weber stood up. 'She is a handsome woman. I think I will enjoy doing this. And the other one?' He grinned. 'She is an even more attractive woman.'

'Yes,' Heydrich agreed. 'I wish to know the moment she returns to Berlin.'

Three

The Route

'Well, look who's here,' Rachel remarked.

'Pound Three,' Joanna said. 'For what it's worth.'

James got up and came round the desk. 'Where in the name of God have you been?'

'Aren't you going to kiss me?'

'I'm tempted to put you under arrest.'

'Oh, well . . .' She sat down, crossed her knees. 'Mom was agitating, so I had to go home for a visit.'

'Just like that? Without letting anyone know?'

'I didn't think you'd be interested in my domestic movements.'

'Your domestic movements, everything about you, are my business.'

'You say the sweetest things. So tell me when the code name was changed.'

'Some time ago.'

'Just like that, and nobody thought to inform me.'

'Nobody knew where you were. But Joachim seems to have found you.'

'So that's what his name was. Funny little fellow. But kind of cute.'

'Oh, my God! You didn't . . .'

'No, I did not. We had a small misunderstanding at first, because we were using different passwords, but once that was cleared up we got on very well. Now tell me, did you get my message.'

'I got a message.'

'And you've put Liane's lot on hold?'

'It wasn't necessary. They're on hold anyway. What was it all about?' Joanna explained. 'Would this be the same source as gave you that incorrect information of a German war with Russia?'

'It was not incorrect information.'

'Have you looked at a calendar recently?'

'It's been put back a month because of this business in the Balkans. It's going to happen mid-June.'

'Does he talk in his sleep,' Rachel asked, 'or only when he's having sex?'

'Wouldn't you like to know.'

'Let me put it to you straight,' James said. 'The brigadier feels you've been stringing us along, and he's not happy. If this latest info isn't correct . . .'

'It's me for the Tower. OK. But it's correct. I'd stake my life on it.'

'You may have just done that. Get the brigadier, will you, Rachel.'

'What about the Gruchys?' Joanna asked.

'You're positive it's a trap? Your source tell you that?'

'No. It's a logical deduction. People don't get released from concentration camps just because someone may feel they're not guilty. Those camps aren't concerned with guilt or innocence. They're for getting rid of people the regime doesn't like.'

'And they don't like the older Gruchys. Why?'

'They're Liane's parents. And Pierre's. And Amalie's.'

'But they're also Madeleine's parents. Isn't her husband big with Hitler?'

'Sure. That doesn't mean he's not keen on getting hold of Liane. And the fact is, Madeleine doesn't count with her family anymore, or they with her.'

'Have you seen her?'

'I call on her whenever I'm in Berlin.'

'And how is she?'

51

'Still carrying a torch. She gives every impression of being a contented hausfrau.'

'Does she have any idea what you're doing?'

'Shit, no! She thinks I'm the ultimate layabout, fiddling while Europe burns. So what are you going to do about the Gruchys?'

'There's not a lot I can do. As I said, Liane's people have been stood down for the moment. Telling them about the return of their parents, with or without your suspicions, is likely to stir them up again, and we don't want that right now.'

Joanna stood up. 'You mean you're saving them for some big deal, and you don't give a fuck about them as people. They're not children. They'll handle it, but they need to know. Liane does, anyway.'

'I'm sure she'll find out in due course.'

'She's in the Massif Central, isn't she? Aren't you in constant touch with her?'

'Where Liane happens to be is classified. As for being in touch, we contact each other when it is absolutely necessary, or when there is an emergency.'

'And you don't call this an emergency?'

'In the context of the war, no.'

Joanna glared at him, and Rachel said, 'I have the brigadier on the line.'

Liane stood on the street outside her apartment, looking up at the windows. She had the strongest temptation to go up and see what was left, if anything. But that would be crazy. If she had made the journey without difficulty, thanks to her black-dyed hair, which Amalie had cut short, and her inconsequential grey suit, provided by one of the women in the village, her low-heeled shoes and her beret, not to mention her carefully forged papers and travel documents, she still knew that the slightest mistake could betray her. The apartment would still be there after the war. After the victory. She had to believe that. But it was still necessary to take calculated risks; she also had to believe that the average Frenchman would not betray her, certainly when he was an old friend.

She turned away and walked towards the river, her heavy satchel bumping on her back. On the left bank she headed for her favourite bar. There were some men seated at a table in the corner; they all turned their heads to look at the pretty woman with the good legs. So did the barman, leaning on his counter; he was a big, roughly good-looking man with lank black hair who needed a shave. Liane leaned on the counter. 'Hello, Achille.'

He stared at her for several seconds; then his mouth sagged open. 'Liane? My God, Liane!'

'Softly. Can we speak?'

'Of course.' He poured Pernod, added water. 'Jacqueline!' he shouted. 'Come in here.' The girl, gauntly handsome with long dark hair, came in from the back. 'Mind the bar,' Achille said, and raised the hatch to allow Liane through.

Jacqueline gave her a hard stare as she went into the back room. 'She's new.'

'There has been a considerable upheaval. But she is all right. She is my sister.'

'I did not know you had a sister.'

'Well, when last you were here, she was a schoolgirl.'

'You must not tell her who I am.'

He grinned. 'I will tell her you are one of my old mistresses.' They gazed at each other, and he flushed; she knew he had always wanted to get his hands on her during those heady days before the war, but had never dared attempt it. That long-suppressed desire was one of her weapons. 'But to see you here . . . You know there is a price on your head?'

Liane sat at the table, drank some Pernod. 'Do you wish to collect it?'

'Of course I do not. I am just afraid of the danger you are in.'

'Did you recognize me?'

53

'Not until you spoke.'

'Well, then, no one else is likely to, either.'

'But why are you here?'

'I am working for the Resistance.'

'The Resistance?'

'You have not heard of it?'

'Well, there are rumours.'

'Which are based on the truth.'

'There is no Resistance here in Paris.'

Liane smiled. 'We are going to change that.'

Achille scratched his head. 'It will be very dangerous.'

'Are you afraid? You will be working with me. If you work with me, I will be your mistress in fact as well as fiction. Would you not like that?'

He licked his lips. 'You would live here, with me?'

'Yes. Starting today. Now, there are people I need to meet.'

Achille had remained standing by the door. Now he came across the room to stand beside her. He took off her beret and ran his hands over her hair and then down to her neck. 'Do you know how I have dreamed of this?'

'I have seen it in your eyes often enough. I will be good, I promise you. But I am here to work, for France. And so must you. Is Laurent still around?'

'Oh, yes. He was in here yesterday.'

'You mean he has not been arrested?'

'Well, the Germans have not yet caught up with him, and the police are ignoring him for the moment.'

'Get word to him that I wish to see him.'

'But you will be my woman.'

'Entirely. I wish him to work for me.'

'You have papers?' Suddenly he was anxious.

'I have papers. How do you think I got here? My name is Sandrine Bouchard. I wish Laurent to forge papers for others.'

'What others?'

'I will tell him as I need them. But he must start work

54

now, making them up, leaving only the descriptions and the place for the photographs blank for the time being.'

'I will bring him to see you.'

'Next, I wish the use of a house.'

'But you will live here.'

'Yes, I will. But I need the house for friends of mine who from time to time may visit Paris. The house must be safe from investigation by the Germans.'

Achille considered, then snapped his fingers. 'Madame Constance.'

'You mean she is also still in business?'

'Oh, yes. She now has the best house in Paris. Because it has been taken over by the Germans.'

'And that is safe?'

'Of course. Don't you see? The Germans have given her a licence, under which she accepts only their officers. They will never search her place.'

'And you think she will conceal my friends under their very noses?'

Achille shrugged. 'That you will have to find out.'

'Then give me her address.'

'I will do this. But first, you will come upstairs.' His hands were coursing over her shoulders and down to her breasts. 'I am on fire.'

He was an earthy man, and so very adoring. But he also took a very long time to get a sufficient erection. Liane supposed this was because he was really very nervous, anxious at once to possess and to please. His hands roamed over her body, from her shoulders to her feet. He made her lie on her stomach so that he could caress and squeeze her buttocks, but he also wanted to play with her toes and stroke her calves. Then he wanted to kiss her all over, suck her nipples, put his head between her legs. Actually, she enjoyed it, although she would have preferred him to be clean-shaven. And at last he made it, and collapsed panting beside her. 'You are magnificent,' he said.

As she had not actually done anything, she considered this might be the easiest part of her mission. 'So were you,' she said, and got up.

'Where are you going?' he asked in alarm.

'I'm going to unpack.' She opened her rucksack, took out the single change of underclothes she had with her, then began removing the various dismantled pieces of equipment.

He sat up to watch her. 'That is a gun.'

'It is a Luger automatic pistol.'

He scratched his head. 'And what are those?'

'When I have assembled them, it will be a radio receiver.'

'A radio?' His voice was high. 'You cannot have a radio. It is against the law.'

'Achille, my being here at all is against the law. Do you wish me to leave?'

He gazed at her naked body. 'No, I do not wish you to leave. But why do we need a radio?'

'It is necessary so that we can be told when my friends are to be expected. The calls will be made either at six in the morning or six in the evening. I will usually be here to take them, but I will teach you how to use it.'

'Will the Germans not be able to trace such calls?'

'Given enough time, perhaps. But it is simply a receiver, not a transmitter, and they will find that very difficult to trace. Now, the calls will always be very brief and in code.'

'What is this code?'

'I will teach you that as well. Enough of it, anyway.' She looked at her watch. 'It is five o'clock. What time does the bar get busy?'

'Half past six, maybe.'

'Then you have the time to get dressed and go out and find Laurent. I wish to see him tonight.'

'And Madame Constance?'

'I will attend to her tomorrow.'

The house was set back from the street, in a large unkempt garden. It was four-square and four-storeyed, with shuttered windows, and sadly needed a coat of paint, but then, so did most of the houses in Paris. The wrought-iron double gate was unlocked; Liane pushed it open and went in.

The house actually looked deserted as she walked up the path to the front steps, but as it was eleven in the morning it was obviously not working hours. She rang the bell, and waited for several minutes, until she heard shuffling steps and a moment later the door swung in to reveal a middle-aged woman in a dressing gown. As she lacked either looks or chic Liane reckoned she was a maid. 'We are not open,' she said, and then realized she was addressing a woman. 'We do not need anyone.'

'I think Madame Constance should be the judge of that,' Liane said. 'I wish to see her. Now.' The sudden authority in her voice made the woman step backwards, and Liane stepped inside and closed the door behind her. The hall was gloomy after the bright sunlight, but she could tell at a glance that it was tastefully furnished, and could be well lit; there was a crystal chandelier, filled with electric light bulbs. On the right, large double doors, presently closed, led to an obvious reception room. On the left there was another, smaller door, and in front of her there rose a wide staircase with a reverse bend halfway up. Beyond the staircase the hall continued for some distance, no doubt to the pantry and kitchen. 'Where do I go?'

'Madame!' the woman called. 'Madame! This woman—'

'Thank you, Marguerite,' a voice said. Liane looked at the stairs, and the woman descending them. She was quite tall, and strongly built, and had handsome, forceful features and a mass of obviously dyed red hair. She also wore a dressing gown, made of silk as opposed to the maid's cotton, and came down the stairs slowly and gracefully. But clearly she liked what saw. 'Well,' she said, 'I have not seen you before.'

'I would like to speak with you. In private.'

'Come into the office.' She reached the floor and indicated the small door. Liane went towards it. 'It is open,' Madame

Constance said, and followed her into the room, where there was, predictably, a desk and two comfortable chairs. Constance seated herself behind the desk. 'You are from Paris?'

'Once upon a time.'

'And now you are back. Your name?'

'Sandrine Bouchard.'

Constance gazed at her for several moments. 'There is something familiar about your face. Have we met?'

'I do not remember doing so.'

'It is not important. As Marguerite told you, we have no need of additional help, but if your figure matches your face I might be able to squeeze you in. Strip off and let me look at you.'

Liane sat down and crossed her knees, her bag on her lap; Constance raised her eyebrows. 'I am not seeking employment, Constance. I am here to employ *you*. If you are suitable.'

'Just who do you think you are?'

'I know who I am. My real name is Liane de Gruchy.'

Constance opened her mouth and then closed it again. Her right hand dropped beside the desk, but before she could either open the drawer or press the bell Liane had opened her satchel and levelled her Luger pistol. 'I took this from the body of a Gestapo officer I killed,' she said. 'It does not actually make a lot of noise. But it does hold nine bullets, and the magazine is presently full. So put both your hands on the desk, and pray that no one comes through that door.'

Constance gasped 'What do you want?'

'You were recommended to me by Achille Custace.'

Constance's eyebrows went up again. 'You wish sex?'

'Not right this minute. I have told you, I wish to employ you.'

'I am fully employed. So are my girls. Every night from six in the evening to six in the morning.'

'I do not wish to interfere with your business, Constance.

I simply wish the use of one, or perhaps two, of your rooms from time to time. As a place to rest for my friends when they happen to be in Paris.'

'Your friends? People who are on the run from the Germans? You must be mad. It is German officers who come here. This house is reserved for them.'

'That is why my friends will be safe here. Are your girls trustworthy?'

'I have not had to trust them with anything like this before. Anyway, I cannot do it. It is too risky. We could all be shot, or sent to a concentration camp. Or even hanged.'

'I would like you to listen to me,' Liane said. 'Very carefully. We are a very large organization, and we have agents everywhere. You need to remember this, that should anything happen to me, my associates have the names of everyone I have seen or will see in Paris, and will pay them all a visit. You also need to remember that when the war is over, and we have won, we are going to remember everyone who assisted us with gratitude, and everyone who did not assist us with disfavour.'

Constance stared at her, but Liane knew that she spoke with such confident authority that the woman could not be sure whether or not she was telling the truth, nor was she in a position to dare risk finding out.

'Now,' Liane went on, 'you will be informed when your guests will be arriving, and when they will be leaving again. Obviously it will be most convenient, and safest, if they arrive during the day, when you are not entertaining. The transfers will be made as rapidly as possible, but sometimes they may have to remain here for two or three days. While they are here you will be visited by a friend of mine who will take their photographs and issue them with papers. If any questions are asked, you will say that he comes to photograph your girls. He will do that as well.'

'It is madness,' Constance muttered.

'Any risk you take will be for France. It will be up to you what you tell your girls, or Marguerite, but they will have to know that these men are seeking refuge from the Gestapo. You will receive a payment of five hundred francs per man per day. I suggest you share that with your people. Once they accept money they are committed, but I also suggest that you tell them what I have told you about the consequences of betrayal. Now, do you speak English?'

'I have some.'

'That should do. It is unlikely that many of your guests, if any, will speak French.' She wagged her finger to and fro as Constance's eyebrows went up again. 'You should not even attempt to think about them. Just conceal them, feed them, and have them ready for collection. Are there any questions?'

'These men, these fugitives, suppose they wish to use my girls?'

'Then they must pay for it. Although I very much doubt that they will be in the mood for sex.'

'They will be clean?'

'When they arrive, probably not. But you can bathe them.'

'I meant, they will not have VD.'

'I very much doubt that, either. But I'm sure you can tell if a man is diseased by looking at his genitals. If anyone should be, then you must forbid him the use of your girls. They will not argue with you. Was there anything else?'

'Yes. You will be back again?'

'Regularly. Both to pay you and to check things out. I may also from time to time have to deliver your guests, and collect them again. But it will not always be me.'

'I need to be able to reach you. Just in case there is a crisis.'

'You must make sure there is not a crisis.' Liane stood up. 'It has been a pleasure speaking with you, madame. I will let myself out.'

Liane's next stop was the Paris office of de Gruchy and Son. She knew the building well, and went up to the reception desk. 'I would like to see Monsieur Brissard, please.'

The woman behind the desk looked her up and down. 'Monsieur Brissard is a very busy man, mademoiselle.'

'He will see me. Tell him I have news of the family.'

Another long stare. 'You know Paulliac?'

'I have just come from there.'

'Wait here.' The woman left the desk and disappeared into the office. From the amount of noise back there Liane decided the business was doing well, even without Papa running things. The woman returned. 'Come with me.' Liane followed her through the office, attracting glances from the clerks seated at the high desks entering invoices. She knew where the manager's office was located, knew the interior of this as well, just as she knew the grey-haired, hunched-shouldered man who sat behind the desk. 'Mademoiselle Bouchard,' the woman said.

'Well?' Henri Brissard asked, without raising his head.

'What I have to say is for your ears alone,' Liane said, speaking very softly. Now Brissard did raise his head, his expression one of incredulity. 'So kindly leave us, madame,' Liane said.

The woman gave her boss an outraged glare, but Brissard was nodding. She left the room, closing the door, and Brissard got up and came round the desk. 'Mademoiselle Liane?' He peered at her. 'My God! It is incredible. Your hair . . .'

She embraced him, kissed him on both cheeks. 'I do not wish to be recognized, except by people I know I can trust.'

'But to come to Paris . . . To come here . . .'

'There is no danger. I am staying with a friend who is absolutely reliable. As for coming here, will you betray me?'

'Of course I will not. But the danger . . .'

'There will be no danger as long as we all keep our heads.'

He guided her to a settee against the wall, and sat beside her. 'You wish money?'

'Yes. How is the business doing?'

'Very well.'

'Who is managing at Paulliac?'

'Jacques Bouterre.'

'I remember Jacques. Is he doing a good job?'

'An excellent job. As I said, we are doing well. There are

61

no overseas sales, of course, but the Germans like good wine. I imagine your Papa will wish to leave Jacques in control, at least until he finds his feet again.'

'I do not understand you. Papa is in prison in Germany.'

'No, no, mademoiselle. He and your mother were returned from Germany two weeks ago. They are back in Paulliac.'

Liane stared at him in utter consternation. From the way he was speaking there could be no doubt that it was true. Which meant it could only be Madeleine's doing. If that were so, she thought she could almost forgive her sister for marrying a Nazi. But . . . 'They are alone there?'

'No, no, mademoiselle. The servants are there.'

'I meant, are there any members of the family with them?'

'Well, no, mademoiselle. With Madame Burstein dead . . . Did you not know of that?'

'I heard of it.'

'So tragic. And then Monsieur Pierre . . . You know he had to flee Paris last October. The Germans say he was operating an illegal radio. But when they went to arrest him, he had disappeared. They think he got into Vichy.'

'What of Madeleine?'

'Oh, well, Mademoiselle Madeleine married a German officer and left the country.'

'You are sure she is not also in Paulliac?'

'I do not think so. I have not heard of it. And frankly, mademoiselle, I am not sure she would be welcome there.'

What to do? If she found it difficult to believe that, having arrested her parents, the Gestapo had decided to let them go, it could only be because of Helsingen's intervention, which, with his reputed close links to Hitler, was entirely possible. Thus they were living in Paulliac under German auspices. Did that make them collaborators, like Madeleine? Would they be so considered after the war? But the only alternative would be to go to Paulliac and get them out of there. To go where? She doubted they would survive in the Massif Central. She wondered if James would be prepared to fly them to England; as far as she knew the family still maintained a flat in Sloane Square, and she knew that Albert de Gruchy had always kept a considerable amount of money invested in England, as well as large balances in various English banks. While Mama, who *was* English, would have all her family and their wealth to support her. That would certainly be the answer. But she had no means of communicating with James until she returned to Moulin's headquarters. The temptation to go back now was enormous. But her responsibilities here in Paris were even more enormous. 'Mademoiselle?' Brissard asked, anxiously.

Papa and Mama would have to wait. They would be quite safe in Paulliac, under German protection, no matter what people might think of them. The war was not going to end this year, that was certain, and she would again be in touch with James long before then. Dear James. He was, or appeared to be, so utterly in love with her. Even if she knew he disapproved of the life she had lived before the war, he still, again apparently, dreamed of marrying her. What would he say of the life she was living now, as the mistress of a somewhat disreputable bar owner? But he was a dream for her too, of peace and security when this was over. And love? She did not suppose that she had ever loved anyone in her life. But he was a man she *could* love. If she ever had the time. 'I'm sorry, Henri.' Brissard was now looking quite agitated. 'I was thinking of my parents. Do you know when I last saw them? The 10th of May, 1940. The day of Amalie's wedding. The day the Germans invaded. That is more than a year ago.'

'A terrible year. If there is anything I can do to help . . .'

'Yes. That is why I am here. As I said, I need money.'

'Of course, mademoiselle. How much money?'

'I need ten thousand francs to begin with.'

'You wish it placed in your bank account?'

'I cannot touch my bank account, Henri. The Germans are certainly keeping an eye on it, and they would know I have been in Paris. It must be in cash.'

'I will arrange it. Will tomorrow be soon enough?'

63

'Tomorrow will be fine. I will then need another ten thousand, perhaps in a month's time, perhaps in a fortnight. I will let you know. These drawings will continue for the foreseeable future. '

Brissard scratched his head. 'It will be difficult.'

'You said the business is doing well.'

'It is. But such amounts will have to be accounted for.'

'Are you not the manager?'

'I am the Paris manager, mademoiselle. The director is Monsieur Bouterre. I can manage to lose ten thousand francs. But ten thousand francs a month, or a fortnight, well, questions will be asked. Eventually.'

'Isn't Bouterre trustworthy?'

'His appointment had to be approved by the local commander, a Colonel Hoeppner. I do not know what passed between Monsieur Bouterre and Colonel Hoeppner, what pressures Colonel Hoeppner may be able to bring to bear.'

'I see.' Liane wished she had been more interested in her father's business when she had had the opportunity. 'How often are the books audited?'

'Every six months.'

'And when last was it done?'

'Actually, only a few weeks ago. It was done when your parents were sent away and Bouterre took over. That was in October. Then it was done again in April.'

'So it will not be done again until October. That is four months away.'

'But it will be done. And then I will be sacked, if I am not imprisoned for embezzlement.'

Liane squeezed his hand. 'By then I will have sorted it out. I give you my word. Now you make the first withdrawal, and I will see you tomorrow.'

The man leaned on the bar counter. 'Laurent sent me.'

Liane drew beer. 'Do you know why?'

'He said it is for France.'

Liane looked over the bar. It was half past five, about the

slackest part of the day; there were only two customers, drinking at a table in the corner, and they were regulars. 'Your name?'

'Andre Voix.'

'And you are prepared to work for France?' she asked in a low voice. 'To risk all for France?'

'I am prepared to risk all for you, Mademoiselle Liane.'

'My name is Sandrine Bouchard. Remember this. Do you have special skills?'

'I work for the post office. I repair telephone lines.'

'I think that may be very valuable, in time. What I wish you to do first, Andre, is meet the Brussels train on Monday. Two of your cousins will be on it, coming to Paris to look for work. They do not speak French, but I will give you their descriptions.'

'They will have papers?'

'I am told so. In any event, Laurent will have fresh papers waiting for them here.'

'I am to take them to Laurent?'

'No. You are to take them to Madame Constance.' Andre Voix rolled his eyes. 'She will be expecting you,' Liane said. 'If any questions are asked before they get into the house, you are taking them there to seek work as gardeners. Once they are inside, you have no more interest in them. You merely go back to work. But come into the bar once a week and see me. Can you do these things for me?'

'I can do anything for you, mademoiselle.'

Liane squeezed his hand. 'That makes me very happy.'

'Pound,' said the brigadier.

'Pound Two,' Rachel acknowledged.

'Put James on.'

Rachel held up the phone, mouthing, 'The boss.'

'Sir.'

'James, at dawn this morning the German army crossed the Russian frontier.'

'My God! But that is tremendous news!'

65

'There are only sketchy reports at the moment, but it does appear as though the invasion is on a massive scale, and that it has achieved total surprise. It seems that Stalin has been caught entirely on the hop. Well, we did try to warn him. From our point of view, it means that Jonsson has justified our trust. The PM would like to meet her.'

'I'm afraid she's not in the country, sir.'

'You haven't sent her off again? I gave instructions that she was to be kept here.'

'I know, sir. But she is very difficult to control, with her family background, and her contacts, and the fact that she is not English, and was never actually inducted into the SIS.'

'What? What do you mean?'

'Well, sir, you may remember that she absconded from our training school because she didn't like the discipline. Then she disappeared for several months, before returning last year with the news of Hitler's intentions. Then she went off again, and returned, briefly, a month ago, to confirm that information. Then she left again.'

'To go where?'

'Officially, to visit her father in Stockholm. I don't expect her to stay there. She's probably back in Berlin by now.'

'That is quite unacceptable. We cannot have a loose cannon like that wandering about the place with her head stuffed full of our secrets.'

'With respect, sir, she knows none of our secrets, other than our password. And she did turn up that vital piece of information, even if Marshal Stalin chose to ignore it. I'm inclined to let her go for the moment. Her heart is with us, and she does seem to have a very potent source in Berlin.'

'Hm. I take your point, but I still don't like it. However, she is your baby, and you will have to carry the can for her.'

'So what's new,' Rachel muttered.

'Now what about the route?' the brigadier asked.

'That has been successfully established. I am informed

that the first two evaders have passed through Paris into Vichy and thence Spain. I have not had confirmation, but they should be in Portugal by now and so will be home in another week.'

'Now that is excellent news. Are you in touch with the people operating it?'

'From time to time, sir.'

'Well, do congratulate them for me. They will be fully recognized when this show is over.'

'Thank you, sir. Am I allowed to ask if there have been any developments in the Hess business?'

'There have been no developments, James. Nor are there likely to be any. The Germans are claiming he's gone off his head, as they would, but we are coming to the conclusion that they may be right. He seems to have been under the impression that because he once met the Duke of Hamilton, if he could get together with him he could sort out the differences between Britain and Germany and end the war. You have to give him credit for being an excellent pilot and navigator. To fly a Messerschmitt single-handed from Germany to Scotland and actually crash it on Hamilton's estate was quite a feat.'

'What will happen to him?'

'He's been locked up, and he will stay locked up, at least until the end of the war. Good day to you, James. And for God's sake, keep an eye on that termagant of yours.'

Rachel replaced the phone.

'What exactly does the word "termagant" mean?' James asked.

'Ah . . . a savage, violent, boisterous, overwhelming woman. I'd say that sums Joanna up, wouldn't you?' James blew her a raspberry.

'Heil Hitler!' said the small, dark man standing in the office doorway. He wore a neat suit and tie, but had a military bearing.

Franz Hoeppner leaned back in the swivel chair behind

the desk and surveyed his visitor. In his early thirties, Colonel Hoeppner was a handsome man, with crisp fair hair, cut very short, and blue eyes. He was normally good-humoured, but this morning he was not. The official communiqué lay on his desk. It seemed that everyone who was anyone was now in Russia. Even his oldest friend, Freddie von Helsingen, was commanding a regiment in the invasion forces. But no one, not even Freddie or Hoeppner's own uncle, the panzer general, had bothered to inform him the war with Russia was going to start. He had been abandoned, stuck in the backwater that was Bordeaux, which was as far away from any fighting as it was possible to get, left to chase smugglers and nursemaid elderly innocents who had found themselves at odds with the Gestapo. He fully intended to correct the situation. He had in fact been in the midst of drafting a letter requesting a transfer to a fighting unit when he had been interrupted.

And now the Gestapo was in his office, which could only be to do with the de Gruchys. It was not a business he understood at all. His sympathies were largely with the family. Brought up as a Nazi, like his friend Helsingen, he firmly believed that Hitler was the only man in the country capable of restoring Germany to her past greatness. That such a course would involve at some stage a confrontation with the democracies who had been so triumphalist in 1918 he had accepted as necessary and even exhilarating. The great victories of the past year had confirmed his faith in both the Führer's ability and his will-power. But he remained very glad that he did not have to exercise such a will, which apparently required the coercion or imprisonment of anyone who opposed the regime. The older Gruchys had not done so; their children had. That Albert and Barbara de Gruchy had had to suffer for the crimes of their offspring he found depressing. But why they should suddenly have been released was totally bewildering. He had no doubt that this loathsome little rat standing before him had had something to do with it: the

Gestapo was fond of playing cat and mouse games with their intended victims. 'Heil Hitler,' he acknowledged. 'Every time I see you, Roess, I feel ten years older. I suppose you have come to arrest the de Gruchys again.'

'By no means, Herr Colonel. The charges against them have been dropped. Did you not know that?'

'I was informed. Am I to believe that you think they have been punished enough?'

'They have not been punished at all, Herr Colonel. They were merely locked up. I trust they are well?'

'If I thought you were trying to be funny, Roess, I would kick you down those stairs. They have been humiliated, half starved, and Albert de Gruchy has been publicly flogged. One of the richest men in France, publicly flogged.'

'Well, he must have broken one of the rules. These prisons have to be run on strict lines. And, Herr Colonel, you must remember that we are national *socialists*. The power of wealth can no longer protect criminals.'

'There are criminals, and criminals,' Hoeppner observed. 'All of whom, hopefully, will one day have to answer for their crimes. I would still like to know why the charges against them have been dropped.'

'I am not fully informed of the facts,' Roess said, stiffly. 'I am here on a different, more important matter. I am acting under the instructions of Colonel Weber of the Sicherheitsdienst. And, I may say, it is a most secret matter as well.'

Despite himself, Hoeppner was interested. If the Gestapo, as the state police, were a law unto themselves, and the SS, as the Führer's own creation, obeyed no laws at all, he knew that the SD, which were personally commanded by Heydrich, were beyond the grasp of even those two terrifying organizations. 'Colonel Weber sent you to me?'

'He sent me to the commandant of the Bordeaux district. But it turns out that you may have a personal interest in this matter. You will remember that it is top secret.' Hoeppner nodded. 'Then I have someone I would like you to meet.'

69

'Very well.'

Roess went to the door. 'Bring in the prisoner.' There was some shuffling outside, and a woman was thrust through the doorway. 'Thank you, Kramer,' Roess said. 'You may close the door.'

'In the name of God . . .' Hoeppner stared at the prisoner. Her wrists were handcuffed behind her back, her dress was torn, her shoulder-length black hair disordered. But the face was very fine, the features close to flawless. 'Christine? But . . .'

'Hello, Franz,' the woman said. 'It's been too long.'

'My dear girl!' He was on his feet and rounding the desk. 'What the devil are you playing at, Roess? Get these things off Fräulein von Ulstein's wrists.'

'I would actually like that,' Christine von Ulstein said. 'Just for a moment.' Roess unlocked the cuffs, and she rubbed her wrists, and then sat before the desk.

'Will someone tell me what is going on?' Hoeppner demanded.

'I am on an undercover mission,' Christine von Ulstein explained. 'I am to infiltrate the guerilla group which we know is hiding in the Massif Central, and which we know was responsible for the train outrage last year. You are involved because your command is nearest to the Vichy border, and besides, the people we are looking for come from this area.'

Hoeppner sat down again. 'You are an undercover agent? For the Gestapo?'

'For the SD. I have worked for Oskar for several years now.'

'But when—'

'All those evenings we danced together, and smooched together? Yes, I was working for Oskar then. But those were my nights off.'

Hoeppner looked at Roess, who smiled benevolently. 'And now you think you can infiltrate a bunch of desperadoes? Those people are killers.'

'That is why I have to be absolutely genuine. I speak French fluently, and English like a native; I spent four years at Oxford University. I have a carefully planned background, which I have memorized. My name is Monica Round.'

'And you think these people will accept you, just like that, for no reason other than you are pretending to be English?'

'They will accept me because, like so many of them, I am on the run from the Gestapo.' She glanced at Roess.

'It is all arranged, Herr Colonel. Fräulein Round was arrested just north of here. The reason for her arrest is information received that she is a British agent, which is what she will represent herself as to the guerillas. Her arrest was carried out in a most public manner, and she was brought here, as you see, handcuffed and generally dishevelled. I have told my men to speak of it in the town, make it known that she is to be interrogated here and then taken away for execution. She will leave Bordeaux in a car with three of my men. On a lonely stretch of road, close to the Vichy border, the car will have an accident, and she will make her escape. There will of course be a hue and cry, but you will make sure that she is not caught. Once across the border—'

'It is up to me,' Christine said.

'It is absolute madness,' Hoeppner declared. 'These people will see through you in a moment, and cut your throat. Look at you. Even when you appear to have been roughed up by the Gestapo you are clearly a lady.'

'I am told that Liane de Gruchy is also a lady, or was before the war.'

'Liane de Gruchy is a cold-blooded killer.'

'Well, I also am trained to kill.'

'You?'

'You should try me sometime, Franz.'

'And you are going after de Gruchy.'

'I am going after all of them. But she is top of the list, yes.'

'I still think you are committing suicide.'

'Because I look like a lady? But even ladies can be British

71

agents. And even ladies can be . . . interrogated by the Gestapo, and escape from them too.'

'Do you think anyone will believe that you have been interrogated by the Gestapo? There is not a mark on your body.'

Christine's mouth twisted. 'There are going to be several marks on my body. I am told Captain Roess is an expert.'

Hoeppner looked at Roess. 'Just a flogging, Herr Colonel. But you understand, her body must be marked, sufficiently to last some days, in case it takes her that long to find these people.'

'You intend to flog Fräulein von Ulstein? I absolutely forbid it.'

'Oh, Franz,' Christine remarked. 'You are so old-fashionedly upright. I shall not mind, even if I scream a bit. You can come and watch, if you wish.'

'In fact, Herr Colonel,' Roess said. 'Your presence as a witness is required by Colonel Weber.'

PART TWO

The Trap

To beguile the time,
Look like the time; bear welcome in your eye,
Your hand, your tongue: look like the innocent flower
But be the serpent under 't.

William Shakespeare

Four

The Agent

'Isn't it a lovely day for a drive in the country,' Rachel said. 'Makes one glad to be alive. Do you realize, sir, that this is the first time we have been out of the office together, in the year we have been in operation?'

'It's not quite a year,' James pointed out.

'Sometimes you can be very pedantic,' she remarked. 'But I suppose it goes with the job. All those Ts to cross and Is to dot.' The ATS private driving the car was obviously listening to the conversation with great relish. But she could only see their heads in her rear-view mirror, and James allowed his hand to drift on to Rachel's knee, slip under her skirt – they were both wearing uniform – and give it a gentle squeeze. She rippled, like a cat, and then pointed. 'The sea!'

They descended the gentle slope from the downs, bypassed Chichester, and as they came up to the little seaport of Bosham were halted by a roadblock. Passes were produced and studied. 'We're actually looking for Commander Lewis,' James explained.

'Yes, sir. The end house, just before the harbour.'

'Thank you. Drive on.' They proceeded slowly over the cobbles. The village, and the harbour, looked somnolent in the July heat, although there were some naval personnel to be seen. 'But no ships,' Rachel complained.

'What do you think those are?' James inquired.

The tide was out, and the tiny harbour was virtually dry. There were several dinghies pulled up on the slip, and in the pool half a dozen fishing boats, either heeled on their sides or standing on legs. Two were fairly large, and even had a cabin. 'They don't look very seaworthy to me,' Rachel observed.

The car stopped outside a building flying the White Ensign, and their door was opened by a member of the shore patrol. 'Major Barron? The commander is expecting you.' He opened the door for them, casting an appreciative glance at Rachel's khaki-stocking-clad legs as she got out.

The house was a typical fisherman's cottage except for the brass nameplates on the doors of what presumably had once been parlours and sitting rooms. The SP opened the door on the left. 'Major Barron, and, ah . . .'

'Sergeant Cartwright,' James explained.

'Major,' said the man inside, wearing naval uniform with the appropriate three bars. He was not very tall, but heavily built with a protruding jaw. 'And you, Sergeant.'

'Thank you, sir.' Rachel followed James into the room, stood to attention.

'At ease, Sergeant. And have a seat. And you, please, Major. Commander Lewis.' James shook hands and sat down. Lewis returned behind his desk. 'Welcome to Operation Windrush. I'm told your people need a month notice.'

'I'm assuming they will have a fair distance to travel.'

Lewis nodded. 'It's still a security risk, revealing our plans so far in advance.'

'These people are absolutely reliable. In any event, only their commanders have the use of our code. The rest will follow where they are led.'

Another nod. 'Very good. We have had a couple of dummy runs, and they have been successful. That is, we have got right up to the French coast, and even put men ashore, and then taken them off again without a shot being fired. Obviously, when we go in in earnest, things won't be quite so easy, but the exercise will be of great importance, not only in pricking the enemy, but in learning about what we might expect when we do the big one. However, as I am sure you will appreciate, operations such as this require spot-on timing, on every side. You must get this across to your people.'

'I appreciate that. Have you got a schedule yet?'

'It is still being worked out. You understand that it depends on the moon and the tides. At present we are thinking of the 7th of August. That gives your people five weeks to be in position. The night will be moonless, the tides at neaps. But you will understand that the date is subject to weather. If the wind is above force six we will have to postpone. Will your people be comfortable with that?'

'They'll have to be. But of course every day they have to be concealed in the neighbourhood is dangerous for them.'

'I realize that, and we will do our damndest to keep to our schedule.'

'I will need the place of entry so that they can start moving right away.'

'St Valery-en-Caux. It's where the Highland Division had to surrender last year, so it seems an appropriate place to return with violence. Your people should be in position no closer than five miles by midnight on the 6th. We will go in at zero four hundred, so their attack should begin at zero three thirty.' He indicated the map on his desk. 'Their target is this power station just outside the town. Knocking it out will be of great value in itself. Assuming we get ashore, we will rendezvous, but this is strictly a raid. We must be in, do as much damage as we can, and be out in an hour. Your people must do the same.'

'To be chased right across France.'

'I was informed that they will all be volunteers and that they can disappear into the population.'

'Most of them. And they will all be volunteers, certainly. May I ask, what craft will we be using?'

'You saw them in the harbour.'

'Those?' Rachel asked. 'Sir?'

'I know they don't look like much, Sergeant. But while they may look decrepit from the outside, they're very well equipped inside. Did I hear you use the word "we", Major?'

'I'll be coming with you.'

'Ah. I would have to get clearance. And I should warn you that this will be a high-risk operation. If Jerry gets one of those bits of wood in his sights, it's curtains. They only have two-inch planking.'

'You are asking my people in France to risk their lives. I intend to be there when they do it. I can join them on land, but that would mean taking something like a month off my other duties, and I'm not sure I'd get clearance for that. This way I shall be away for one night, right?'

'Or forever,' Rachel muttered.

'As you say, Sergeant Cartwright,' Lewis agreed. 'But you'll have your berth, if you really wish it, Major. Now, you'll stay to lunch, of course.'

'You are stark raving mad,' Rachel declared when they regained the office. She had clearly been simmering all afternoon, but had managed to keep quiet while they were being entertained by the navy, or in the presence of the driver on the way home. 'Do you really want to get killed?'

'I don't think any of Liane's lot want to get killed either,' he pointed out. 'Or any of these Commandos. It's a job of work.'

'But it's not *your* job of work. Your job is to be here, pulling strings. Not dangling out there at the end of one of them.'

'I'm going as an observer. It is necessary, if I am to carry out my job efficiently, that I should know the conditions in which my people are operating.' He took her in his arms. 'It will only be for one night.' She allowed herself to be kissed and then carried into the bedroom and laid on her back to be undressed. 'I've always wanted to strip a woman in uniform,' he said.

'And I always knew you were kinky. As well as barmy.

80

But then, I suppose that goes for all men. Oh, James,' she sighed, 'if you get your head blown off, I don't know what I'd do.'

He caressed her breasts and slid his hand down to her pubes. 'I think I am more likely to be drowned. And you would go to some other intelligence officer who would treat you much better than I do.'

'I like the way you treat me best. Oh, James, James, James!' She subsided, and lay still for some moments, panting, while he rolled off her and lay on his back as well. 'I suppose the real reason you want to go is that you'll be seeing Liane.'

'Liane is in Paris.' He got up. 'Back to work. We have to encode a message for Moulin.'

Jean Moulin stood between Pierre and Henri to watch the men coming through the trees. 'Monterre?' he asked.

'And friends,' Pierre said.

'We knew they were coming,' Henri reminded him.

Moulin nodded. 'But do we really wish them?'

'There are twenty of them,' Pierre pointed out. 'That just about doubles our strength.'

'It also doubles the number of people we have to feed and arm. And they will cause trouble. They always do.'

Pierre grinned. 'You are prejudiced.'

'Perhaps I am. I spent a great deal of time in Chartres combating the activities of these people.'

'Well,' Henri said, 'I don't see how we are going to get rid of them. So we may as well use them.'

'As you say.' Moulin went forward, his two aides to either side. Amalie watched from the entrance to the cave. 'Welcome home, Monterre. I see you have been recruiting.'

'These men are all volunteers, Monsieur Moulin. They wish to fight the Boches.'

Moulin surveyed the new recruits. They were mainly young, and they looked fit and tough. There could be no doubt that they would make good fighting men.

Pierre was thinking the same thing. 'I think James would approve,' he muttered. 'Especially in view of what we have coming up.'

'Yes. They will have to accept my discipline, Monterre.'

'Of course, Monsieur Moulin. They have been commanded to do so.'

'By Marshal Stalin?'

'Of course, Monsieur Moulin.'

'And will they continue to fight with us, and obey my orders, when Marshal Stalin and his government have been defeated and destroyed by the Nazis?'

'Of course, Monsieur Moulin. But that is not going to happen, is it?'

'That is a matter of opinion. Well, billet your people. I will speak with them later. Their training will commence tomorrow.'

They watched the men as Monterre spoke with them. 'Do you think we should inform James?' Pierre asked.

'I do not think that is necessary,' Moulin said. 'Recruitment is our business. All he wants is to have sufficient men on the ground when he needs them.'

Amalie was in charge of the camp radio and the code book. When she was finished taking down the Morse message she decoded it and took the sheet to Moulin and her brother in their makeshift office at the mouth of the cave. The prefect stroked his chin. 'Berkeley Square. That completes the message. St Valery. That is a considerable distance.'

'And in five weeks,' Pierre said. 'But that is sufficient time, if we move in ones and twos.'

'You also have to get back,' Moulin pointed out.

'We'll make it. Some of us, at any rate.'

'I will come,' Amalie said.

'Don't be ridiculous. Your place is here.'

'Because I am a woman? Or because I am your sister?'

'Because you are our radio operator.'

'But you will require Henri to go.'

82

'I will take only volunteers. But Henri will wish to volunteer. Where is he, anyway?'

'He went into town with Etienne. He should be back by now.' She went outside, looked down the hillside, and saw her husband coming up, accompanied by several men, all talking excitedly, and . . . a woman? Amalie squinted at the black hair floating in the breeze. The woman wore a dress, which even at a distance Amalie could see was torn in several places. She had no shoes, and limped; indeed her whole movements were indicative of pain. As she approached, Amalie could see a steel band on each wrist. 'Henri?' she called. 'Who is that?'

He came closer. 'A British agent.'

'A what?' Pierre hurried out of the cave, followed more slowly by Moulin. 'An agent? That is impossible.' He stared at Christine. 'What is your name?'

'Monica Round.' Her voice was low.

'And you say you were sent by the British? We were not informed of this.'

'I was not sent to you. Please . . . I am in such pain. May I sit down?'

'You are wounded?' Moulin was solicitous.

Christine shook her head. 'I have been walking barefoot for two days. And I have been beaten. I spent four days in the hands of the Gestapo.' She held up her wrists. 'Do you think someone could take these off?'

'And you escaped? That is impossible,' Pierre repeated.

'Let her sit down,' Moulin said. 'Etienne, fetch a file. Amalie, some wine.'

Amalie poured a cup of wine and gave it to Christine, who gulped it. 'Tell us what happened.'

'I was put ashore on the beach, from a British submarine. My instructions were to make contact with certain people in the Bordeaux area, but I had only been ashore for just over a day when I was arrested by the Gestapo. I think I was betrayed, but I do not know by whom. I think it must have been someone in England.'

Moulin and Pierre exchanged glances, while Amalie poured some more wine. This time Christine sipped. Etienne knelt beside her and started sawing away at the handcuffs. 'Go on,' Moulin invited.

'I was taken to Gestapo headquarters in Bordeaux, and questioned. It was terrible. I fainted several times, but they revived me by throwing water on me.'

'What did they do to you?' Moulin asked.

'They stripped me naked and placed me on an iron frame, spread-eagled and tied at wrist and ankle, and then they flogged me. The room was crowded with men. Even the commander of the Bordeaux district came to watch. They laughed at me and abused me in between strokes of the whip. I screamed, and as I said, I fainted more than once.' She raised her head and looked around their faces. 'But I did not tell them anything. I swear it.'

The first cuff parted, and she rubbed where it had been. Etienne began work on the second. 'What happened after your interrogation?' Moulin asked.

'When they realized they were not going to get anything out of me, they decided to send me to Paris. There were four of us, three Gestapo agents and I, in a command car. For some reason they took a circuitous route out of Bordeaux, but a few kilometres north of the city the car skidded. There had been rain and the surface was slippery. Anyway, it went right off the road and rolled over. I was thrown clear, and so were two of the Germans, but they were unconscious. Maybe they were dead. I do not know. Anyway, I crawled away. But I knew I could no longer continue with my mission, so I went to the border. I got across at night. I found a rock and managed to break the chain for the cuffs, but I was starving, and when I came to a farm I asked the farmer to help me. He said he could not, but he knew people who might. So he hid me, and then he brought this man to me.' She gazed at Henri, and again rubbed her wrists as Etienne removed the second cuff.

'That is true,' Henri said. 'I was in the village with Etienne, and this man told us there was a woman concealed in his barn. So we went with him, and when she told us she was a British agent, we brought her here.'

'Just like that,' Pierre said. 'You revealed our location to a complete stranger.'

'But if she is a British agent . . .'

'Do you have any proof that she is telling the truth?'

'Well, what about the handcuffs?'

'That is proof?'

'Do you have any identification, mademoiselle?' Moulin asked.

'The Germans took all of my papers when they searched me. That search . . .'

Amalie squeezed her hand. 'I have been searched by the Gestapo. It was the most horrifying experience of my life.'

'Then you understand. It was terrible.'

'If you are working for the British,' Henri said, speaking English, 'then presumably you speak English.'

'Of course I do,' Christine said, in English, and smiled. 'I am English.'

Henri looked at Pierre. 'That proves nothing,' Pierre said. 'You speak English, Henri, and you have never even been there.'

'Her accent is very good.'

'So no doubt she has studied at a university there. It is all too pat.'

'What are we to do with her?' Moulin asked.

'We have absolutely no proof that anything she tells us is true,' Pierre said.

'Would you like to see the marks on my body?' Christine asked, angrily.

'There are marks on your body?'

'Where I was whipped. I am scarred for life.'

'Do you expect us to believe that?'

'I will show you.'

'No,' Moulin said. 'You cannot undress before these men.

Go with Amalie and let her inspect you.' Amalie was still holding her hand.

'Are they going to kill me?' Christine asked as she followed Amalie into a recess of the cave.

'Not if you are telling the truth. I am sorry my brother is so suspicious. But you understand that if the Germans were to find out exactly where we are they could wipe us out.'

'Even in Vichy?'

'I should think they would obtain permission easily enough. Did you know that they have forced the government to start rounding up Jews?'

'I did not know that. But that man who came to my help—'

'My husband. Yes, he is a Jew. But they cannot reach him while he is with us. Here we will be private.'

The light was very dim. Christine took off her dress, and then what remained of her petticoat. She wore no knickers. 'The Germans took them away from me,' she explained.

'I know,' Amalie said. 'They did that to me too.'

'You were captured by the Gestapo?'

'Yes.' Amalie peered at Christine's back. Although she reckoned they were several days old, the weals were still very visible, one or two quite deep and showing signs of festering. 'These are terrible. But I have some medication to put on them. You are a very brave woman.'

'Did the Germans flog you as well?'

'No.'

'You escaped them?'

'No. I was rescued.'

'That must have been very exciting. Please tell me about it.'

'Some other time. It is a long story.'

'They called you Amalie.'

'It is a common name. I will go and fetch something for your back. And a pair of my knickers.'

She rejoined the men. 'Well?' Pierre asked.

'Her back is torn to ribbons.'

'Then I shall apologize.'

'We will have to find something to do with her,' Henri said.

'We must first of all find out what her mission was,' Moulin said.

'Why is she skulking back there?' Pierre asked. 'Tell her to come here and we will see if we can help her complete her mission.'

'She is staying back there because she has no clothes on. I will put some salve on her back; then she will dress and rejoin us.' Amalie drew a bowl of water from the vat outside the cave, collected the first aid box, and returned to where Christine sat on the floor of the cave. 'My brother sends his apologies for distrusting you. Now he wants to help you to complete your mission.'

'I told him, I told you all, my mission cannot be successful now, with the Gestapo hunting for me.'

'Nonetheless, we may be able to help you. Lie on your stomach.' Christine obeyed, and Amalie knelt beside her. She first of all cleaned the open wounds as best she could. 'This will hurt,' she warned.

'If it makes me well again, it will be worth it.'

Amalie applied iodine, and Christine gave a little moan. Then Amalie added lint and sticking plaster. 'That should do the trick.'

'I feel better already. Amalie . . . Was there not an Amalie de Gruchy, a daughter of Albert de Gruchy, the famous wine grower?'

'Yes. I am she.'

'But I was told you committed suicide.'

'I pretended to.'

'And ran away to join the Resistance? That is incredibly romantic.'

'Not really. I ran away with my sister.'

'The famous Liane?'

'I suppose she is famous. But how did you know of us?'

Christine began to dress. 'My mission was to contact Monsieur and Madame de Gruchy.'

'What did you say?' Amalie cried. 'You came to France to make contact with Mama and Papa? But why?'

'Your father has been a British agent for a long time. Did you not know that?'

'Of course I did not. Oh, if only I had. But you are too late. They were taken by the Gestapo last October.'

'I know this. But it has been reported, by one of our agents in Germany, that they have been released and sent back to their home in Paulliac.'

'Mama and Papa? Back in Paulliac? I cannot believe it.'

'Well, I cannot swear it is true. But my superiors in England believe it is true. That is why I was sent to contact them.'

Amalie scrambled to her feet and ran to the mouth of the cave. 'Pierre! Henri! Mama and Papa are back in Paulliac. They have been set free!'

Pierre frowned at her. 'That is not possible.'

'It is true. Mademoiselle Round was sent here by the British government to contact them.'

'She told you this?' Pierre looked past his sister at Christine.

'Yes,' Christine said. 'Because it is the truth.'

'If that could be true . . .' Henri said.

'And what did the British government wish with my parents?' Pierre asked.

'They wish to reopen contact with them. They have acted as our agents for some time. Since before the war.'

'Did you know of this, Pierre?' Moulin asked.

'No,' Pierre said. 'No, I did not know of it.' Could it be true? If it were, while he could understand Papa's refusal to confide in any of his family before the war, why had he not confided in *him*, when he had returned from England last year, an accredited English agent? Father had agreed to help him, but had said not a word of his own involvement. On

88

the other hand, it had been impressed upon him when he had been training in England, and by James afterwards, that in their business one was never supposed to know the identities of any other agents, or seek to find out. Papa was certainly the sort of man who would follow such a directive to the letter. 'What instruction were you to give my father?' he asked.

'I do not know. I was told to give him a sealed packet, but when I was captured and searched, the Gestapo found it.'

'You must eat, and then rest while your back heals up,' Amalie said.

They went off with Henri, and Moulin and Pierre were left alone. 'What do you think?' Moulin asked. 'If her back really is scarred . . .'

'She is telling the truth, or she is a very dedicated woman.'

'Sent here to destroy us? So she has managed to discover where we are. As long as we do not let her leave us again, she cannot give that information to anyone.'

'And if she finds out where we are going?'

'Again, while she is here, she cannot interfere.'

'But she will have to be watched, day and night, to stop her from using the radio. And most of us are leaving.'

'I will be here. And Amalie.'

'It will still be an unnecessary burden. It would be far simpler to execute her.'

'I cannot consider that, Pierre.'

'Because you accept that she is a British agent.'

'Because I have no proof that she is not. I will not execute an innocent woman.'

Pierre sighed. 'You are too decent a man for this business. I wish Liane were here.'

'Meaning that you think she would shoot her.'

'Meaning that she would know, better than either of us, what needs to be done.'

'Well, there is one way of finding out the truth: we can contact Barron.'

'Our instructions are explicit: no radio contact until after the raid, or it is aborted.'

'Except in the event of an extreme emergency. Would you not so describe this business?'

'I doubt that Barron will consider it more than a domestic problem. I suppose it had better wait until we return.'

'And your parents? Do you really think they are British agents?'

'You have known them longer than I, Jean. And probably more intimately.'

'I have never seen or heard the slightest indication of it. Your mother used to visit England regularly before the war, but as I understood, it was either to see her family or the girls when they were at school there, or for shopping. I suppose she could have been carrying information, but what information could Albert have been obtaining, spending most of his time in Paulliac? Do you believe what the woman said, that they are back there now?'

'I find that also inexplicable. But I would like to find out.'

'Simply because they are your parents?'

'Is that not a good reason? I would like to get them out of there. Because if the woman is telling the truth, and she *was* carrying some kind of incriminating letter, they are in danger of being arrested all over again. That would kill them.'

'If that is true, as the Gestapo have the message sent to them, they will have been re-arrested already. For you to attempt to get to them would be extremely dangerous. And if you succeeded in getting them out, what then? I imagine they are finding life in Paulliac far more comfortable than anything we could offer them here. Anyway, that also will have to wait. Barron's message said that you should leave immediately.'

Pierre sighed, 'You are asking me to abandon my parents.'

'If they are there. We do not know that. Even this woman does not know that for certain.'

Pierre nodded. 'You're right, of course. I will summon Jules and Etienne and Henri as soon as we have eaten, and we will plan our move.'

Oskar Weber lowered himself into the chair in front of Heydrich's desk. 'She is there. She made her escape a week ago, and has not been heard from since.'

'She could be lying dead in a ditch. Have you any means of getting in touch with her?'

'You know that is impossible, Reinhard. Her business is not, under any circumstances, to give herself away, but to be in there, and, shall I say, stir them into unwise activity. We must be patient.'

'I put your woman in, Oskar, because I want these people cleaned up at the earliest possible moment. They are almost certainly recruiting, and if they are left unchecked they will grow into a formidable organization. What about the de Gruchy parents? Do you suppose these people know they are back?'

'Christine will certainly make sure they know of it, so we may expect some developments there also.'

'I hope so. Was there anything else?'

'Three things which may interest you.' Heydrich lit a cigarette while he waited. 'One concerns British airmen.'

'Is that our business?'

'It could be. These people come over and bomb us, and suffer casualties. But only a few are destroyed in the air. In several cases their planes are badly damaged, but they attempt the return journey, obviously. Those who don't make it come down either in the North Sea, or in Belgium or Holland. In most cases the crews parachute and are picked up by our people when they land, but quite a few manage to evade capture, sometimes for a couple of days. Their idea is to reach the coast and hope to find a fishing boat which will carry them to England, and needless to say they are assisted by the local population. I may say the success rate from their point of view is very low.'

91

'Isn't this a Gestapo matter?'

'It is, on the surface. However, over the last month there have been a couple of disquieting events. We have positive information that the crews of at least two aircraft have come down alive and uninjured, and have simply disappeared.'

'Well, tell the local Gestapo commander to make it quite plain that anyone found hiding British aircrew will be shot. And then shoot a few.'

'I will certainly do that. But it is not as simple as you think. I have just received a communication from one of my people in Lisbon. My team there watch all arrivals and departures, either by sea or by air, and they are certain that two men seen boarding a steamer for England last week were British aircrew.'

'You mean they were in uniform?'

'No, no. But that is in itself a clue. My people got close enough to them to hear them speaking. Not only did they talk like airmen, but they were both obviously well-educated men, public school types, yet their clothes were ill-fitting, their shoes down at the heel. They were also accompanied and being seen off by a man who we know to be in the employ of the British government, but who is not on the embassy staff.'

Heydrich stubbed out his cigarette. 'You are saying that they may have made their way the length of France, across Spain, and into Portugal? Isn't that rather far-fetched?'

'It is quite feasible, if they were assisted.'

'That is also rather far-fetched. The journey must have taken several days. They must have been very fortunate to find so much assistance. Once or twice, perhaps. But every day for a month? And without papers and travel permits? It is simply not possible.'

'That is exactly my point, Reinhard. These people must have *had* papers and travel documents. And they must have known where to go and when and for how long to wait while further travel was arranged. Their escape was not a matter of good luck. It was carefully planned and orchestrated,

92

obviously by a well-organized group of people who are taking their orders from London.'

'We will have to do something about that. *You* will have to do something about that.'

'Unfortunately, my people are stretched a little thin on the ground. I think it would be best if we put Gestapo head-quarters in Paris on to it. If they don't already know it's happening they are incompetent.'

'You mean that idiot Kluck? We *know* he is incompetent.'

'I was thinking of Roess. I have mentioned him to you before. He is one of Kluck's aides, and is the best of the lot. He has monitored the placing of Fräulein von Ulstein in the midst of the guerillas, and appears to have handled it very successfully. I would like him placed in command of a special unit whose sole task will be the finding and destruction of this escape route.'

Heydrich nodded. 'Have the order drawn up and I will sign it. You said there was something else?'

'Indeed. The woman Jonsson is back.'

Heydrich sat up. 'When did she arrive?'

'In Berlin? A week ago.' He held up his hand as Heydrich looked about to explode. 'I know. It is sheer incompetence. She came in from Sweden, as usual, but while the people at Lubeck noted her entry it went on an ordinary report and did not reach my desk until yesterday. I immediately called for a report from the team maintaining surveillance on Frau von Helsingen, and they say that Jonsson did pay a call on her, four days ago.'

'You mean virtually the moment she arrived in Berlin. And you were not informed immediately?'

'Again, it was a bureaucratic fuck-up. The team makes a report once a week. Jonsson visited Helsingen in the middle of their week, so it was not reported until yesterday.'

'What a way to run a security service,' Heydrich grumbled. 'Right. Bring her in. There is no need to make a fuss about it. Arrest her, rough her up just enough to scare her

– we do not want any permanent bruises – and then let her go with a warning.'

'Unfortunately, she is no longer here.'

'*What?*'

'Another report I only received this morning. She left yesterday, by train for Zurich.'

'Oh, for God's sake, Oskar. Your people need overhauling.'

'I said, she only left yesterday. And this was reported immediately. With her American passport there was no way she could be stopped.'

'And why has she gone to Switzerland?'

'I have no certain knowledge of this.'

'There has to be a reason. I think this is a line of inquiry worth pursuing. And the third matter?'

'That is probably the most disturbing of all. The Wehrmacht have captured a senior Russian intelligence officer. Someone quite close to the top. He was of course handed over to my people, and under interrogation claimed that Stalin was informed by the British – he said by Churchill personally, although I doubt that; the two men hate each other – last December, that we intended to invade Russia, but that he discarded the warning as British propaganda. In the context of what is happening, this is not relevant. However, in the context of what *might* have happened, had Stalin believed the British warning . . . *Were* there plans to invade Russia last December?'

'The plans were actually drawn up last October. But they were absolutely top secret. Only the Führer's innermost circle and the top brass at OKH knew of them. Even I was not informed until the new year.'

'Well, then, someone in the inner circle, or at the top of OKH, is a traitor.'

Heydrich studied him for several minutes. Then he said, 'That is a very serious accusation.'

'It is a very serious business. Tell me, where is Helsingen at this moment?'

94

'God knows. They are advancing so fast he could well be in Smolensk.'

'But in such an advance, there will be very little opportunity for sending or receiving letters, and none at all for leave. I would like your permission to arrest Frau von Helsingen.'

'You are determined to play with dynamite, Oskar.'

'Just consider for a moment. Stalin was warned by the British. The British could only have obtained that information from one of their agents here in Berlin. But it is not possible for the British to have an agent in the top ranks of OKH or in the Führer's inner circle. At least, I hope it is not. But someone must have let something slip to someone. Now, who do we know who is a member of the Führer's inner circle, who is married to a French wife, a wife whose siblings are wanted outlaws, and who is good friends with an American journalist who comes and goes from Germany as she pleases?'

'My God!' Heydrich said. 'This is a matter for the Führer.'

'I do not think that will be necessary, yet. Let me arrest her for questioning as to the activities of Jonsson. There need be no rough stuff. I do not think any will be necessary; I do not think she is a very strong character. If she has no information for us, we will apologize and let her go. But I would estimate that we may well glean something of value.'

'And if it is her who is the traitor, and you find this out?'

Weber smiled. 'Well, then, Herr General, we will be in the position of a man playing a rubber of contract bridge who is dealt thirteen cards of the same suit.'

'Where are they going?' Christine asked as the men assembled. Everyone was heavily armed and carried a fortnight's rations of bread and cheese; they would expect to obtain extra supplies en route. Henri carried a small radio set.

'It is a secret,' Amalie explained. 'No one knows where they are going, except Pierre, Henri and Jules.'

95

'But *you* know where they are going. And Monsieur Moulin.'

'Well, yes. But we are the only two others.'

'Meaning that you do not trust me.'

'I am sorry, Monica. I must obey orders.'

'The British trust me.'

'I am sorry,' Amalie said again.

'But you must obey orders. I understand. What I do not understand is how they propose to get where they are going – I presume it is in the occupied territory – carrying all those guns and ammunition and equipment, and not expect to be found by the Germans. Or are they going to attack something in Bordeaux?'

'They are not going to Bordeaux. They will split up into small groups, and move only by night. Then they will rendezvous on an appointed date.'

'And will your sister be joining them?'

'No, no. I told you, Liane is in Paris.'

'You mean she is living there? She has abandoned you?'

'Good lord, no. She is working for the Resistance, setting up an organization in Paris.'

'But is that not terribly dangerous? Isn't there a price on her head?'

'Isn't all war dangerous? Wasn't it dangerous for you to be landed on the beach? If that car hadn't skidded, and you had been taken to Paris, they would probably have hanged you.' Amalie squeezed her hand. 'It is better not to think about it.' She ran down the hillside to say goodbye to her husband.

Thirty men went with Pierre. Six remained, with Etienne, the two women, and Moulin. Although her back was still very sore, as were her feet, Christine insisted on playing a full part in the life of the little community, going with Amalie to the stream to draw buckets of water to empty into the vat, and helping with the cooking. 'She is a treasure,' Amalie told Moulin.

'A very pretty treasure. The lads are quite smitten.'

96

'Do you still not trust her?'

'Pierre is the one who does not trust her. I am keeping an open mind. Anyway, she can do us no harm while she is here, and she is certainly pleasant company. Just make sure she is never left alone with the radio.'

'It must be terrible for you,' Christine said the next morning as they went down the slope with their buckets, 'knowing that your parents are only a few miles away and being unable to visit them and make sure that they are all right. Aren't you going to try?'

'Pierre says we must do nothing until he gets back.'

'Pierre, Pierre. Always Pierre.'

'Well, he is the head of the family. At least, when Liane is not here.'

'I would really like to meet Liane one day.'

'Well, perhaps you will.' Amalie frowned. There was a road about a mile away at the foot of the hill, but as it led to the border it was very seldom used. Yet now there was a vehicle proceeding along it, driving very slowly.

Christine had seen it too. 'Do you think it is the gendarmerie?'

Amalie put down her bucket and ran up the hill. Christine followed. At the camp Etienne and Moulin had also seen the stranger. 'What do you make of it?' Moulin handed Amalie the binoculars.

She focussed. 'An open car, with one person. Can it be . . . a woman?'

'Another strange woman,' Etienne remarked, glancing at Christine. 'Will she be a friend of yours, mademoiselle?'

'Of course she is not,' Christine snapped.

It was Amalie's turn to glance at Christine, in surprise at her vehemence. Then she levelled the glasses again. 'She's stopped. She's getting out.' Etienne took the binoculars.

'Perhaps she has broken down,' Moulin suggested.

'She is leaning against the door. She is using glasses to examine the hills. She is looking for us!'

97

'She must be eliminated,' Christine said. She couldn't imagine what was going on, but she certainly did not want any other agent muscling in on her territory and perhaps giving the whole game away.

'I think she should be investigated,' Etienne agreed. 'I think the best thing, if she is looking for us, would be to let her find us.'

'If you do that, you will not be able to let her go again,' Amalie told him.

Etienne pointed at the smouldering fire, from which wisps of smoke were rising. 'If she has seen that, and she is actually looking for us, then she has found us anyway.' He looked at Moulin.

He nodded. 'That is true. Go down and see what she wants. Do not give yourself away. If you consider it necessary, bring her up here. But Etienne, do not harm her, unless you have to. She may be entirely innocent.'

Etienne nodded, and picked up his tommy-gun. 'I will come with you,' Amalie said.

'And I,' Christine volunteered.

'Well, be careful. She may be armed.'

They lost sight of the road as they descended the hill. 'She will probably have driven away again by the time we get there,' Amalie panted.

'Not if she is really looking for us,' Christine said. 'And wants us to find her.'

'There!' They had reached a crag, only about a hundred feet above the road, and Etienne pointed.

The car was still there, and the woman had got back behind the wheel and was smoking a cigarette.

'Oh, my God!' Amalie cried. 'It is Joanna!'

Five

The Crisis

'Who is Joanna?' Etienne asked.

'An old friend of the family,' Amalie told him. 'She and Liane were at school together.'

'And she knows you are here?'

'Well . . . she must do.'

'How?'

'I have no idea. But we must get down there. She may have a message.'

'A message from whom?'

'I don't know. Perhaps Liane.' She stood up and waved. Etienne stood also. 'Well, as she is there . . .'

Joanna was waving back. 'Come along, Christine,' Amalie said. 'You'll love Joanna. She's a bundle of fun.' She frowned. 'Are you all right? You've lost all your colour.'

'I feel a little faint,' Christine acknowledged. 'I have still not properly regained my strength.'

'You have been doing too much too soon. You stay here. We'll bring her up.'

She ran down the hillside, Etienne beside her. Christine sat on the ground and watched them. Shit, she thought. Shit, shit, shit! Of all the absolutely incomprehensible bad luck! She had actually met the Swedish-American on two occasions, at soirées in Berlin. And now she remembered that she had seen her speaking with Madeleine von Helsingen, but it had not occurred to her that she might be a friend of the de Gruchy family. Weber would be interested to learn that. He would be even more interested to learn that she

99

was in contact with these guerillas. Now, how could she have learned their whereabouts except through either Madeleine or Liane? Which had to mean that she was in touch with Liane – the most wanted woman in France! But to use those two priceless pieces of information she had to survive this meeting. She had to rely on the fact that there was very little similarity between the rag doll she had allowed herself to become and the sophisticated, immaculately groomed woman Joanna might remember.

She began to descend the hill.

'Joanna!' Amalie cried, running forward for an embrace. 'It's so good to *see* you.'

'Snap.' Joanna looked past her at Etienne.

'This is Etienne,' Amalie explained. 'One of us. But however did you find us?'

'I have friends who tells me things. But no one knows for sure where you are. I've been looking for three days. You wouldn't have anything worth drinking?'

'No. But we have something.'

'And a bath?'

'You'll have to use the stream. Come along. Jean will be so pleased to see you.'

'Jean?'

'You must remember Jean Moulin. He was the prefect of Chartres.'

'And he is here with you? Good Lord!'

'He is our leader.'

'Your leader? I thought . . .' She checked at the sight of Christine coming towards her.

'This is Monica,' Amalie explained. 'She was captured and tortured by the Gestapo. But she escaped and joined us.'

'Hello, Monica.' Joanna shook hands, frowning.

'Is something the matter, mademoiselle?' Christine asked.

'There's something . . . We haven't met, have we?'

'I do not think so, mademoiselle. Perhaps Oxford University, before the war.'

'Nope. I never made any university. Never tried.'

'Monica is a British agent,' Amalie said proudly. 'That is why she was captured by the Gestapo.'

'A British agent,' Joanna commented. 'Gee whiz! I have always wanted to meet a genuine spy. But I thought you guys spent your time *not* being arrested by the Gestapo?'

'I was betrayed,' Christine said. 'By somebody in England.'

'I can believe it. They're an untrustworthy lot.'

'My God!' Joanna said. 'Jean? What did they do to you?'

'They tortured him too,' Amalie explained.

'But I survived,' Moulin said. 'As did Monica.'

Joanna hugged him. 'They sure don't seem to be very competent. But I'm real glad you got out, Jean. Now listen, where is Liane? And Pierre? I was told you were together.'

Amalie was pouring wine. 'Well, we are, usually. But Pierre is off on a mission. With Henri. The British are going to raid St Valery, and our people are going to help them. They reckon they'll be away about a month.'

'Amalie!' Moulin protested.

'Oh. Joanna's one of us. Aren't you, Joanna?'

'Of course I am.'

'Just as long as you're not going to rush off and print any of this in your newspaper.'

'No way. But where's Liane?'

'Liane's in Paris. She's setting up an escape route for Allied airmen who get shot down.'

'You let Liane go to Paris? There's a reward out for her.'

'She'll be all right. She's totally disguised. We cut her hair short, and dyed it black. And she's going to move in with her Left Bank friends.'

'I still think it's criminally dangerous.' Joanna glanced at Christine, who had been a silent observer of the discussion.

'I agree with you,' Christine said. Her brain was racing. This whole thing was falling into her lap more quickly than she could have dreamed, every bit of information she had

101

been sent to discover. This over-the-top woman was obviously *not* in touch with Liane, but what Amalie had so carelessly revealed was an absolute bombshell. It had to be got to Franz, just as rapidly as possible. But how? There was no way these people would let her leave this encampment, and if she just stole away she would never be able to come back. Was the information she now possessed sufficiently important to blow her cover? Would Weber think so? He was the only man in the world of whom she was truly afraid.

'The reason I'm here,' Joanna was explaining, 'is to warn you about your parents. Holy shit!' She had drunk some wine.

'You'll get used to it,' Amalie said. 'What about Mama and Papa?'

'Did you know they're back in Paulliac?'

'Yes. Monica told us.' Joanna gave Christine another look. 'That is why she is here,' Amalie explained. 'She was sent by the British to make contact with them. Papa is a British agent. Can you imagine? And we never knew.'

Joanna drank some more wine, wrinkling her nose. 'No, I cannot imagine. Who told you this?'

'I did,' Christine said. 'As Amalie said, I was sent to reopen contact with them. But the Germans caught me before I could reach them.'

'How annoying for you.'

'They tortured her terribly,' Amalie said, sensing Joanna's disbelief. 'You should see the marks.'

'I should love to do that sometime. What I want to know is, have *you* made any attempt to see them.'

'Well . . .' Amalie flushed. 'I wanted to. They don't even know I'm alive. They think I drowned in the river last year. I would so like to see them. But Liane wasn't here, and Pierre said to do nothing until he came back from this mission. He felt there was something suspicious about them being released.'

'And he was absolutely right. They are the bait of a trap to lure you out of these mountains, to lure you across the

102

border into the occupied territory.' Amalie clasped both hands to her neck.

'Do you know this for a fact?' Moulin asked.

'I keep my ears open in Berlin. It's my job.'

'Do *they* know it?'

'Almost certainly not.'

'Then what are we to do? If they were sent here to entrap Pierre and Liane, and no notice is taken of them, they could be re-arrested.' He preferred not to mention Pierre's fear that that would happen anyway, should the Germans be able to decode Monica's message.

'Oh, my *God!*' Amalie cried.

Joanna appeared to consider. 'It is a tricky one,' she said. 'But listen. I can at least see them and tell them the situation.'

'You?'

'I am on a driving tour through the south of France, reporting on conditions for my newspaper. No one stops me from going anywhere I please. I'm an old friend of your family, and the Germans are making no secret that your parents have been released. In fact, they're giving it maximum publicity. So, as I happen to be in the Bordeaux area, what would be more natural than for me to pay Paulliac a visit, see how they're getting on – and put them in the picture.'

'Oh, that would be marvellous,' Amalie cried. 'I wish I could come with you.'

'That would be far too dangerous. But . . .' She looked at Christine. 'You could come. To complete your mission. I'd bring you back here afterwards.'

Christine could hardly believe her ears. She was being offered an out! Did she dare take it? And then get back in again? It could be done. 'I would like to do that,' she said. 'But I have no papers.'

'There is a spacious boot in that car. You can hide in there.'

'It is too dangerous,' Amalie protested.

103

'Not for Monica,' Joanna pointed out. 'From what I've read, an agent's life is nothing but risk. Right, Monica? Besides, I'll take care of you.'

'Of course you will,' Christine said.

'There is no need for you to go into the boot until we're close to the border,' Joanna said, cranking the engine. She had had a meal and a hasty dip in the cold water of the stream.

'I am in your hands,' Christine agreed, getting into the front and waving to Amalie and Etienne, who were watching them from up the hill.

The engine started. Joanna waved as well, and got behind the wheel. 'I don't know much about this neck of the woods, so you'll have to map read. It's in the glove compartment.'

Christine took the map out, opened it, and pressed it flat on her knees to stop it from flapping in the breeze. She was wearing some of the clothes accumulated in the camp, trousers and a blouse and canvas ankle boots, and looked like a scarecrow beside Joanna's chic dress. 'This road goes right up to the border, as long as we don't take any turns off.'

'And how far is it?'

'It looks like . . .' She tried to relate the distance to the scale at the bottom of the map. 'Maybe sixty kilometres.'

'So even on this surface we should do it in a couple of hours. There by six.'

'There will be a curfew.'

'Sure, but it's not going to get dark much before nine. We'll be in Paulliac by then.'

'You have been there before? You know the way?'

'Sure. But you must know it too.'

'I have never been there.'

'But you must know the district, where the de Gruchys live. How were you supposed to contact them?'

'I had a map, like you. But the Germans took it.' They were now down from the highland and driving between fields of sunflowers. Without warning Joanna pulled into the side of the road and braked. Christine had to throw up her hands to avoid hitting her head on the dashboard. 'What has happened?'

Joanna switched off the ignition. 'I just felt that you and I should have a chat.'

'I do not understand you.'

'Come on. You're not a British agent.'

'You are calling me a liar? Why do you think the Gestapo tortured me?'

'Did they? What exactly did they do to you?'

'They flogged me. Would you like to see the marks?'

'I gather you showed them to Amalie, so I'm quite sure they're there. But that doesn't necessarily prove anything, save that maybe you're a masochist. What is your code name?'

'I am not going to tell you that.'

'Would you like me to beat it out of you?'

'I would be amused to have you try.'

They gazed at each other. Joanna was the bigger woman, and she had immense confidence in her training, her skills. But for the first time in her life she had an unexpected spasm of uncertainty. If this woman *was* a British agent, working for some other control, she would have received the same training, perhaps at the same school she had attended, briefly, before absconding, from the same instructors as herself. If, on the other hand, she was a *German* agent, her training would have been entirely different, her skills of a different calibre . . . and superior? In any event, supposing she did take her on, and got nowhere, however victorious, what would she tell Amalie and Moulin, who obviously trusted the woman? She temporized while she considered the situation. 'Suppose I were to tell you that I know for a fact that Albert de Gruchy is not and never has been a British agent?'

'How can you know such a thing?'

'I'm a newspaper reporter. I get confidences from people. It's my business.'

'And you think a man like de Gruchy would confide in you?' Christine's tone was contemptuous.

Pressing any further could well mean Joanna admitting that she was a British agent. 'Have it your way,' she agreed, and got out to crank the engine. They drove in silence for another twenty kilometres, passing a couple of horse-drawn carts but no traffic, then Joanna braked again. 'Time for you to disappear, I think.'

Christine got out without a word, raised the boot lid, and crawled in, pulling the lid down on top of her. Joanna resumed driving. The French border post was perfunctory. If anyone was so misguided as to wish to enter the occupied territory from the relative safety of Vichy it was not their business to do anything more than wonder. At the other end of the short road two German soldiers, a private and a sergeant, tommy-guns slung on their shoulders, waited for her. A third stood by the lowered barrier. They inspected her approvingly, then the sergeant said, 'Papers.'

Joanna opened her bag and handed them over. He studied them with great care, turning the pages of the passport one by one, then raised his head. 'You are going to Bordeaux?'

'I have friends there who I am going to visit.' He looked at his colleague, who shrugged, and handed the documents back. Then he waved to the man at the barrier, who leaned on the broad base to lift the horizontal bar. 'Thank you,' Joanna said, engaged gear, and suddenly there was a loud sneeze. All the men reacted immediately, and she faced three tommy-guns, which ended her immediate inclination to gun her engine and get away. So she braked again.

'Switch off the motor.' Joanna obeyed. 'Now get out. The keys.'

Joanna gave him the keys. 'It's not locked.' She wondered what was likely to happen next, how far she could go in defending Monica. How far she *wanted* to go.

One of the soldiers kept his gun pointed at Joanna. The

106

sergeant opened the boot. 'Out, out,' he commanded. 'Get out.'

'That is what I am doing,' Christine replied in German. 'What is this?'

Christine stretched. 'That woman is a spy. Arrest her.'

'What the shit . . .'

The soldiers were equally confused. 'You are German?' the sergeant asked.

'My name is Christine von Ulstein.'

'My God!' Joanna muttered.

'You have papers?'

'No, I do not have papers. Your commanding officer is Colonel Franz Hoeppner, right?'

'That is correct.'

'I am a personal friend of his. You will take me to him, now, and you will place this woman under arrest.'

The sergeant goggled at her. 'The woman is quite mad,' Joanna said. 'I picked her up a few kilometres back. She said she had to get into the occupied territory, but that she had no papers. I agreed to smuggle her across the border. It was foolish of me, I know, but she was such a decrepit-looking creature . . .'

'Ha!' Christine commented.

'This is very strange,' the sergeant observed.

'It is not strange at all. Listen, you have a telephone in that box. I can see the wires. I wish you to telephone Colonel Hoeppner. Tell him my name, and ask for instructions.'

The sergeant nodded. 'That is the best thing. Hans!'

'Christine von Ulstein,' Christine reminded him.

'You cannot hold me,' Joanna said. 'I am a neutral, and I have committed no crime.'

'You have just admitted attempting to smuggle someone across the border, Fräulein.'

Joanna bit her lip, and looked at Christine. 'I am going to break your lousy neck.'

'It is your neck you should think of, Fräulein.'

Hans reappeared. 'Colonel Hoeppner has left his office.'

'Then ring his home, you idiot,' Christine shouted.

Hans, clearly offended, looked at the sergeant. 'Do it.' He went off again.

The two women had to wait over an hour, while the evening slowly drew in. They were allowed to sit on the bench outside the post, and were given water to drink. 'What's your plan when this Hoeppner character says he has never heard of you?' Joanna asked.

'Franz and I are old friends. We have even been lovers.'

Joanna stared at her. 'My God! I remember you! Berlin!'

'As I remember you, Fräulein Jonsson.'

Joanna had nothing to say. She could only wonder what James's reaction would be when he discovered that she had compromised the guerillas. But of course she hadn't. This woman had already infiltrated them, prepared them for destruction. Her business was to prevent that from happening. If she could.

At last two cars approached the post, and the soldiers stood to attention. Several men got out, but only one came forward. Franz Hoeppner was in evening dress and did not look very pleased. But he brightened up when he saw Christine, before frowning again. 'What has happened?'

'I will tell you when we are alone. But first, this woman must be arrested.'

Franz looked at Joanna. 'We have met.'

'In Berlin, yes. Then you know who I am.'

'Fräulein Jonsson, the journalist. I do not understand. What are you doing in Bordeaux?'

'She is in league with the guerillas,' Christine said.

'I don't know who this woman is,' Joanna said. 'But she is stark staring mad. I picked her up on the road, and she asked me to smuggle her into Bordeaux. So I hid her in the boot of my car. I know it was a stupid, perhaps a criminal thing to do, but she looked such a pitiful wreck . . .'

'I must speak with you, Franz. I have vitally important information.'

'But this woman—'

'Must be kept under close arrest until after we have spoken.'

'You would not dare!' Joanna snapped. 'I am an American citizen. My papers are in order.'

'But you have admitted to breaking the law,' Franz said. 'The matter will have to be investigated. Sergeant!'

One of the men waiting by the cars came to him. 'Herr Colonel!'

'This woman is under arrest. Take her to headquarters and hold her there until I can interview her.'

'Buster, you are going to be cashiered,' Joanna said. 'I wish to speak with the American consul. No, on second thought, I wish to make a phone call to the ambassador in Paris.'

'All in good time, Fräulein Jonsson. You will go with the sergeant, please. If you attempt to resist, he will be forced to handcuff you.'

'I would do that anyway,' Christine recommended. Joanna gave her a last look, and allowed herself to be led away.

'Now you come with me.' Franz showed Christine to his car, and got into the back seat beside her. 'Tell me what has happened.'

'It is a long story.'

'And I am going out to dinner.'

'So where are you taking me?'

'A hotel?'

'Like this? Besides, I do not wish anyone to see me. I also want a hot bath and some decent food and drink. Take me to your apartment.'

'It will be a pleasure. Are you still on duty?'

'I am always on duty. Are you still going to your dinner party? What I have to say is most important.'

Franz considered, and then smiled. 'I think I had better stay with you.'

Christine soaked in Franz's tub, a glass of champagne at her elbow. 'So there it is.'

Franz had taken off his jacket and was leaning against the wall, looking at her. 'It is a confusing picture.'

'It is not in the least confusing.' Christine got out of the bath and dried herself. 'I have told you where the main part of the guerillas will be in three weeks' time, and that they will be assisting the British in an assault upon St Valery.'

'But you do not know the exact date.'

'Three weeks' time, Franz. All you have to do is give Weber that information and he will take care of it. But the other information is even more important.'

'That Liane de Gruchy is in Paris? It is a very large city.'

'She is going to be associating with her old Left Bank friends. And she is there for a purpose. Weber will know how to handle it.'

'And you? You have broken your cover.'

'I do not think so. If I return to the guerillas explaining how we were arrested, and how I managed to escape, they will accept me back. Moulin and Amalie de Gruchy, certainly. They are trusting people, and Amalie likes me. The important thing is for this Jonsson woman not to be able to get back to them to tell them what really happened.'

'That is a tricky one. I believe she is very well connected.'

'Weber will tell you how to handle it.' Christine went into the bedroom, lay on the bed. 'Why do you not call him now? I am very tired, and would like to be able to relax.' She rolled on to her stomach.

'My God!' he said. 'Those scars . . . You are marked for life.'

'They will fade. Would you not like to stroke them for me, Franz?'

'It is all falling into our lap,' Weber told Heydrich. 'That girl is brilliant. I have alerted our people in Normandy, and also Roess in Paris.'

'You think this de Gruchy woman is connected with this escape route.'

'That is what Christine says. Somehow I doubt it. She is

110

an assassin, not an organizer. But if she is in Paris, it is for some reason. We will find her. Now there remains the question of Jonsson.'

'My original orders stand. Rough her up a little, apologize, and let her go.'

'Let her go? That will compromise Ulstein. At the very least she must be deported from Europe.'

Heydrich shook his head. 'That would cause difficulty with the United States. They are already virtually at war with us, with their ships attacking our submarines, and the amount of matériel they are pouring into Great Britain. The Führer does not wish, at this time, to give them an excuse to claim the mistreatment of one of their citizens. Besides, she will be more useful to us here, now that we know she has links with the guerillas.'

'It will mean endangering Ulstein's mission. Her life.'

'Not unless Jonsson manages to return there, or get in touch with the guerillas. That is up to you to prevent.'

'I do not like it.'

'I have never known you so agitated. Is this Ulstein a friend of yours?'

'She is one of my best people. I would like to pull her out.'

'After going to such lengths to establish her?'

'Reinhard, if this information she has provided is accurate, her mission has been completed. When we have destroyed the main body of the guerillas—'

Heydrich held up a finger. '*If* we destroy the main body of the guerillas.'

'We will. But also, if we manage to lay hands on Liane de Gruchy—'

'Again, it is a case of if you manage to do so. No, no, Oskar, I think your little friend will have to remain *in situ* until we are certain of success. You tell me she is eager to continue. Humour her. Just make sure than Jonsson cannot again interfere. It will be quite simple. Have Hoeppner apologize for his mistake in arresting her and return her to

Berlin. Once she is here, you make sure she does not leave again until we have destroyed these vermin. You know how to handle it. It should only be a matter of a couple of weeks. It will be interesting to see if she contacts Madeleine von Helsingen. What is the situation there, anyway?'

'I put it on ice, as we agreed, until we discovered what Jonsson was up to. Now that we know . . .'

'Do not arrest her.'

'But you said—'

'Circumstances have changed. I have discovered that she is pregnant, and there is a rumour that the Führer has agreed to be godfather to the child when it is born. However, I think you could pay her a visit. Right now, with her husband far away and her belly full, she will be even more vulnerable than usual. But you are not interrogating her. Make sure she understands this. You are attempting to enlist her help in discovering just what Jonsson is up to. As I have said, I think she is in a fragile state. She may well reveal a great deal, especially if you make her feel that we, you, the SD, are entirely on her side in wishing to protect her from such a dangerous and undesirable acquaintance.'

'Monica! Oh, Monica!' Amalie embraced her friend, and then stood back to look at her. As on the occasion of their first meeting, Christine looked like a rag doll that had been rolled in the dust. 'What happened?'

Christine sat down, struggled to her feet again as Moulin appeared. 'Monica? Where is Mademoiselle Jonsson?'

Christine sat down again. 'May I have some wine?'

Amalie hurriedly poured, and Christine drank deeply. 'Did you get to see my parents?' Amalie asked.

'We never even got to Bordeaux. We were arrested.'

'They recognized you?'

'I don't think so. It was Joanna they were after.'

'Why?'

'I don't know. But they had a photograph of her pinned to the wall of the border station, and one of the men recognized her. They placed her under arrest. They paid no attention to me, so I slipped away and hid. I got back across the border and have been walking for two days.'

'My God! You poor woman,' Amalie said. 'I will get you something to eat.'

'But I don't understand,' Moulin said. 'Surely Joanna cannot be arrested? She is an American citizen.'

'I do not know the reason,' Christine insisted. 'I only know that they had a wanted picture of her.'

'Do you know what happened to her?'

'No. As I said, I escaped.'

Moulin looked at Amalie. 'What are we to do?'

'What can we do? Joanna is a journalist, and as you say, an American. Her own people will have to help her. We must just be happy that Monica has got back to us.' Christine hugged her.

Joanna got out of the police car and the hotel doorman hurried forward to greet her. 'Fräulein Jonsson! How good to have you back.' He picked up her bag.

'My room still there?'

'Of course, Fräulein. Exactly as you left it.'

'Thank God for that.' She looked along the street, the bustling, chattering, smiling people. 'Everyone seems happy.'

'Well, of course, Fräulein. The news is all good, eh? The Russian army has been entirely destroyed. We shall be in Moscow in a fortnight.'

'Great stuff.' She went to reception.

'Fräulein!' The clerk frowned. 'Are you all right?'

'Not as right as I am going to be after a hot bath and a drink. Send up some champagne.'

'Of course, Fräulein.' He took the key from the pigeon hole, and with it an envelope. 'There is a telephone message for you.'

Joanna put the envelope in her shoulder bag and went to the lifts, followed by a bellboy with her suitcase. She was keeping herself carefully under control, as she had done for the past week. But when she had closed and locked the bedroom door behind the boy, she threw herself across the bed and lay there for several minutes, fists clenched. When there was a knock on the door, she got up, opened it, signed the chit. The waiter opened the bottle and left. Joanna kicked off her shoes, poured herself a glass, drank, and turned on the bath. While it filled, she dropped her clothes on the floor, emptied the contents of the suitcase on top of them. She did not wish to see any of them again, certainly not until they had been laundered at least twice.

Then she stood in front of the mirror, again for the first time in a week. She was staring at a stranger. She touched her hair, which was both untidy and dirty. Both of those were about to be put right. But she could still feel the fingers being thrust into it, still feel the tugging of the roots as her head was forced forward and downwards. 'Bend, Fräulein, bend.' The words hummed in her ears. She touched her breasts, ran her fingers down her sides to her hips, then in front to sift through her pubes. She had nothing to show for what had happened, not a single bruise. They had been almost gentle with her. Yet she felt filthy, and in all the fifteen years of frenetic sexuality she had enjoyed since her sixteenth birthday, which had encompassed both men and women and some pretty wild sessions, she had never felt filthy before.

The envelope had fallen to the floor. She picked it up, slit it with her thumb. *I must see you. It is terribly important. Madeleine.*

There was no date. Joanna switched off the water and rang the desk. 'Fräulein Jonsson. The telephone message for me. When was it made?'

'Yesterday morning, Fräulein.'

'Thank you.' She sank into the tub with a great sigh of relief. So they were getting to Madeleine, too. But they couldn't know anything about Madeleine's treason, or she would hardly be making telephone calls. She washed her

114

hair, again and again, then got out of the bath, dried herself, wrapped her head in a towel, picked up the phone, and put it down again: Madeleine's line was almost certainly being tapped, as was the hotel's, no doubt. On the other hand, Madeleine's apartment was being watched. So what the hell? All she wanted to do was go to bed for a week, at least after she had got back to Stockholm . . . and that was actually more important than contacting Madeleine. She telephoned the travel agency she always used. 'Hermann? Fräulein Jonsson. I want a seat on the next train to Copenhagen.'

'Ah . . . I am sorry, Fräulein. There are no seats available to Copenhagen. There is some kind of security problem.'

'Don't tell me the Danes are acting up. Oh, very well, find me a passage on the next ship direct to Sweden.'

'I am sorry, Fräulein. There are no berths available for Sweden.'

'Oh, for God's sake, Hermann. You are starting to annoy me. All right, I'll go to Switzerland.'

'I m sorry, Fräulein, but—'

'There are no trains to Switzerland. You are a shitting asshole, Hermann. You can close my account. I won't be using you again.'

'I have already closed the account, Fräulein.'

Joanna slammed the receiver into its holder so hard she thought for a moment that she had broken it. Then she picked it up again, hesitated for a moment, and called the Swedish embassy – it would be better not to involve the Americans unless she had to. 'The ambassador, please.'

'Is he expecting your call?'

'Tell him it's Joanna Jonsson, and it is urgent.' She tapped her fingers on the table as she waited for the man's voice. 'Sven!'

'Joanna? My dear girl. Are you in Berlin?'

'I am at the Albert.'

'Of course. But are you all right? You sound upset.'

'I am upset. I have been arrested.'

'*What*! Here in Berlin?'

'No, it was in the south of France. I was following a possible story, and I appear to have broken one or two rules.'

'They did not hurt you?'

'No. They were most apologetic when they realized their mistake, sent me back here in a first-class compartment, had me met at the station and delivered here . . . But it is humiliating to be locked up, even for a couple of days. I want to go home.'

'Of course. Would you like me to make an official protest?'

'I would like you to get me out of here.'

'I don't understand. You mean you are still under arrest? I will soon sort that out.'

'I am not under arrest, Sven. At least officially. But I am confined to Berlin. I can't get a train, and I can't get a booking.'

'Is there a reason?'

'There is nothing available anywhere, they say.'

'Hm. That is very strange. Leave it with me. I'll have a word with Ribbentrop and sort it out.'

'Thank you. Would that be today?'

'Well, that will depend on how soon I can get hold of him. Give me a day or two.'

Joanna stared at the phone. But if the Gestapo were listening, to press too hard might be dangerous, especially as she did not know how much *they* knew about her real activities. 'OK,' she said. 'But make it as quick as you can. I really would like to get out of this place.' She replaced the receiver, gazed at the wall. She knew exactly what was happening. The Germans wanted her kept in Berlin until they had been able to act on that bitch's information, both as regards countering the guerilla move towards St Valery – and preparing the defences there for a British attack – and had closed the net on Liane. And if she tried to send a message to England from inside Berlin, they would then

116

have her arrested as a spy, lock her up until they were ready, and then deport her, permanently.

But they didn't know about Joachim. So he was only to be used in the direst emergency. But if this wasn't a dire emergency, she didn't know what was. His address was locked in her jewel case, which appeared to be untouched. She got dressed, brushed her hair, added make-up and felt a whole lot better . . . and the phone rang. She ran to it, picked it up. 'Sven? So quickly? You are a darling.'

'Joanna? Did you get my message?'

'Oh, shit,' Joanna remarked, and sat on the bed.

'What did you say?'

'How nice to hear your voice, Madeleine. Yes, I got your message. I was coming to see you tomorrow.'

'I said it was urgent.'

'Nothing has happened to Freddie, I hope?' Chance would be a fine thing.

'No no. Not as far as I know. I have been visited by the secret police.'

'You have been visited by the Gestapo?'

'Not the Gestapo!' Madeleine's voice became almost a wail. 'The SD.'

'Shit! What did they want?'

'They wanted to talk about you. They think you're connected with the Resistance in France.'

'Good Lord! How absurd can you get?'

'They say you have just been in France. In the south. Where the guerillas are.'

'Of course I have just been in the south of France. I went to see your parents, as nobody else seems interested in them.'

'Oh. And how are they?'

'I have no idea. I was arrested before I could get to them.'

'You have been arrested by the Gestapo?'

'Not the Gestapo. The Wehrmacht. Your old friend Franz Hoeppner. He was most apologetic, but he would not let me visit Paulliac. So he sent me back here.'

'Oh. What are you going to do?'

117

'Go back to Sweden, as soon as I can get a passage. There seems to be some kind of fuck-up at the moment. Look, I have a lot to do. I'll see if I can get round to you tomorrow. Take care.' She hung up, and found she was sweating. But at least that conversation should keep whoever was listening happy.

She had lunch, and then went out. It was broad daylight, but she felt safer in the light; it was easier to tell if she was being tailed, and although she had no doubt she was – if only to prevent her from simply going to a railway station and seeing how far she could get – as it was a Sunday afternoon the streets were busy. Even so she doubled back on her tracks several times while steadily leaving the centre of the city to delve into the side streets until she reached the address she wanted.

It was a cheap lodging house. The front door was open, and the hall stank of stale tobacco and unwashed human bodies. The things I do for England, she thought. But she was doing this for Liane more than England.

As she closed the door, a man came out of one of the downstairs rooms and peered at her, taken aback by her expensive clothes as well as her extravagant good looks. 'You have business?'

'With Joachim.'

The man looked her up and down again. 'You could do better, Fräulein. Third floor.'

He watched her climb the stairs, studying her silk stockings. She ignored him, went up the three flights, arriving only just out of breath. There was only one door, and when she tried the handle it was unlocked. She opened it, and there was startled movement from the gloom. Joachim sat up, while his partner slipped down under the bedclothes. 'What the fuck . . . ?' Joachim complained.

'Get her out of here,' Joanna said.

Now the partner also sat up. 'Who the hell are you?' he demanded.

'His wife.'

'You bastard,' the young man snapped at Joachim.

'She's not . . .'

'In this country,' Joanna remarked, 'homosexuals get sent to concentration camps. Are you going to leave, or am I going to call a policeman?' The man scrambled out of bed, began putting on his pants. Joanna gathered up the rest of his clothes and threw them into the corridor. 'You can finish dressing out there.' The man staggered out of the room, and she closed and locked the door. Then she advanced to the bed. 'You are a shit!'

'I . . . I . . .'

'Was I dreaming, or didn't you once make advances to me?'

'It's the job. Not you. You're beautiful. But . . .'

'Are you telling me he's one of us?'

'Well, no, but . . .'

'He knows who you are?'

'No, no. You see . . .' He got his nerves under control. 'What are you doing here? It is against all the rules, except in the most extreme emergency. You are risking both of our lives.'

Joanna sat on the bed beside him. 'This *is* an extreme emergency. I want you to earn your pay. I have to get a message to England not later than tomorrow night.'

'That is not possible.'

'You had better make it possible or it's the high jump for you. Now listen very carefully. The message will read: St Valery blown. Abort. Liane blown. Recover. Group penetrated. Warn. Now repeat that.'

'Can you not write it down?'

'That would compromise both you and me. Repeat.' Joachim repeated the message. 'Good boy. I'm sorry I interrupted your fun.' She gave the lump under the sheet a squeeze. 'Now, I am leaving. You jerk off to clear your head; then go find your courier and send him on his way. Come to see me as soon as it's gone to confirm. If that

119

message doesn't get through, I am going to return here and personally castrate you . . . with a blunt knife.'

She closed the door behind herself. Joachim sat still for several moments, then got out of bed and dressed himself. His hands were trembling and it took him a little while to fasten his buttons. Then he checked his kit, took out the capsule, regarded it for a few moments. He hated carrying it, in case he made a mistake. But if he was going out on a job . . .

He inserted it into his mouth, between the inside lip and his teeth, pulled on his coat, and there was a rap on the door. 'Fritz!' he asked. 'Is that you?' He opened the door, and received a thrust in the chest that sent him staggering backwards across the room. Two men came in, closing the door behind them. 'What do you want?' he gasped.

'Tell us about the lady who was just here.'

'The lady? Oh, Lili. She is just a friend.' He knew he was finished. She was finished. They were all finished. Simply because she had broken the rules.

'A friend. A rich and well-known American woman is a friend of a two-bit crook like you, Joachim? You will have to do better than that. You will come down to headquarters and tell us all about her.' Joachim drew a deep breath.

'He should be searched,' said the other man.

'If he had a weapon he would have used it by now.'

'His mouth, you fool. His mouth.'

'Open your mouth,' said the first man.

Joachim sucked the capsule between his teeth, and bit.

'Would you believe it,' Weber said. 'The fools began to question him before they searched him.'

'Who was he, anyway?' Heydrich asked.

'Oh, some petty crook who also pimps, so far as we have been able to ascertain. Name of Joachim Schmitt. But he had a cyanide capsule. This is not normal equipment for a petty crook. It *is* standard equipment for enemy agents. Any agents. We issue them to our own.'

'You are saying that this "petty crook" was actually a British agent?'

'It looks like it.'

'Living and operating in Berlin, under our very noses, and no one knew of it?'

'These people are very difficult to find, unless their cover is blown. This fellow's cover was blown simply because Jonsson paid him a visit, and my men were tailing Jonsson.'

'And instead of merely keeping an eye on this fellow they went barging in. The quality of the people we are forced to employ appalls me.'

'On the other hand,' Weber argued, 'we now surely have sufficient evidence to arrest Jonsson.'

'What evidence? That she paid a visit to a thief and a pimp. Maybe she felt like a fuck.'

'That she paid a visit to a suspected enemy agent.'

'On the basis of one cyanide capsule? It won't work, Oskar. Do you know that there are already rumours circulating in the States about atrocities being carried out in our prison camps? God knows who is spreading them.'

'But they are basically true.'

'That may be, but we do not want the world to know about it yet. Certainly not America.'

'Why are you so afraid of America? You know we are going to have to fight her eventually.'

'Eventually. When the Russian campaign is completed, which will be by the end of this year. Then we will have all Europe west of the Urals.'

'Save for Great Britain.'

'Great Britain is not a part of Europe. It is an offshore island which has a habit of interfering in European affairs. Once Russia is gone, Great Britain will become an irrelevance. But until then, we keep the Americans happy, and we will not do that by arresting one of their better-known citizens without sufficient evidence to prove our case. In any event, she is better off where she is. Let us suppose you are right and this Joachim is a British agent, and let us

121

suppose that Jonsson is also a British agent. Why did she go to see him immediately on being returned from the south of France? It has to be because of Ulstein. She knows what Ulstein has discovered, and has to warn her people in England so that they can take the appropriate steps. As she does not know that Schmitt is dead, she will assume that whatever message she told him to transmit has gone. You found his transmitter?'

'No, because there wasn't one. He must use a courier.'

'Well, that is someone else for you to find. The important thing is, as I say, that Jonsson will assume that her message has been delivered, and do nothing more about it. When she is allowed to leave Berlin, it will be too late. It is all in your lap, Oskar. I look forward to hearing that you have captured Liane de Gruchy. In fact, do you know, I look forward to meeting the famous lady. Tell your men not to tarnish her beauty until I can get there.'

Six

The Decision

The clicking of heels on the pavement penetrated the closed window of the bedroom. Liane was instantly awake and sitting up. 'Soldiers!'

Achille rolled over, lazily. 'They are up early.' He put his arms round her waist to draw her down to him. She had shared his bed now for nearly a month, and he still could not keep his hands off her.

'They are on our street. They are coming here.'

'Why should they do that?'

'Because we are next on their list. Yesterday they raided two houses in the Rue Saint-Alor, and the day before in the Rue Vincennes.'

'I know of this. They are looking for someone.'

'They are looking for me.'

Now Achille also sat up. 'Nobody knows you are here.'

'Several people know I am in Paris.' She got out of bed.

'None of them would betray you.'

'I know. It is routine.' The boots had stopped. Liane moved to the window, stood against the shutter to look down. 'Fuck it!' There were two soldiers in the alley behind the bar. She was surprised at her agitation. She had always known this had to happen, had always known the way to handle it. She drew a deep breath to get her nerves under control.

'What are we going to do?' Achille was now also nervous.

'Nothing. We are in bed together. Asleep.' She listened

to the banging on the street door. 'Now we are awake. Go down, and do whatever they wish.'

'Suppose they search the place. The radio! The gun?' He looked at her shoulder bag, hanging on the hook behind the door.

Liane also looked at the bag; her capsule was in there. 'They will not search the place, if we handle it correctly. Go down or they will break the door.' The banging was getting louder. Achille pulled on his pants and went to the door. Liane got back into bed, pulled the sheet to her throat. The voices were coming closer, and she could hear feet on the stairs. Achille was protesting. Then the bedroom door was thrown open.

Liane sat up with an exclamation of alarm, the sheet still held to her throat. Achille was thrust into the room, followed by an officer and four soldiers. The officer gazed at Liane, then looked down at a piece of paper in his hand. Liane felt a sudden rush of relief. The only portrait of her they possessed, the one they had used on the wanted posters, was a blow-up of a photograph they had taken from her flat last year. That photo had itself been a year old, and was of an immaculately dressed woman, shoulder-length yellow hair perfectly groomed, classical features flawlessly delineated by her make-up . . . There was obviously no way he could relate his print of the picture, which was in any event dog-eared and beginning to crack, with this somewhat unkempt woman with short black hair and not a trace of either rouge or lipstick 'Your name?'

'Sandrine Bouchard.' Liane spoke in a low voice, the one thing she could not adequately disguise. But there was no possibility that any of these men could ever have heard her speak.

'You are this man's wife?'

'I am at this moment in this man's bed. He allows me to do this while I try to find a place of my own.'

'You are a whore.'

'I am trying to stay alive.'

124

The lieutenant snorted, and turned to the door, but one of his men remarked, 'As she is a whore, Herr Lieutenant, should we not have a closer look?'

'A look,' the officer said.

The soldier came to the bed. Liane made herself keep calm, slowly lay down again. There was nothing she could do about what was about to happen. She just had to endure it and wait for them to go away again; she had experienced this before, in the village north of Paris in the first week of the war. But then Joanna had been with her, sharing the burden.

The soldier grasped the sheet and jerked it away. Liane lay absolutely still. 'There's a sight,' commented another of the men. Even the lieutenant came closer to look at the magnificent body lying before them.

'Very good,' he said. 'You have had your look. Now let us be about our business.'

The first soldier was still staring at Liane's pubes. 'Herr Lieutenant.'

'Have you never seen a cunt before?'

'The hair is pale, sir.'

'So?'

'The hair on her head is black. Are we not looking for a blonde woman?' Liane attempted to sit up, and was thrust flat again.

'By God,' the lieutenant said. 'You are a genius, Gruber. Up, Fräulein. You will come with us.' Liane looked from face to face, and realized she was panting. She was finished, all because of that careless slip. Hands grasped her arms to pull her from the bed, and the bedroom exploded.

The five Germans had ignored Achille, standing by the door, in their desire to look at Liane's body. He had reached into her shoulder bag, drawn the Luger, and emptied the nine-shot magazine. He was no marksman, but in the confined space he could not miss. Even Liane could not suppress a little shriek as bodies fell about her; the man who had revealed her secret actually fell across the bed, spewing blood. 'Achille!' she gasped.

'I could not let them take you.' But he too was aghast as he looked from the pistol in his hand to the five men. He dropped the gun on to the floor. 'Now they will hang us together.'

'Get this thing off me,' Liane commanded. Achille held one of the man's arms – he was certainly dead – and dragged him off he bed. Liane wriggled out from beneath the blood-soaked sheet, used it to wipe the blood from her stomach and breasts and shoulder, and reached her feet, listening to a groan. The lieutenant, although he too was bleeding, was moving, trying to reach his holster. Liane stooped beside him, drew the pistol, then looked at Achille. 'There must be no more shooting. Use a bayonet.' Achille swallowed, knelt beside one of the soldiers, and drew the bayonet from the sheath on his belt. Then he hesitated. 'Do it,' Liane said. 'We must hurry.' Achille drew a deep breath, and drove the bayonet into the lieutenant's chest. More blood gushed, and his body sagged. Liane checked the other bodies. 'And this one.'

Achille again obeyed. 'You are a terror,' he muttered.

'That is what the Germans think, and that is what they will continue to think.'

She took the spare magazine from the lieutenant's cartridge pouch, dropped it and the pistol into her shoulder bag. Then she got dressed, pulled the radio from its hiding place, and took it apart with expert speed. This also she stowed in her bag. 'What are you doing?' Achille asked. 'We may as well shoot each other.'

'We must get out of here.'

'People will have heard the shots.'

'At this hour? They will have heard distant sounds. Tell me, what of Jacqueline?'

'She does not come in until ten.'

'I know that. Will she be able to handle this?'

'She will be horrified.'

'That will be ideal.' She slung her bag. 'Let's go. There won't be anyone on the streets at this hour.'

'Go? But go where? They will tear the city apart to find us.'

'So we must go to the one place they will not look.'

'Are you stark raving mad?' Constance demanded. Dragged out of bed by a terrified Marguerite, only an hour after saying goodbye to her last client, she was a long way from her normal chic.

'It is my business to preserve both the route and our lives,' Liane said. 'If the Germans had taken me to Gestapo headquarters and tortured me, I would have told them everything.'

'So you decided to put all of our lives at risk.'

'Constance, all of your lives have always been at risk. Your survival depends upon my survival. And if you are thinking of any treachery, just remember two things. One is that as you have already entertained several evaders, you are as guilty as anyone. The other is that my friends are still out there, and they will avenge me should anything happen to me.'

'But for you to stay here . . .'

'We will be no trouble. Nothing will have changed, save for my headquarters.'

'Next thing you will want to set up a radio.'

Liane patted her bag. 'I have it here.'

'Oh, my God! And when they trace the calls . . .'

'They will not trace the calls, because I will not be making any. This is a receiving set, not a transmitter.'

'Just to own a radio carries a prison sentence.'

'So don't tell anyone we have one.'

'I have always wanted to live in a brothel,' Achille said.

'Well, I am sure you will be very happy here. But they may expect to be paid.'

'I have no money, save what I took from the till.'

'Money!' Constance said. 'You will have to pay.'

127

'Haven't I always paid?'

'But you cannot leave the house. They will be looking for you everywhere.'

'That is not a problem. I will give you a note so that you, or one of your girls, can go to Gruchy's and see the manager, Monsieur Brissard. He is our paymaster, and he will hand over the money on my instructions.'

'We are all going to be hanged,' Constance muttered.

'Not as long as we all keep our heads,' Liane told her, with more confidence than she felt.

Oskar Weber did not like Paris, mainly because he did not like the French. This afternoon he thought it the most disgusting place on earth. 'I would like you to repeat that,' he said, his voice ominously quiet.

'It was a routine matter, Herr Weber,' Kluck explained, his voice a mixture of irritation and apprehension. This man had no superior rank, yet he was the deputy – and actual – head of the security service, and more importantly, he was a close personal friend of Heydrich's. 'On the instructions we received from Berlin, we –' he glanced at Roess, standing impassively beside his desk – 'began a street-by-street search of the Montmartre area for the woman de Gruchy, investigating all the places she is known to have frequented before the war. These searches were carried out by a squad of four men, under a lieutenant. They had been proceeding for several days, without any sign of the woman, until the day before yesterday they visited the bar owned by Achille Custace. We do not know what actually happened there, but . . .'

'I presume these men were armed?'

'Of course they were armed,' Kluck snapped, even more irritated at the absurdity of the question.

'So you are saying that four armed German soldiers and an officer entered this bar and were shot and stabbed to death. How many people lived in this bar?'

'As far as we know, only this man Achille Custace, the owner. And his mistress.'

'And none of the neighbours heard the sounds of this battle? Your report says nine shots were fired.'

'It was only five in the morning, Herr Weber, and, well, the people have become accustomed to minding their own business.'

Weber looked at the report again. 'The bodies were not discovered until ten. Why is this?'

'Well, no one knew where they were. It was remarked that they were late returning to barracks, but it was supposed there was some reasonable explanation. No one could imagine that they had all been killed. This man Custace must be a devil incarnate.'

'Or his mistress is,' Roess said quietly.

Weber turned his head. 'What do you mean?'

'Five men have been killed, Herr Weber, with absolute cold-blooded ruthlessness, following which the assassins left the scene, apparently with utter calmness. I remember, just about a year ago, that a Gestapo officer was killed, again with cold-blooded ruthlessness. That assassin was Liane de Gruchy. On instructions from you, Herr Weber, these men were looking for Liane de Gruchy. I believe they found her.'

'My God!' Kluck muttered.

Weber was inclined to feel the same way. 'How many people know of what happened?'

'Well, the regiment, of course. And the neighbours will have seen the ambulances and our people searching the bar . . .'

'Very good. First, the name of Liane de Gruchy must not be mentioned in this matter.' Both policemen raised their eyebrows. 'This woman is already a heroine to the French people,' Weber said. 'We do not want to turn her into a legend as well. Our people were massacred in an ambush organized by French Resistance fighters, who will be exterminated. Understood?' They nodded. 'Secondly, if it was known that Custace was living with his mistress, there must be people around who have seen this mistress.'

'Of course. There is Custace's sister, for a start. The one who found the bodies.'

'Would you mind saying that again. Custace's sister found the bodies?'

'Yes. She went to the bar, where she helps out, at ten in the morning to prepare for opening at eleven. The door was unlocked, so she went in, and when she did not see her brother, she went upstairs.'

'Well, that is something. Bring her to me.'

'She is not here.'

'Kluck, are you saying that this woman is not in custody?'

'Well, she had nothing to do with what happened.'

'God give me patience. She is Custace's sister, you say. She works in the bar, you say.'

'But we are sure she had nothing to do with the killing. She was horrified by what she found. She ran into the street in hysterics.'

'Kluck,' Weber said, with great and obvious patience. 'She knows who Custace's mistress is. She will be able to describe her. I want her arrested and brought here, now. And God help you if she has also managed to get away.'

While he waited, Weber telephoned Berlin to put Heydrich in the picture. 'This is quite unacceptable,' the general said.

'I agree with you entirely. May I remind you that it was your decision to leave the matter in the hands of the Gestapo?'

'I am aware of that, Oskar. Kluck will have to go. I should have listened to you long ago. Tell him he is sacked and should return to Berlin. We will put him behind a desk somewhere. Promote Roess to colonel and give him the local command. Tell him that if we do not get results he will go the same way.'

'I will do that. However, although we will do all we can to keep the details secret, and especially the identity of de Gruchy, the business itself is already widely known. Five German soldiers have been murdered by this so-called

Resistance. Everyone will be privately exultant, even if they dare not be so in public.'

'I understand this. They will be not so happy when we bring Custace and de Gruchy to justice.'

'As they have vanished into thin air, that may take a little while. And all that while other hotheads will be dreaming of doing something similar. That would be very bad for morale.'

'Certainly. But there is not a lot we can do about it.'

'I would like your authority to take hostages.'

'You think that will bring de Gruchy in?'

'Probably not. But if she does not come in at a stated time, we will shoot them. Ten men for each of ours killed, and ten men for any more acts of terrorism that may occur.'

'Hm. Yes. I think that might be very productive. However, there will undoubtedly be protests from people like the Americans and the Vatican. I will have to obtain clearance. Put the idea on hold and I will come back to you.'

Weber replaced the receiver, listened to a knock on the door. 'Come.'

Kluck entered. 'We have the Custace girl.'

'Excellent. Bring her in. By the way, Kluck, you are relieved of your duties.'

'Me? You have no authority to do that, Herr Weber.'

'I am acting on the authority of General Heydrich, with whom I have just spoken. You are to return to Berlin immediately, and report to Gestapo headquarters for re-assignment. Roess, you are promoted to colonel, and will take over command of the Paris station.'

'Yes, *sir.*' Roess could not resist a triumphant glance at Kluck, who was speechless.

'Now,' Weber said. 'Let us have a look at this woman. Not you, Kluck. You had better be on your way.' The colonel looked as if he wanted to protest, then changed his mind and left the office. In his place two Gestapo officers pushed

Jacqueline into the room. She was clearly terrified, was having trouble with her breathing. 'Good morning,' Weber said. 'You are Mademoiselle Custace?'

'Yes, sir.'

'Well, sit down.' Jacqueline sank into a chair. The two guards stood behind her; Weber stood before her. 'What is your given name?'

'Jacqueline.' She spoke in a whisper.

'What a pretty name, for a pretty girl. How old are you, Jacqueline?'

'I am sixteen, sir.'

'So all of your life is in front of you. Isn't that exciting? But I understand that you have had a horrifying experience.'

'It was terrible. All those bodies . . .'

'Murdered by your brother.'

'Oh . . .' Jacqueline bit her lip.

'You don't think your brother could have done such a thing?'

'Achille is such a gentle man.'

'I am sure he is. But somebody shot and then stabbed those soldiers. Do you think it was his mistress?'

'Sandrine? But she is so . . . so . . .'

'Go on.'

'Well, sir, she is such a lady. She doesn't look it; her clothes are poor, but everything about her, the way she moves, the way she talks, the way she eats her food, shows that she is a lady.'

'Yet she is your brother's mistress. Do you not find that strange?'

'Well, I think they knew each other before the war.'

'Ah. Now, describe her to me.'

'Well . . .' Jacqueline licked her lips. 'She is medium height, with a good figure, very pretty.'

'What colour hair?'

'Black.'

'And eyes?'

'Blue.'

132

'That is a strange combination, is it not? Now tell me where they will have gone.'

'I do not know, sir.'

'I am sure you do, Jacqueline. Or you have an idea. Tell me your idea.'

'I do not know, sir. If they are not in the bar, well . . . I do not know where they could have gone.'

'But they have friends, surely.'

'My brother has no close friends, sir. Only the people who come to the bar.'

'You are Achille's only sister, is that right? And your parents are dead. So you are his closest living relative.'

'Yes, sir.'

'And you are trying to say that you do not know where he will have fled? That you have no idea?'

'I . . .' Another quick circle of her lips.

Weber put his face close to hers. 'Jacqueline, if you do not tell me where they are, I am going to be angry. And when I am angry I hurt people. Do you want me to hurt you?'

Jacqueline's lips trembled. 'Please don't hurt me, sir. I don't know where they have gone. I swear it.'

Weber straightened. 'You have a room?'

'Of course,' Roess said.

'Let us go there. Have my equipment taken down.'

Weber snapped his fingers, and the two guards grasped Jacqueline's arms and lifted her from the chair. Tears rolled down her cheeks. 'Please, sir, are you going to hurt me?'

'Yes,' Weber said. 'I am going to hurt you very much, unless you tell me what I wish to know.'

'But I don't *know,*' she wailed.

'Shut her up,' Weber said. One of the guards swung his fist and struck Jacqueline in the stomach. She gasped and almost choked, continued to pant as she was forced to stumble down the stairs, past inquisitive eyes, and into the cellar. She shivered and wept as she panted, blinked at Roess, who was already there, with two other men.

Weber closed the door, and looked around the room. It

133

was a typical, to his mind primitive, Gestapo torture chamber; on the walls hung an array of whips and irons, an iron frame leaned beside them, and in the centre of the room there was an interrogation stool, bolted to the floor, a single narrow seat only a foot high, with a back rising another two feet. Around it, set into the floor, were several iron rings. There was also a table against one wall on which there was a gramophone and also a large square box with a lid. 'Strip her,' Weber commanded.

Jacqueline panted and tugged on her arms, but she was helpless as the men tore her dress and petticoat into strips, then pulled off her drawers and stockings, threw her shoes into a corner.

Weber was aware of that peculiarly exultant surge of sexual fury that always overtook him when about to torture a woman. How he dreamed of having Joanna Jonsson in this position. Or better yet, Liane de Gruchy, a woman he had never seen outside of a poor photograph, but who, simply because of her reputation, he desired more than any other woman in the world. For the moment, this girl would have to do. She was not beautiful. She was not even hand-some, although she might become so, given the chance. But right now, with her long straight black hair, her small breasts and narrow hips, her thin buttocks and slender legs, she could only be described as piquant. Yet still enjoyable. 'Put her on the stool,' he said. 'Stretch her.' The guards made Jacqueline sit on the stool; she no longer attempted to resist them. They pulled her arms behind her and to their widest extent and secured them to the appropriate rings. 'Legs up, but spread,' Weber commanded.

Jacqueline's legs were pushed up until her thighs almost touched her breasts, and then pulled apart, her ankles also secured to the appropriate rings so that she was utterly exposed, and unable to move more than her head. Roess watched with interest. 'We usually flog them first,' he remarked. 'In fact, it is seldom necessary to do more.'

'And they are reduced to gibbering wrecks. You should

come up to date, Colonel.' Weber touched the box on the table. 'This allows you to apply as much pain as you think necessary, and to end it at the flick of a switch. It leaves no mark, yet is so intense as to be irresistible. And it is so interesting to use.' He opened the box, took out an inner case, which was a good foot square and six inches deep. From it extended three cables, one ending in a plug, the other two in alligator clips. Attached to one side there was a small handle, such as that used on a telephone. 'Socket.' One of the guards plugged the machine in.

'Now, we begin softly.' Weber lifted the box from the table and laid it on the floor behind Jacqueline. He extended one of the leads and clipped it to the forefinger of her hand and then did the same to the other. Then he knelt on one knee beside her head; she was again panting and rolling her eyes. 'When I crank my machine,' he explained, 'electricity will run from one finger to the other. It will travel up your left arm, across your shoulders, and down your right arm to the negative pole. It will feel exactly as if your skin is being opened by a sharp knife the whole way. And if that does not persuade you to tell us what we require, I shall then attach the clips to your toes. Then the charge will run up one leg, through your groin, and down the other. If that does not work, I shall attach the clips to your tits. That is very exciting. And if that doesn't work, I shall put one clip up your ass and the other into your vagina. That is the most exciting of all. Do you understand me?'

Jacqueline panted. 'Please . . .'

'So why do you not save yourself a lot of agony and tell me where your brother and his woman may have gone?'

'I do not know, sir. I swear I do not know.'

Weber moved behind her. 'Put on the gramophone.'

Roess cranked that machine, and a moment later Wagner filled the room. Weber then cranked his own device.

Joanna paced up and down her hotel room. Never had she felt so frustrated. She kept telling herself to keep calm, but it was now over a week since she had seen Joachim, and he had not come to confirm that the message had been sent, and even longer than that since she had asked Sven for help. As far as her getting out of Germany was concerned, she knew the regime well enough to be sure that if they intended to keep her here, they would, no matter what representations might be made. There remained of course the American embassy, but she was still inclined to keep that as a last resort. But the message . . .

She came to a decision, left the hotel and went to Joachim's lodging house. This was a weekday, and she did not suppose he would be home, but she might be able to find out where he worked. As usual, the street door was open, and as before her entry was overseen from the downstairs apartment. 'You,' said the man. 'You have the nerve to return here?'

'Do my nerves have anything to do with you?' Joanna asked. 'Is Joachim here?'

'Are you pretending you don't know?'

'Don't know what?' She kept her voice even, but suddenly she felt sick.

'Joachim is dead. He died the day of your last visit.'

'Oh, Jesus!' she muttered. 'How?'

'Your friends came to see him, and he died. No one knows how.'

'My friends?'

The man stared at her. 'You should go away,' he said. 'We do not wish you here.' He stepped back into his flat and closed the door.

Joanna wanted to bang on the door and get him back out, but she didn't suppose she would get much more information, and she didn't wish to create a disturbance which might involve the police. But what to do? Her 'friends' could only have been the Gestapo. Poor Joachim. But the important point was that her message had not been sent. Had he told his interrogators about it before he died? If he had, they would surely have arrested her by now. So they couldn't know why she had visited him, only that as a result of that

136

visit he had killed himself. But the message! It was now more than two weeks since that woman Christine von Ulstein had been able to report. Two weeks in which the Germans had known Liane was in Paris and why. Two weeks in which she had been in deadly danger. Equally, the projected attack on St Valery had to be only days away. With the Germans waiting for it!

But there could be no doubt that in addition to tapping her phone, the Gestapo were also tailing her. Waiting for sufficient proof to arrest her? Or waiting for her to betray another British agent? She felt quite flushed with heat although her hands were cold as she hurried back to the hotel. One thing was for sure: the bastards were not going to beat her. She telephoned the Swedish embassy first, and not very hopefully. Correctly. 'Joanna!' the ambassador said. 'I should have called you before, but I have been rather busy.'

'Can I get out?'

'Ah! I had a word with Ribbentrop, who promised to look into it, and as a matter of fact he had me in two days ago. He told me that it was not considered safe for you to leave Berlin right now. He said it would only be a matter of another couple of weeks; then you would be free to go wherever you pleased.'

'And you accepted that?'

'Well, he is a difficult man. You know how he looks at you with those cold fish eyes of his. And frankly . . . You haven't been doing anything stupid, have you?'

'Of course I have not. And supposing I had, wouldn't they have arrested me and deported me, rather than keep me here?'

'That's true. Well, there it is. I protested of course, and he noted my protest. I don't think there is anything more I can do. After all, if it is only to be a couple of weeks more . . .'

'Well, thanks for trying anyway. I'm grateful.'

She telephoned the American embassy. She had met the ambassador, but unlike Sven she knew he was a somewhat heavy-handed character who on being told that an American citizen was virtually under house arrest in Berlin would probably raise the roof and get too many people interested in her. On the other hand, her getting out was now of secondary importance to her message getting out, fast. So she asked for George Munday. George was actually younger than her, but they had met on several occasions and she knew he would like to get together. He was her best bet. 'Hi,' she said. 'Remember me?'

'Joanna? Say, what a pleasant surprise. I didn't know you were in Berlin.'

'I've been here a couple of weeks, and I'm feeling bored stiff. How would you like to have dinner with me?'

'Gee. Well, that sounds great.'

'We can eat right here in the hotel. I'll see you at seven.'

That should give the phone-tappers a giggle.

George was a decently tall young man, which Joanna, with her height, always regarded as a bonus. 'Tell me what you've been doing,' she suggested.

'Well, not a lot.'

'You got a line on the Russian situation?'

'Oh, sure. They're licked.'

'I know that's the German slant. But is it for real?'

'There is no nation in history that's taken such losses as the Soviets and survived. The regime, anyway.'

'You happy about that?'

'They had it coming. The Reds.'

'But if the Nazis win there, what happens next?'

'Looks like curtains for England.'

She finished her dessert. 'Shall we go up to my room?'

'What about the house detective?'

'If any goddamned Kraut house detective tries to muscle into my business I'll wring his fucking neck. Rudolf!' She summoned the maître d'. 'My friend and I wish for a little privacy. Send up some coffee and two glasses of Hine Antique.'

Rudolf bowed. 'Right away, Fräulein.'

They went to the lifts. 'You're terrific,' George murmured.

138

'Keep saying things like that and you may have an enjoyable evening.' She led him along the corridor and into her room, closed the door. 'Now kiss me.'

'Eh?'

'Don't you want to kiss me?'

'Well, sure I do. But I mean, gee . . . just like that?'

'Just like that.' She put her arms round his neck kissed him and hugged him, then slid her mouth round to his ear. 'I think this room may be bugged,' she whispered. 'And I have something very important to say to you.' She let him go, and he goggled at her. 'Let's sit down.' She held his hand and led him to the settee. 'Put your arms round me and hold me close.' He obeyed, and she rested her head on his shoulder. 'Please don't make any stupid remarks or exclamations,' she whispered. 'Just listen, and say yes or no, as appropriate. Your diplomatic pouch goes to London every couple of days, right?'

'Yes. But—'

'Just listen. I would like to send a message to London, very urgently. Could you get it into your bag for me?'

'Well, yes, I suppose so. But—'

'There's the door.' She got up, allowed the waiter into the room. 'Thank you. I'll just sign, shall I?' She took the chit to her desk, signed it. The waiter left, but Joanna remained seated at her desk. 'I'll just enter this up.'

'You on some kind of expense account?'

'Mom likes to know how I'm spending her money.' She wrote:

Unable to make St Valery. All booked up with people I don't like. Do tell the others. Liane has a problem. Paris very unhealthy at the moment. See if you can persuade her to move. Love JJ

She took out an envelope, wrote down James's address. This was a serious breach of security, but she was in the business of saving lives. She did not seal the envelope, returned to sit beside him, laid the letter on his lap, and again rested her head on his shoulder. 'You can read it.'

He did so, frowning. 'You want this sent to England, in our diplomatic pouch?'

'Yes, please.'

'Is it a code?'

'Does it read like a code? I arranged to meet some friends in St Valery, and now I have decided I can't make it.'

He hugged her. 'Joanna, I think you are the most exciting woman I have ever met, but I'd also hate to think that you consider me a fool. Do you seriously expect me to believe that you arranged to meet some *English* friends in St Valery, which is in German-occupied France, and which is in any event a prohibited area, being a seaport on the Channel?'

She nestled against him. 'Will you send it?'

He looked at the envelope. 'Who is this person Pound?'

'I can't answer that.'

'Are you working for the British?'

'I am a reporter. I happen to have got hold of a story which my editor commissioned, but which I know the Germans would not let me publish. In fact, the reason they are keeping me here in Berlin is just so I can't get the story out until it is stale news.'

He breathed into her hair. 'You are being kept in Berlin against your will?'

'Yes, I am. They tell me it is only for a couple more weeks, but that's too long.'

'Well, we'll soon see about that.'

'No, you will not see about that. Too much fuss and they'll deport me and not let me in again. Just let's be smarter than them. If I can get that message out, I won't care how long they keep me here.' He did not reply for several moments, so she finally asked, 'Will you do it?'

'It could cost me my job.'

'Oh, don't tell me you guys don't use the pouch for personal correspondence.'

140

'So it happens. Nobody is supposed to know. And if this is some seditious or illegal material—'

'No one is ever going to find out. Listen, George, this means a whole lot to me. If you'll send it, well . . .' She lifted his hand and placed it on her breast. 'Maybe you could stay the night.'

'Now stop looking like a long streak of misery,' James suggested. 'I'll be back tomorrow.'

'Or not at all,' Rachel pointed out. 'And you're going to be seasick. You told me you're always seasick.'

'One of those things. If I can stand it, so can you.'

'Oh, you . . .' She handed him various items. 'Haversack. I've been right through it and it's got everything you'll need. Gas mask.'

'For God's sake.'

'You never can tell. Anyway, it's required gear. Revolver. Box of cartridges.'

'I imagine I'll be given a tommy-gun.'

'Again, required gear. Well . . .' They gazed at each other, and then were in each other's arms. 'Just come back,' she whispered.

'That's what I have in mind.' He kissed her and left the little flat.

Rachel sat at the desk and gazed at the closed door. She sometimes found it impossible to accept that she had spent most of the last year in this room, with James, waiting for news of death and destruction, condemning other human beings to risk that death and destruction simply to thwart the ambitions of other men and women who she had never seen. Because they were evil, she had been told, and believed. It had all been jolly hockey sticks two years ago, when Britain had gone to war in defence of Poland. Just how England was going to defend Poland, with the two countries separated by the width of Europe – including Nazi Germany – had never been adequately explained, but the war had come as a welcome end-of-season diversion to the

141

bright young things of her then set, the products of schools like Benenden and Roedean and Cheltenham, who spent their summers drifting from Ascot to Wimbledon to Henley, vying to see whose photograph would most often appear in *Tatler*.

Rachel liked to feel that she had, even then, been seeking some more serious aspect to life, but she knew she had not considered the call to arms as more than another social adventure. She had been one of the first volunteers for the newly formed ATS. She had actually had little choice about this. Her father was a general and he had quickly intimated that he expected her to do her bit. Mum had been appalled at the idea of her daughter having to share a barracks with a bunch of shop girls. Rachel had also been appalled, less at the prospect of slumming it, which she found rather amusing, than at having to exchange her silk lingerie and stockings for the coarse cotton of the army.

The work itself she had found boring and repetitive. As an avid amateur aviatrix, she had hoped to become a driver, and had instead wound up in the typing pool. Thus when the call had come for volunteers for special training she had jumped at it, and with both feet, into a world she had never supposed to exist, from dawn rising and cold showers, always shared with half a dozen other girls, to ten-mile runs before breakfast, to intensive training in unarmed combat, to a study in cyphers and undercover activity of all sorts. That had certainly been interesting, even if she had had no idea where it might all be leading. It had led here, to this somewhat claustrophobic office which reminded her of a spider's web, but in which she was at least the assistant spider.

It had also led her to James. When she thought of all the bosses she could have wound up with, the moustache twirlers, the bores, the misogynists who regarded women in uniform as monstrosities, the homosexuals, the lechers . . . Was James a lecher? Of course not. She had seduced him, because she had found him at once attractive and exciting, and because she had been, and remained, on an euphoric high at being at the very centre of the great game that was being played all over Europe and indeed all over the world. James had allowed himself to be seduced. Sharing so much at work, spending so much of their time exclusively in each other's company, it would have been unnatural had it not happened. It was only after it *had* happened, and she had realized that she was falling in love with him, that she had discovered he was already in love with somebody else, the Frenchwoman Liane de Gruchy, whose life he now controlled.

Oddly, learning about Liane had not affected their relationship. Rather, it had come as something of a relief. While she knew she was in love with James, she was also level-headed enough to understand that it was an emotion created by the war and their special circumstances that could well dwindle with the return of peacetime routine. Not to mention the enormous difficulties that would lie in the way of a marriage between upper and lower middle class. James's father was a schoolmaster; hers came from a long line of generals. So when it was all over, he would go looking for his French inamorata – a woman she had never met – supposing, in view of the life she was leading, she was still around – and she would go looking for . . . what?

She went out to lunch, came back to a thoroughly boring afternoon, springing up every time the radio crackled. At six she decided to call it a day. James would have embarked by now. All she could do was wait. She was billeted at an ATS hostelry not far from the office, but she rather felt like going home tonight. Mum understood that she was engaged in top-secret work without having a clue what she was actually doing. She never asked questions, but was always glad to see her, and she felt like enjoying a decent meal off decent crockery and with a decent bottle of wine. She closed down the radio, put on her hat – she wore civilian clothes when on duty – and turned as there was a rap on the door. 'Mrs Hotchkin, Miss Cartwright.'

'Come in. I'm just packing up.' She frowned. 'Is there anything wrong?'

'This letter.' Mrs Hotchkin, a Dunkirk widow, short and plump with an almost uncontrollable moustache, might also not know exactly what her tenants were up to, but she also knew it was top secret. 'We've never had a letter before. But it says Pound.'

Rachel took the envelope. 'And our address. That's not good. Thank you, Mrs Hotchkin. I'll deal with it.'

Mrs Hotchkin withdrew, as reluctantly as ever; she was dying to be involved. Rachel waited for the door to close, then went to the desk, sat down, drew a deep breath, and slit the envelope. It was so unusual she had simply had no idea what to expect.

She looked at the signature first. Oh, the silly bitch! Sending a letter . . . But by hand? Revealing the address to everyone? Then she read the text, and suddenly felt quite cold. Joanna was telling them both to abort the raid and to recall Liane from Paris. But Joanna did not *know* about the raid, or that Liane was in Paris! Yet somehow she had found out. She grabbed the telephone, gave the brigadier's number 'Pound. Is Pound there? Pound Two speaking.'

'I am afraid he has left the office.'

'Look, this is most urgent. Will you give me the number of Commander Lewis in Bosham?'

There was a brief hesitation, while the woman, hopefully, looked it up. But she was looking up her instructions. 'I'm afraid that number is not available at this moment. If you wish, you may try again tomorrow.'

When the raid would have been completed. 'Tomorrow will be too late. Look, this is Pound Two. We are involved.'

'I am sorry, miss.'

Rachel drew several deep breaths to stop herself from screaming. 'All right. Will you tell me how I can get in touch with Pound.'

'You can reach him in this office tomorrow morning.'

'That will be too *late*!' Rachel shouted. 'Look, can *you*

144

get in touch with him.' Silence. 'I will take that as yes,' Rachel said. 'So will you please do that, now, and ask him to call me. Tell him it is a matter of life and death. A whole bunch of lives and deaths.'

She hung up. Going home was obviously out of the question. So was going out to find a bite of supper. So was having a drink to calm her nerves. And there were no cigarettes available; James did not smoke himself and did not like them used in the office.

She went into the bedroom, lay on the bed, and actually fell asleep, to awake with a start when the phone rang. She dashed into the office, nearly dropped the receiver. 'Pound Two!'

'Pound,' said the brigadier. 'Is there something the matter?'

'Yes, sir. I have received this message.' She read it out.

There was a moment's silence. Then he said, 'That means of communication breaks every rule in the book.'

'She obviously feels the situation is desperate, sir.'

'How did she know of these operations, anyway? I hope James did not confide in her.'

'No, sir, he did not. But the fact that she *does* know of them leads me to believe that her source in Berlin confides them to her, which means that somehow Jerry has learned of them.'

'Hm. Yes. There will have to be a full investigation of this business.'

'Yes, sir. But what about our people?'

'Yes. What a goddamed shame.'

'Sir? Aren't we going to abort?'

'That is not an option.'

'Sir?'

'It's past midnight. They will be nearly across the Channel by now, and the French people will be about to launch their attack. To attempt to abort now would lead to the most tremendous snafu, even if we could get in touch with everyone in time. Bury that report, Sergeant.'

'But sir, the people—'

'People get killed in war, Sergeant. Let's hope some of ours get back. Kill that report. That is an order.'

PART THREE

The Survivors

Against the hour of death.

The Book of Common Prayer

Seven

The Invitation

Rachel stared at the phone in disbelief combined with anger. Past midnight. The brigadier, having sent his people into battle, had obviously gone out to dinner. No doubt he would say that as there was nothing he could then do, his best course was to do nothing. She supposed it was a testimony to his dedication that he had troubled to check with his office at all before going to bed.

But if he had stayed in that office instead of going out she would have reached him in time. Now . . . She did not know the call sign for the Commando boats, and even if she did, to recall them on her own initiative would lead to a court martial. But she did know the call sign used by the Resistance group, and she knew Liane's call sign too. She could still save some lives, perhaps. Liane, she knew, would only listen at six in the morning and six in the evening, She would have to wait. But the others . . .

She switched on the radio, selected the required wavelength. 'Pound Two,' she said. 'This is Pound Two. Come in please.' There was no reply.

'Perfect night for it, what?' Lewis asked, standing beside James in the little wheelhouse, immediately behind the helmsman. The wheelhouse was situated right aft in the thirty-foot boat; forward was filled with uniformed Commandos, crouching with their weapons. To either side, another fishing boat kept pace with the leader. 'I mean,' Lewis said. 'No moon, flat calm sea . . . I say, old man, are you all right?'

151

'No,' James gasped, opening the door and almost falling outside to hang over the side. Lewis waited for him to return, but made no comment. 'Happens every time,' James said, wiping his lips. 'The sea and I just don't get on. Don't worry; I'll be all right when the show starts.'

'Of course you will, old man. Nelson was always seasick.'

'Do you know where we are?'

'Oh, yes.' Lewis bent over the little chart table, which was illuminated by a pencil-thin ray of light from a small lamp. 'Twenty miles off.'

James peered through the salt-encrusted windscreen at the utter darkness in front of them. 'How can you be sure?'

'Dead reckoning, old man. We take the speed of our boat, the rate and directions of the tide, any leeway caused by the wind, which isn't a factor tonight, calculate our position, and mark it off on the chart.' He indicated the last little pencilled X.

'And it really works?'

'I guarantee that we'll hit the beach within a hundred yards of where we want to be.' James scratched his head, but he didn't really doubt it. Lewis was about the most confident man he had ever met; it was reassuring to suppose that every officer in the Royal Navy was, by training and experience, similarly endowed. 'Fifteen miles.' Lewis opened the door. 'Have your men standing by, Captain.'

'Right away, sir,' replied Captain Cooper.

'You'll be going ashore?' Lewis asked James.

'That is my intention.'

'Very good. We'll have to stop short of the beach itself, so you'll have to wade. But we'll be waiting for you.'

James nodded, took off his cap and put on his steel helmet, again peered into the darkness . . . which was suddenly illuminated by a star shell, fired to hover immediately above the three little ships. 'What the shit . . . ?' Lewis shouted.

'MTBs to port,' the helmsman snapped.

The outside of the three vessels had also seen the approaching little warships, and now she altered course

152

violently, forcing the two other fishing boats to do the same. 'What now?' James asked, lumps of lead gathering in his stomach.

Lewis grabbed the radio microphone. 'Abort,' he said. 'Return to base.'

'But the French!' James protested.

'It can only be the French who have betrayed us,' Lewis snapped. 'I must save what I can.'

But it was by now academic. The MTBs had opened fire, after sending up more star shells to illuminate the night. One of the fishing vessels was already sinking. Now a shell ploughed into the flagship, forward, bringing shrieks of agony and despair.

'We're going down,' shouted the helmsman.

'Then you'll have to make the beach,' Lewis told him. 'Can you swim?' he asked James.

'Some.'

'Well, your Mae West should keep you afloat.'

'And on the beach?'

'I wish you luck.'

Machine-gun bullets were still slashing into the hull, and the bows of the fishing boat were dipping under; the surviving Commandos were already in the water. James could see lights ahead of him now; he did not suppose they were in any way indicative of help or support, but they at least suggested that the land was not very far away. He looked back at Lewis, who had taken the helm himself and was trying to control the sinking ship, and felt a sudden numbness in his leg. Oh, shit, he thought, and fell over the side into the surprisingly cold water, remembering the destroyer in which he had been evacuated from Dunkirk disappearing beneath his feet; the sea and I do not agree.

Pierre looked at his watch. He could not believe the operation had gone so smoothly. Every one of his thirty-man squad had arrived at the rendezvous on time and in perfect

153

shape – and he had had serious doubts as to the reliability of the Communists. 'Five minutes,' he told Henri. 'Pass the word. And remember, we stick together, for greater fire-power. Equally, when we destroy the power station, we withdraw, together, regardless of what the Brits may be doing.'

'Understood.' Henri crawled away to speak with the various section commanders. Pierre checked his watch again, counting the seconds. The Commandos must be very near the beach by now. But as he had been a soldier all of his adult life, he knew that precision and timing was every-thing in an operation like this. Two minutes. Henri had returned. 'They are ready.'

'Then—' Pierre watched the star shell arcing over the sea beyond the town. 'What the shit . . . ?'

'They are signalling us.'

'That was not in the plan! Listen!' The sound of firing was clearly discernible across the stillness of the night.

'They must have landed already,' Henri said. 'So much for their schedule.'

'They have not landed,' Pierre said. 'They are being destroyed.'

Henri gulped. 'Can we not help them? It is time for our attack.'

'It is a trap,' Pierre said. 'Get the men out. Tell them to scatter and return to Vichy as best they can.'

'But . . .'

'Do it. I am placing you in command. Go, go, go. Leave me Jules.' Henri hesitated, then crawled away. Pierre stared at the town, which was now a blaze of searchlights sweeping the approach roads, the low hills surrounding the town, and the beaches, turning the night into day. Had that star shell been fired two minutes later, his entire squad would have been caught in those lights and cut to pieces.

Jules arrived beside him. 'We have been betrayed. The fucking British . . .'

'I do not think it was the British, as such. They would hardly sacrifice their own men to destroy us.'

'Then who?'

'There is a traitor somewhere; that is certain. Let's move.'

'Behind the others?'

'Down to the beach.'

'With respect, Monsieur de Gruchy, that beach is going to be crawling with Nazis.'

'That is why they will not be expecting us.'

'But what can we do?'

'We came here to help the Commandos. If we can help even one we must do it.'

Jules sighed. 'As you say, sir.'

'Pound Twelve,' Rachel said. 'Pound Twelve.'

'Pound Twelve,' Liane replied, frowning. This was not her usual contact.

'Pound Two. You have been betrayed. Leave Paris immediately.'

'Your news is a little out of date.'

'Oh, my God! What has happened?'

'To the route? Nothing, so far. It is still operable. Let me speak to Pound One.'

'I think Pound One is dead.'

Liane stared at the set for several seconds. 'Say again?'

'He has also been betrayed.'

'And the others?'

'We have no news. None of our people have returned. There is no word of yours.'

'That is very serious.'

'Yes,' Rachel said. 'I am so terribly sorry. For both our sakes. But you must leave Paris and return to Vichy.'

'My business is here. With the route.'

'The route must survive without you for a while. Have you no one to take your place?'

Liane considered. 'Yes. It can operate without me. For a little while.'

155

'Then see that it does. Your immediate business is to return to Vichy and reorganize your group. That is an order.'

'Understood,' Liane said. 'Over and out.' She replaced the mike, lowered the aerial, and closed the cupboard in which the radio was situated. For a moment she couldn't think, because she didn't want to think. James was dead! Oddly, it was something she had never expected to happen. But she had not even the time to give way to personal grief, and in any event, her feelings for him, although she had enjoyed moments of great passion in his arms, had always been ambivalent. She found herself wondering about the woman on the radio. Pound Two had to be his second in command. Pierre had told her, when he had visited James's office before being returned to France, that there had only been a staff of one, a young woman he had described as quite attractive, named Rachel. Could this be her? She had certainly sounded fond of her boss.

But that was really irrelevant. The important catastrophe was the suggestion that the guerillas had been wiped out. Pierre would have been leading them, and Henri would certainly have accompanied them. Were they both dead? Amalie would be devastated. And was she not devastated? But again, more important than personal grief, there was the group, now without a leader. Moulin was a splendid organizer, and he had the prestige, but because of his injuries he could not lead in the field, and without someone to do that the group would disintegrate. Pound Two had recognized that; hence her orders, which had to be obeyed. She didn't want to leave Paris. Or the brothel. She was enjoying herself, even if it was irksome being unable to go outside. But inside . . . She had even on occasion visited the bar, and been in instant demand. Once, she had been told, she had even serviced a very high-ranking Gestapo officer. Constance hadn't known who he was – he was apparently only on a visit to Paris – but the other officers had all clearly been in awe of him. He had been a good

156

lover, too. But if there was any risk of the group ceasing to exist . . .

The door opened. 'That was a long conversation,' Achille said. 'It is dangerous to talk for so long.'

'It was necessary. I must leave.'

'Leave? To go where?'

'There has been trouble in the south. I must sort it out.'

'But you cannot leave. Who will command here?'

'You. Or if you cannot, Constance. She is a treasure.'

'But what of Jacqueline?'

Liane sighed. 'Achille, Jacqueline is gone. She is in a concentration camp.'

'She may come back. Your parents came back.'

'If she comes back, I am sure it will make you very happy. But my being here, or not, will not affect that. I must go.'

'How can you go? The Germans are looking for you everywhere.'

'The Germans have been looking for me for more than a year, and now they do not even know what I look like.'

'Jacqueline will have told them. They will have tortured her, and she will have told them. Your name, too. Oh, my poor baby sister.'

Liane held his hand. 'I am so terribly sorry. But you are quite right. I must go and have a talk with Constance. One of her girls can fetch Laurent to make me a new identity card and a travel document. And she will take over the local running of the route.' She kissed him. 'Don't worry. I will come back. As soon as I have sorted things out in the south.'

'What a fuck-up,' Heydrich remarked, throwing the report across his desk. 'I thought you said Roess was a good man?'

'He is,' Weber insisted. 'This is not his fault. He had to apply to the local commander for men to carry out his mission, and once that idiot heard what it was about he insisted upon taking over.'

157

'Roess should have applied to you, or me, for overriding authority.'

'Agreed. But he was new to the job and was uncertain as to what powers you might have over the Wehrmacht.' Heydrich raised his eyebrows. 'Well,' Weber said defensively, 'not everyone realizes who you are. Anyway, the operation was not that much of a failure. The entire British force was wiped out. All the boats were sunk, and out of an estimated one hundred men only eight made the shore. They are now in captivity.'

'You are positive of these figures?'

Weber made a face. 'There are some indications that one or two others may have reached the beach. The tides are strong in the English Channel, and it is possible that a few men might have been swept away from the harbour. But even if they made the shore, they have nowhere to go. They will be picked up,'

'So the affair will be trumpeted as a great victory. Three little fishing boats and perhaps a hundred men. I wonder how many fishing boats Churchill has at his command? We know he has getting on for a million men. Do you really suppose this minor mishap is going to cause him to lose five minutes' sleep? The object of the exercise was to destroy the Gruchy guerilla group, and this has not been done. Has it? Have you any evidence that they were even there?'

'They were there all right. Roess combed the countryside after the battle, found evidence of a group of people having camped within a few miles of the port.'

'But they never attacked.'

'Well, as you say, the navy jumped the gun. I would assume the guerillas were to attack the moment the British hit the beach. They must have seen, or heard, the naval attack, and decided to withdraw.'

'I assume Roess mounted a pursuit?'

'Yes, but he has not found anything. These people just melt into the local populace.'

'So, you accept that from our point of view the operation has been a complete failure.'

Weber sighed. 'We must accept that, yes.'

'And the search for Liane de Gruchy and her lover?'

Weber sighed again. 'They have vanished into thin air.'

'Did you get nothing out of the sister?'

'The name de Gruchy is currently using. But I imagine she has, or can obtain, another identity.'

'And a description?'

'Oh, yes. She claims the woman she knows as Sandrine Bouchard has short black hair.'

'But you are still convinced it is de Gruchy?'

'Hair can easily be cut and dyed. The ruthlessness of the killings makes it seem certain. And we know she is in Paris.'

'On your woman's say-so, nothing more. It is a very good thing that we are not living in a society where we have to prove our cases in an impartial court of law. This one, certainly, would be thrown out. Where is this woman Jacqueline Custace now?'

'In a concentration camp.'

'And she gave you nothing more than a description of this woman? You are losing your touch. What did you do to her?'

'I used electricity.'

'Do you know, I have never seen that method employed. Was it . . . interesting?'

'Very. Especially as we went the whole way. She kept shrieking that she did not know her brother's whereabouts. Actually, I very rapidly believed her. But we went on asking her anyway, until she passed out.'

'I can see that must have been enjoyable. Have you taken those hostages?'

'Oh, yes.'

'And shot any of them?'

'I shot all of them, when it became obvious that neither de Gruchy nor Custace were going to surrender.'

159

'So what are you going to do now?'

'We shall keep looking. I intend to return to Paris myself for a while.'

'Cannot Roess be left in charge?'

'I will not interfere. I just feel I should be there.'

Heydrich regarded him for several moments. 'I thought you hated France. And the French.'

'I do, as a people. However . . .' Weber actually flushed.

'Out with it.'

'Well . . . Roess took me to a house there.'

'You mean a brothel.'

'True. But it is the best house I have ever been in. And the madam – she calls herself Constance – is an absolute delight.'

'And this house is safe?'

'Oh, indeed. It is reserved exclusively for German officers.'

'Therefore you are not likely to pick up any information on the whereabouts of de Gruchy or her boyfriend.'

'Well, no. But a man cannot work all of the time.'

Heydrich lit a fresh cigarette. 'I object to no man seeking pleasure, as long as it does not interfere with his duty. I would just like to make a couple of points. I handed this business over to the SD because the Gestapo was getting nowhere, and, I admit it freely, you came up with some very good ideas. Unfortunately, none of them have worked. The senior de Gruchys have been back in Paulliac for more than two months, and no attempt has been made by any member of their family to contact them. Your woman does seem to have penetrated the guerilla group, but her information has been mishandled and squandered. Have you any means of contacting Ulstein?'

'None. We have to wait for her to contact us. And after what has happened, she will have to regroup, as it were.'

'But she did manage to contact Hoeppner. Did she pinpoint the guerilla position?'

'Of course.'

'That is something. We must act on it.'

It was Weber's turn to raise his eyebrows. 'You will need authority.'

'I will get authority.'

'I will look forward to that.' Weber stood up. 'And Jonsson?'

'She cannot interfere now. Let her go to Sweden, if she wishes.'

'Do you not suppose that could be dangerous? She knows that Ulstein is our agent. If she has any means of getting in touch with the guerillas . . .'

'What do you propose?'

'I have some ideas. Will you leave it with me?'

Heydrich stubbed out his cigarette. 'Just remember to be careful.'

'Good morning, sir.' Rachel stood to attention as the brigadier entered the office. After three days of utter despair, she was freshly bathed and dressed, her hair arranged in its normal bun, her spectacles firmly on her nose. She had no idea what was going to happen. She did not care.

The brigadier gazed at her for several seconds. He was a stockily built man with receding dark hair, and wore a neatly trimmed military moustache which quite betrayed his three-piece suit. But then, his bearing also did that. Now he moved about the office, looking at various things. 'What have you been doing?'

'Waiting, sir. Listening.'

'Any word from Jonsson?'

'No, sir. The unorthodox manner in which she conveyed her information makes me think that she is under some kind of restraint.'

'Or something has happened to Joachim Schmitt. We haven't heard from him for a while, either. Mind you, I always had doubts about employing that sort of fellow. He was established by my predecessor, you know. Before the war.'

Rachel had a sense of bemusement, that this so aloof man who had usually in the past treated her as if she

161

wasn't there was discussing confidential departmental matters as if she were *his* private secretary. But that he was doing so made her sense of despair grow. 'Is there no news, sir?'

The brigadier sat behind James's desk. 'Jerry is claiming a "great victory in the English Channel". I am quoting. Their communiqué says "three English warships sunk and their crews killed or captured".'

Rachel's heart leapt. 'Captured?'

'They claim to be holding eight of them.'

'Have they . . . ?'

'No names have been released as yet. However, from our point of view, it makes no odds whether James was killed or captured.'

I suppose not, you old bastard, Rachel thought. But she said, 'Yes, sir.'

'Do you wish to take a vacation?'

'I would like to stay here, sir. In case something comes in. And until we hear from the guerillas.'

'Ah. Yes. Oddly, Jerry hasn't claimed any destruction of a guerilla force. He may be keeping that under wraps for the time being, of course. Or he may have learned of the impending raid but not of the guerillas' intended part in it. Or of course, they may just not have shown up. Yes.' He was thoughtful. 'You have their call sign?'

'At the Vichy base, yes, sir. I also have the call sign we were to use on the road.' She decided against telling him that she had already tried that one.

'Hm. I think you could try calling the base, just to see if they have any information. Do not tell them what has happened.'

'Yes, sir.'

'What about Paris?'

'I called Pound Twelve and told her to get out. She already seemed to know the situation, and indicated that she was getting out anyway.'

'Does this mean the route is blown?'

162

'I told her to make sure it continued, even in her absence. She seemed confident of this.'

'Well, let us hope she is right. Very good, Sergeant. You will carry on here until further notice. I will immediately begin locating a suitable replacement for Major Barron.'

'With respect, sir, there can be no replacement who will possess such an intimate relationship with the guerillas.' Or, she thought, be in love with their leader.

'Well, he will have to cultivate such a relationship. He will inherit you, at least for a while, so you will have to give him all the help you can. And for God's sake, Sergeant, cheer up. So you've lost a respected boss—'

'Who was also a friend, sir.'

'Yes. Well, that is the way it goes. Keep me informed of the situation in Vichy. And you know that I am always here if there is a problem.'

'Yes, sir.' But when there was a crisis, she thought, you were out to dinner.

Joanna's morning paper was delivered, as always, with her breakfast. She had had a bath, but again as always, breakfasted in her dressing gown, spreading the paper in front of her while she buttered toast. Then she paused, the knife upright in her hand. Her blood seemed to have turned quite cold.

GREAT BATTLE IN ENGLISH CHANNEL. ENGLISH INVASION FLEET DESTROYED. MANY CASUALTIES.

She continued to stare at the headline for several seconds; then she got up from the table and poured herself a glass of cognac, although it was nine in the morning and she had an empty stomach. Keep calm, she told herself. You must keep calm. But keeping calm was impossible. She picked up the phone, gave the number of the American embassy. 'Is Mr Munday in yet?'

'I'll just see. Who is calling, please?'

'Joanna Jonsson.'

'If you'll hold the line, Miss Jonsson. I think he's just come in.'

'Joanna! Lovely to hear from you.'

She had to assume her room was still being bugged. 'How would you like to join me for lunch?'

'Ah . . .'

'I really would like to see you, George. One o'clock? And I tell you what: bring a copy of today's paper with you. There's an interesting story I'd like to discuss.' She replaced the phone, drank the rest of the cognac, went back to her breakfast and drank ersatz coffee. Her nerves were settling. She was quite sure that George, who was a very good fellow – if a very poor lover, but perhaps that had been her fault – would have had the message delivered. So James had decided to ignore it. Then the bastard had got what was coming to him. But the thought of all those men killed . . . And where did that leave Liane? If he had not acted on half of the message, he was very unlikely to have acted on the other. What a fuck-up.

The phone rang. 'Joanna? I didn't wake you, I hope?'

'No, I was up, Sven.'

'Well, I'm happy to tell you that the travel ban has been lifted, and that you are free to go wherever you wish, whenever you wish. It seems to have been an administrative mix-up. When people are at war they do seem to become absolutely paranoid.'

'Well, thanks for your help, Sven.'

'Will you be leaving immediately?'

'I imagine so.'

'Would you like me to arrange it for you?'

'That would be very kind.'

'I'll call you back.'

Joanna replaced the phone. Talk about shutting the stable door . . . Except that it was opening the stable door. After what? Well, presumably when she got to England, she'd find out what really happened. Or what had not happened

164

at all. She got up, went to the drinks table, regarded her empty glass, and decided against refilling it. Getting blotto in the middle of the morning was not going to help. Instead she ate some toast.

There was a tap on the door. 'Who the fuck,' she muttered, and opened it, regarded the heavy-set, black-haired man who stood there. He wore civilian clothes, but that made him even more identifiable. 'Don't tell me,' she said. 'Your machine has broken down.'

'Fräulein?'

'Aren't you Gestapo? You look like Gestapo.'

'I am not Gestapo, Fräulein. I see you are not dressed. Would you like me to come back in fifteen minutes?'

'Why should you come back at all?'

'I would like to speak with you on an important matter.'

Joanna considered. But with her skills she was not afraid of any man, and he might turn out to be interesting; in any event, the fact that he could obviously tell she was wearing nothing under the dressing gown gave her an advantage, if only because he would be permanently distracted. 'You can come in now.' She stepped back, returned to the table. 'Drink?'

'Perhaps later. My name is Oskar Weber.'

'Pleased to meet you, Oskar. Have a seat and tell me what's on your mind. What did you say you did?'

'I didn't.' He sat on the settee.

Joanna took the chair, crossed her knees, allowing the dressing gown to fall away from them. 'You know something, Oskar, I hate word games and mind games. And the people who play them. You don't want me to wind up hating you, do you?'

'I am sure that would be traumatic, Fräulein. Let us say I work for the government.'

'Doesn't everyone in this country? Everyone who isn't in a concentration camp, that is.'

'You are very witty, Fräulein. However, I am in a senior position. I do not obey the rules. I make the rules.'

'I'm impressed. But as I am a singularly unimportant

165

person, I don't see how I can interest you.' But her heart was pounding. Could this rather sinister man know what she really was? How? Had that louse Schmitt written something down?

'You underestimate yourself, Fräulein. You are a very successful journalist.'

'I get by.'

'I have also got the impression, from your reports, that you are sympathetic to our ideals.'

'They're better than a lot of others.'

'That is a very mature judgement. You are also in the happy position of holding both American and Swedish passports, is that not so? This enables you to travel freely throughout Europe. From one combatant state to another, without hindrance. You even, I understand, have links with the French Resistance movement.'

'Shit!' Joanna muttered. 'You planted the Ulstein dame.'

'Christine works for me, yes. I am sorry you and she fell out. But you will understand that she is in a very delicate position. If her true identity were to be discovered by the guerillas, it could turn out very badly for her.'

'I reckon they'd roast her over a slow fire.'

'You put things so imaginatively.'

'She had me locked up by your thugs. You have any idea what happens to you when you are arrested by the Gestapo? Oh, I forgot; you make the rules.'

'You were not arrested by the Gestapo, Fräulein. You were taken into temporary custody by the Wehrmacht. Who then apologized for their mistake.'

'Big deal. '

'I would have thought you were big enough to overlook the incident.'

'Give me time. And tell me why you are here.'

'As we are agreed, you are a very successful journalist, your success being based on the inside pictures you draw for your American audience. Were you unable to provide those pictures, would you still be successful?'

166

'Are you threatening to deport me?'

'I should hate to have to do that, Fräulein. It merely occurs to me that, knowing so many of our secrets already, you might like to know more.'

'You've lost me.'

'Very simply, Fräulein, I am inviting you to work for the Third Reich.'

Eight

The Homecoming

Joanna blinked. 'Would you say that again?'

'I think it would be advantageous to all of us.'

'To you, maybe. I can't imagine how it would be helpful to me. What do you want me to be? A spy or something? Or to help turn in my friends?'

'I will tell you what I wish you to do when you have agreed to work for me.'

Joanna's mind was tumbling. How she wished she could contact James, because this could either be something very big or something disastrous. But her instincts were telling her that to agree, just like that, would be a mistake. If he wanted her, Weber would have to bully her, or coerce her, and that might be interesting, not to say amusing, if only because he might tell her something of value – to James. 'And suppose I don't reckon that would be quite my scene?'

'I think you will find it necessary to make it your "scene", as you so quaintly put it, Fräulein. Shall I put certain facts to you? I have been investigating your background. You are an old and very close friend of the de Gruchy family, are you not?'

'I know them.'

'Come now, did you not go to school with Liane de Gruchy?'

'Finishing school, in Switzerland. Liane was there at the same time, sure. But so were another hundred and eighteen girls.'

'But you were very close to Liane. Were you not?'

'We were friends.'

'You were expelled from that school, Fräulein Jonsson. So was Liane de Gruchy, at the same time. You were found guilty of breaking the same rule. What rule was that?'

Joanna gazed at him. 'You tell me, seeing as how you seem to know everything.'

'You were found in bed together, performing certain carnal acts. Am I correct?'

'So you like creepy-crawling about under carpets. Are you trying to blackmail me?'

'I would not dream of it. I am not here to criticize your sexual habits. I find the consideration of them very evocative. I am merely suggesting that once upon a time you must have considered yourself in love with Liane, and as you have kept in close contact ever since, it is reasonable to suppose that you are still in love with her.'

Joanna's nostrils dilated. 'Women outgrow schoolgirl crushes.'

'Not all women,' Weber argued. 'Were you not staying with the de Gruchys in their Chartres home, in May of last year?'

'I was attending the wedding of Amalie de Gruchy. So were more than a hundred other people, although I will admit that not all of them were staying in the de Gruchy house. The ceremony was interrupted by your invasion.'

'Wars are no respecters of occasions, Fräulein. And the day after the wedding you and Liane de Gruchy drove north of Paris. Was that not a very odd thing to do, with a battle going on only a few miles away?'

'We did not realize how close the fighting was. Liane's brother Pierre wished to rejoin his regiment, as did an English officer who had also been a wedding guest, and as we knew the trains would be clogged, Liane offered to drive them up to the Belgian border. I went along for the ride.'

'You wished to share an adventure with your lover.'

169

'I'm a journalist, Herr Weber. I thought there might be a story.'

'So you dropped Pierre de Gruchy and this English officer . . . What was his name, by the way?'

'How on earth do you expect me to remember that? I only met him for a couple of hours. I think he may have been called Tommy or something.'

'All British soldiers are called Tommy, Fräulein.'

'So maybe I'm mistaken.'

'It is not important. Do you have any idea what happened to him?'

'None. Maybe he got away at Dunkirk; maybe he didn't.'

'And he was a friend of Liane's?'

'He was a friend of Pierre's,' Joanna said, as carelessly as she could.

'Very good. And what happened to Pierre?'

'I have no idea. Maybe he got away at Dunkirk, too.'

'Yes, he did get away at Dunkirk. And returned to France a few months later as a British secret agent.'

'You're kidding me. Pierre? He's not the type.'

'He pretended to have escaped the collapse of the French armies, and returned to Paulliac. Then he persuaded his father to make him manager of the Paris office of de Gruchy and Son. Having established himself in Paris, he set up a secret radio station to transmit information to the British SIS.'

'Good Lord!'

'He was traced by the Gestapo, of course, but he managed to make his escape, and reached the guerilla encampment in Vichy, operated by his sister, who was already wanted for murder.'

'Which sister are we talking about?'

'Liane, Fräulein, as you well know. As you have known everything I have been saying. Because you were in that camp hardly more than a week ago.'

'As Christine will have told you. What if I was? These people are old friends of mine. I wanted to see if I could help them. I had intended to pay a call on Barbara and Albert, but your thugs prevented me.'

'But while there, you met Pierre?'

Joanna hesitated, fatally.

'You did not meet Pierre,' Weber said, gently, 'because he was not there. He was carrying out a mission for the British.'

'You'll have to ask Christine about that. She seems to know all the answers.'

'And you did not meet Liane either, because she was not there. As you say, Fräulein, we know all the answers. With one exception. How did you know the location of the guerilla encampment?' Again unable to think of an immediate answer, Joanna merely stared at him. 'It seems to me that there are only two sources from which you could have obtained that information. One is Madeleine von Helsingen, who you visit so regularly, and who no doubt manages to keep in touch with her family.'

'You would not dare arrest Madeleine.'

'Because her husband is a favourite of the Führer, and he has agreed to act as godfather to her child? Let me tell you something about the Führer, Fräulein. He is a man of extremes. When he likes someone, he does so extravagantly. Nothing is too good for his friend. But when he discovers that the friend has turned against him, or betrayed him, he hates with a similar extravagance, and the results can be terrifying.'

Joanna breathed deeply. Never had she felt in the presence of so much cultivated evil. 'Madeleine is not in touch with her family. They have disowned her.'

'Then your only other source would be the man Schmitt. We know you visited him on the day he committed suicide, and returned the following week.'

'Schmitt? How could he know anything about the guerillas? Surely you know that he was nothing more than a pimp?'

'We know he was a pimp, certainly. But for some time

171

we have had suspicions that he was more than that. Unfortunately, he killed himself before we could bring our investigations to a conclusion. And immediately after a visit from you. Now tell me, why should you, a wealthy and well-known woman, visit a pimp?'

Joanna took another deep breath, and held it long enough to force some colour into her cheeks. 'For those very reasons. Together with your earlier suggestions.'

'I do not follow you.'

'For God's sake, Weber, I'm a lesbian. I have been all my life. But here in Nazi Germany it's not done. And I can't take the risk of being blackmailed, because, as you say, I'm both wealthy and well known. Schmitt provided women for me. Women I could . . . love, without risk of repercussions.'

Weber regarded her for several seconds. 'And why did he commit suicide?'

'I found him in bed with a man. He was afraid I would denounce him.'

'But then he would denounce you.'

'So I would have been shamed. Perhaps even deported. Nothing more. But for him . . . Do you not send homosexuals to concentration camps?'

'It is considered the most appropriate place for them, yes. Well, I am sure that this confession will make it easier for us to come to an agreement. Although I will admit that I find it difficult to decide whether you are a very emotionally disturbed young woman or the most consummate liar I have ever encountered. However, you have yourself eliminated every possible link with the guerillas except through the de Gruchys themselves. So tell me when last you spoke with Liane.'

'I have not seen Liane for over a year. Not since I left Paris last July.'

Again he gazed at her for several moments. 'Then how did you know where to find the guerillas?'

'I was told where they were, roughly, by a Swedish journalist, who visited them early this year. He wouldn't tell me how he knew, but he showed me the area they were located on the map and said if I drove around there I would be sure to encounter them, especially if I was known to the de Gruchys.'

'And of course, Amalie, the supposedly dead sister, was there. Together with Jean Moulin, the supposedly dead prefect of Chartres.'

'Yes.' There was no point in denying what Christine von Ulstein would have told him.

'Very good. Now tell me your plans.'

'I am returning to Sweden.'

'And?'

'I intend to remain there.'

'That would be a waste. There is no problem in getting from Sweden to England, surely.'

'It takes time. Why should I wish to go to England?'

'Because you are now working for me.'

'Am I? Simply because you know about my private life? Once I leave Germany you cannot touch me. And what you may publish about me is irrelevant. Outside of Germany.'

'What a defiant creature you are, Fräulein. You are going to work for me, because if you do not, I am going torture your lover to death, very, very slowly.'

Joanna's head jerked. 'What a charming man you are, Weber. But surely even you have to arrest Liane before you can torture her?'

'Liane de Gruchy is in our Gestapo cells in Paris at this moment, awaiting interrogation. I received the news yesterday, but I commanded the local commander, Colonel Roess, not to proceed until I had spoken with you. I was already planning this talk, you see.'

'You expect me to believe this?'

'Why do you not check it out? Here is the number to call.'

Joanna took the card. 'I will be allowed to speak with her?'

'Certainly. But I must tell you that she resisted arrest,

173

and is not in good condition. We are doing our best to put her back together, but these things take time . . .'

Joanna picked up the phone, asked for the number. It took some time to get through, during which Weber smiled at her benevolently. When she was connected, and asked for Colonel Roess, there was more delay. But at last a man said, 'Roess.'

'I have a Herr Weber with me. I have been told that I may speak with Fräulein de Gruchy.'

'I would have to receive that instruction from himself, Fräulein.'

'He wishes to speak with you.' Joanna handed over the phone.

'Ah, Roess. Yes, it will be in order for Fräulein Jonsson to speak with de Gruchy.' He smiled at Joanna. 'She works for us, but as you know, the two ladies are acquainted.' He handed the phone back.

'If you will hold on.'

There was another wait, and then a woman's voice, speaking very low, said, breathlessly, 'Yes?'

It was impossible to identify Liane's voice: the speaker was clearly under a great deal of stress. 'This is Joanna.'

'Joanna? Oh, my God, Joanna! Joanna . . .'

'Are you all right?'

'I . . .' The voice hesitated, and Joanna supposed Liane must be looking at the men to either side of her. 'Yes. I . . . I am all right. But Joanna, can't you help me? As you helped me at Auchamps?'

Joanna frowned. 'I'll try,' she said. 'But in Auchamps we had Aubrey to help us, remember?'

'Ah . . . yes, I remember. Oh, to have Aubrey here to help me again. I love you, Jo. I have always loved you. I will always love you.'

'As I will always love you,' Joanna said. 'I'll be in touch.' She replaced the phone. 'Looks like you hold all the high cards, Weber. What do you wish me to do?'

'Just two things. The first, as I have said, is to tell no

one, however remotely connected with the war, who and what Christine von Ulstein is. Just forget she exists. At least for another month. Now, is that difficult?'

'It doesn't sound so. And the other?'

'This will be your real task from now on. I will give you an envelope to carry with you to England. Once there you will mail it. Nothing more than that. The address is an accommodation, but will reply to . . . I assume you stay in a hotel in London?'

'I use the Dorchester.'

'That is capital. Nothing could be better. Then there is no need to write anything. Just place the envelope I shall give you in one of the Dorchester envelopes and mail that. Then bring the reply back to Berlin.'

'You mean you are employing me as a courier.'

'Yes. We know that the British MI5 open all mail going in or out of the country. But if you mail something from such a reputable hotel, to an address within England, and receive a reply to that address, no one will think twice.'

'And if I were to be found out?'

'You would be deported. They would not dare harm a prominent American citizen, any more, well . . .'

'Than you would. And my reward is Liane's freedom?'

'Well, no, I cannot promise that, at least not immediately. She is a sworn enemy of the Reich. But I can promise you her survival, until this war is over, when you and she will be able to resume your lives together.'

'You think she will be able to survive a concentration camp?'

'She will not be in a concentration camp. You have my word. As long as you play straight with us, we will play straight with you. '

'And you say this is for a month?'

'As a courier? Why, I would hope for an ongoing situation. The month applies to Christine.'

'You intend to take her out of there in a month?'

'Ah . . . yes. The matter will be sorted out in a month.'

175

Joanna appeared to consider. Then she sighed, and said, 'OK, Herr Weber. I'll play your little game for you.'

'Excellent. Now you may ring down for a bottle of champagne and we will celebrate our partnership. And as we are going to be partners, why do you not take off that dressing gown? I have always wanted to share a bed with a lesbian.'

'Joanna!' Madeleine said. 'I have been trying to get hold of you for days, but you are never there.'

'I was there.' Joanna, having embraced her friend, stepped back to look at her. 'You're looking swell. But shouldn't you be bigger?'

'No, no. It is my first, and I am only just coming up to six months. Come and sit down. Hilda! Coffee.'

Joanna sat beside her on the settee. 'I've actually come to say goodbye. I'm leaving tomorrow. For Sweden.'

'Oh! Will you be coming back?'

'It's possible. Now tell me, any news from Russia?'

'Oh, yes. I had a letter only a couple of days ago.'

'And is all going as well as it says in the news bulletins?'

'Oh, yes. They still reckon on being in Moscow in another month. But Freddie says the weather's not so good; it's raining a lot of the time, and the transport keeps getting bogged down. But what have you been *doing*? You say you've been at the Albert all this time, and haven't been able to speak to me?'

'There's been a lot going on. Have you ever heard of a character named Weber? First name Oskar.'

'I don't think so. Don't tell me you've got a boyfriend.'

'You must be joking. But he thinks he's got a girlfriend.'

She waited while Hilda brought in the coffee, and as usual opened the door after the maid had left. Madeleine watched her with a quizzical expression. 'Now, Joanna—'

'Keep your voice down.' Joanna sat beside her. 'He's some kind of super-secret policeman.'

'You mean Gestapo? Oh, my God! They're on to you. To us.'

176

'They're not on to anything. He's not Gestapo. He's more important. When he snaps his fingers, the Gestapo jump.'

'The SS! They're worse. What have they done to you?'

'Do I look as if anything has been done to me? Except for being fucked by that creep.' Madeleine's mouth made a huge O. 'Oh, yes,' Joanna said. 'He exercised some kind of *droit de seigneur* because he reckons I'm working for him. I could have rung his neck, but I figured it wouldn't be politic.'

'You, are working for the Nazis?'

'I said, he thinks I am. And he has some fairly conclusive arguments. So what's more powerful than the SS?'

'Only the SD.'

'Say again?'

'The Sicherheitsdienst. They're the ultimate. No one even knows who belongs to it, except I suppose Hitler and Himmler. And perhaps Heydrich. If you're involved with them . . .'

'Let me worry about that. Have you been to Bordeaux to visit your parents?'

'Well, no. I'm not sure they want to see me. I did write them, but they never replied.'

'I think you should go down there. Now.'

'In my condition?'

'Pregnant women do travel, you know. And you'd be going first class the whole way.'

'Well, I'll think about it.'

'I want you to go. Right away.'

'Why is it so important? I should have thought it would be better to wait until after I've had the baby. That would give me a real reason for going.'

'We can't wait that long. You have to be there by the end of next week at the latest.'

Madeleine stared at her. 'You're up to something. You're trying to make me commit treason again. Well, I won't do it. I told you, I'm finished with that.'

'Madeleine darling, you are committing treason, to France,

177

every day that you sit here in this lovely apartment being a German aristocrat.'

'Oh, you . . . you are so hateful.'

'I'm trying to save your family from destruction. Now listen. Are there people, servants or employees, in Paulliac who are trustworthy?'

'Well . . . I suppose so.'

'Right. I will draw you a map.'

'Of Paulliac? Don't be absurd. I was born there.'

'Of a certain area at the south end of the Massif Central. That is where Amalie and Pierre are living, with Jean Moulin and a group of patriots.'

Madeleine's eyes were enormous. 'Amalie? But . . .'

'She is not dead. She pretended to commit suicide, and then went off with Liane.'

'But she was in Paulliac.'

'So was Liane, briefly, only no one knew it, except Amalie. It's a long story, and I can't go into it now.'

'And she is with Liane and the bandits who blew up that train?'

'She is with her brother and sister. *Your* brother and sister, Madeleine. Now, from what Weber told me, I am pretty damned sure that the Germans intend to raid that camp and wipe them out.'

'But the Massif Central is in Vichy.'

'Sure it is, but I'm also pretty damned sure that when push comes to shove Vichy will do no more than protest at a German raid into their territory, especially if, as it will be, it is represented as the necessary elimination of a bunch of terrorists. You have got to get a message to them warning them of their danger, and telling them to move out and go some place else. I do not think the raid is going to take place for a month, so you have time, just.'

Madeleine stared into her coffee cup. 'You are asking me to betray Frederick again. Betray the Reich.'

'I am asking you, I am begging you, to warn your own family of their danger.'

'They are terrorists. You said so yourself.'

'I said that is how the Germans will describe them. They are still your flesh and blood. And you will not be betraying Germany. What real harm can a handful of outlaws do to the mighty Reich?'

'Suppose they blow up another train?'

'Is that likely? It is nearly a year since they blew up the last one. It was an act of defiance. Now they are wanted men. And women. Will you not allow them to survive?'

Madeleine sighed. 'I will be taking a great risk.'

'You? What risk can Madeleine von Helsingen possibly take?' Joanna put her arm round her and gave her a hug. 'I knew I could rely on you.'

'You look pleased with yourself,' Heydrich remarked. 'How did you get on with your American friend?'

'Very well. She is now working for us.'

'Indeed? Did you persuade her to keep quiet about Ulstein?'

'She fell for my ploy. Would you like to hear about it?'

'Not particularly. How is she working for us?'

'As a courier. She is the perfect material. She leaves for Sweden today, and thence England, taking a letter for Burton.'

'And you really think you can trust her? Burton is a good man. I would not like to lose him.'

'I believe I can trust her, because of the hold I have established over her. But Burton is in no danger, because I am taking no risks. The letter she is carrying is a blank sheet of paper except for the words "reply in kind". If she brings a reply, we are in business. If she does not . . . well, she knows the consequences. Or she thinks she does.'

'If she betrays us, the British will watch the accommodation address until he turns up.'

'And if they arrest him, what have they got? A blank sheet of paper, which is hardly incriminating. There is not a shred of evidence to suggest that the letter she mailed came from anywhere but the Dorchester Hotel. But I repeat, I am quite sure she will not betray us.'

179

'Very good. I will take your word for it.'

'And, of course,' Weber said, 'once she carries out this mission, she is ours completely. Even the Americans will disown her if they were to find out, or be informed, that she is a German agent.'

'You could be right. Anyway, her importance ceases to exist in a month's time. Monsieur Laval has agreed to our removing the guerillas from Vichy territory.'

'That is splendid.'

'Yes. But it is also delicate. The Vichy government must not be involved in any way; it appears that there is a considerable anti-German sentiment, and Laval fears civil unrest if it were known that he was collaborating in the elimination of these thugs. This means that our government cannot be involved either. Thus we are talking of a wholly covert and indeed illegal operation. All we have been able to obtain from Laval is a promise that his government will do nothing more than formally protest at our action, and that, should anything go wrong and any of our people be arrested by the Vichy police, they will be returned to us as rapidly as possible, without being brought to trial. Our people must go in, complete the job, and be out again in five hours.'

Weber nodded. 'The commander of this force will have to be very carefully briefed.'

'That is what I have just done.' Weber sat up straight. 'I am not asking you to go in with guns blazing,' Heydrich said. 'Unless you feel like doing so. But I am placing you in overall command of the operation, and I require you to be on the scene, even if discreetly in the background, to make sure that the job is properly carried out. Laval will keep his promise, I am certain, but there will still be considerable adverse publicity. It took me some time to get permission. Heinrich was uncertain. Fortunately the Führer was for it, but equivocally so. What I am saying is that we are being given this one opportunity. Therefore it must be a one hundred per cent success.'

'I understand. What do I have? Gestapo people?'

'No. I have no confidence in their ability to carry out something like this. You are being given a company of the SS.'

'A company.'

'There are, so far as we know, only thirty-odd of these creatures. You will also have support from the Wehrmacht. You will liaise with the local commander, Colonel Hoeppner. But your people will not wear uniform. Apart from this, I leave the details up to you. Requisition whatever you need, but get the job done.'

Weber nodded, thoughtfully. 'And the date?'

'That is your decision. We wish the business completed by the end of September.'

'That is five weeks away.'

'It is also seven weeks after the St Valery raid. We must give as many of the guerillas as possible time to get home.'

'Understood. However, I will leave for Bordeaux the day after tomorrow.'

'Just remember, Oskar, that no one is to know of this raid until it takes place. You will inform Hoeppner personally, and the SS unit will be on a training exercise. My secretary will give you the necessary written instructions to show to their commanding officer when you choose, but you should leave it as late a possible. And remember also that anything less than the total destruction of these people, in a single five-hour period, will be regarded as a failure.'

'Well,' Rachel said. 'Look who the cat brought in, sir.'

Joanna, standing in the doorway of the office, looked from face to face. 'Say again?'

'I say,' remarked the man behind the desk. 'Who is this woman? And how can she come barging in like this?'

Joanna stared at him in stupefaction. His voice was a trifle high, he was slightly built and not very tall, he had sandy hair and a small sandy moustache . . . Anyone less like James Barron could not be imagined. Rachel got up from her desk. 'This, sir, is Joanna Jonsson. Pound Three.

Jonsson, this is Major Herbert Lockridge. Our new Pound One.'

'Pound Three,' Lockridge said. 'The brigadier mentioned her. Said she was . . . ah . . .'

'A loose cannon, is his usual description, sir.'

'Where is James?' Joanna inquired.

'Ahem,' Lockridge remarked.

'Major Lockridge,' Rachel explained, 'wishes our affairs to be conducted in a proper fashion, remembering always that we are a military establishment. He does not regard the use of Christian names in the office to be conducive to discipline.'

'Look,' Joanna said. 'Cut the bullshit.'

'Here, I say.'

'We have got to move very fast,' Joanna said. 'Now tell me where James is.'

'Major Barron is listed as missing in action,' Rachel said.

Joanna stared at her. 'Missing in action? Oh, Jesus! Don't tell me he went on that raid?'

'Yes, he did.'

'I say,' Lockridge protested. 'That is classified.'

'So am I,' Joanna told him. 'Didn't you get my message?'

'Yes,' Rachel said. 'But there was no means of aborting.'

'You mean the Resistance bought it too?'

'We don't know. We have heard nothing from them since.'

'Holy shit!' Then what she had sent Madeleine to do might be a total, and dangerous, waste of time.

'Now look here,' Lockridge said in an effort to take control. 'How do you know all of this stuff? And why are you here?'

'I am here, Major, because I have vital information to give you.' She looked at Rachel. 'You can just stand there, cool as a duck, and tell me that James could be dead and all his people wiped out? You!'

Rachel bit her lip. 'I feel like shit.' She glanced at Lockridge. 'I am sorry, sir. But Major Barron was my friend. I felt like shit at the time, and I still do. But we don't know for certain that he is dead. I felt I had to carry on.' There were tears in her eyes.

'OK,' Joanna said. 'You're a gutsy chick. Now tell me about Liane. Were you able to contact her?'

'I spoke with her the morning after the raid.'

'You told her she'd been blown?'

'She gave me the impression that she already knew that.'

Joanna frowned. 'But she sounded all right?'

'Who is this woman Liane?' Lockridge inquired, now starting to sound plaintive.

'Pound Twelve, sir,' Rachel explained.

'Did she sound all right?' Joanna shouted.

'She sounded perfectly calm. As I said, she almost seemed to know it already.'

'Shit, shit, shit.'

'Here, I say.'

But both women were now ignoring him. 'Don't you think she got away?' Rachel asked.

'The Gestapo claim to have her in custody.'

'Liane? Oh, my God! You don't think they had her when I called? I used the JJX call sign. That would mean the entire route is blown.'

'I don't think the route is blown,' Joanna said thoughtfully. 'Otherwise I am sure they would have told me. Therefore they must have got her after your call. If they have got her.'

'Do you mind if I interrupt?' Lockridge said coldly. 'Are you saying that you have a contact inside the Gestapo?'

'Yes. Me.'

'What?' Lockridge and Rachel gasped together.

'They have suborned me into working for them by offering to spare Liane's life if I cooperate.'

'But you're Pound Three!' Lockridge protested.

'They don't know that. They just know me as an American journalist who has links to the French Resistance. So to convince me to play ball, they had me speak with Liane.'

'You saw her?' Rachel was again aghast.

'No. I spoke with her on the phone. That in itself was suspicious.'

'But was it Liane?'

'I don't know. The voice sounded very tired and pretty scared, which figures if she was in a Gestapo cell. And she was well briefed, reminded me of our experience when we were captured by German soldiers in Auchamps.'

'What experience?' Lockridge asked.

'We were gang raped.'

'Here, I say . . .'

'But I tried a curve ball of my own. I reminded her how my brother Aubrey had helped us to escape.'

'And she didn't remember that?' Rachel asked.

'Oh, sure she remembered it. The point is that my brother Aubrey wasn't there. He'd been killed two days before when we were strafed by German fighters. Why do you think I'm working for you guys?'

'Oh! I'm so terribly sorry. I didn't know. But it was a brilliant idea. So you think it wasn't actually Liane at all.'

'I don't know for sure. They said if I'd play ball they wouldn't torture her. But suppose they already had? Sleeplessness, disorientation, electric shocks, none of those leave any visible signs, but they can drive someone out of their mind, cause them to forget things . . . We have to find out. If Liane got out of Paris, she'll have returned to Vichy. When last did you speak with the group?'

'Well,' Rachel said, 'not for several weeks.'

'Why not?'

'Our instructions,' Lockridge said, 'are to maintain complete radio silence as regards this "group" until Operation Windrush has been completed.'

'But they were all shot up a fortnight ago.'

'We don't know that. They are to call us.'

'Well, we can't wait for that. I have a notion that the Germans intend to take the group out, sometime very soon.'

'A notion?' Lockridge inquired. 'Is this also from your

Gestapo friends? They seem to be an awfully confiding lot.'

'They don't confide anything they don't want to. One listens, and makes deductions, and then draws conclusions.'

'But that would mean invading Vichy territory,' Rachel said.

'I don't think that's going to concern them too much. So let's get on the radio and warn them. Just keep all reference to me out of it. Unless Liane happens to be there.'

'I'm afraid that is quite out of the question,' Lockridge said. Joanna glared at him, and his colour deepened. 'We are under orders not to contact the de Gruchy group until and unless they contact us. I cannot contemplate seeking a change in orders on the basis of a "notion" suggested by an agent whose behaviour is, to say the least, of an irregular nature.'

'You, buster, are looking for a punch on the nose.'

'Now look here. I'll have you arrested.'

'Try another one.'

Lockridge's mouth opened and shut again.

'Ah,' Rachel said, endeavouring to keep the peace, 'you said the Gestapo blackmailed you into working for them. To do what?'

'I'd forgotten about it.' Joanna opened her handbag and handed her the letter. 'I'm to mail this from the Dorchester, and wait for a reply, which I'm to take back to Germany with me.'

'The Dorchester?' Lockridge demanded. 'Why should you mail it from the Dorchester? That's a very expensive hotel.'

'It's also where I happen to be staying.'

Lockridge did another of his fish-out-of-water acts, and looked at Rachel for an explanation. 'Jonsson always stays at the Dorchester when she's in England, sir.'

'Good God!'

'This letter, sir. I would say it's an MI5 job. They handle internal security.'

185

'Aren't you even going to open it?' Joanna demanded.

'It would have to be steamed open and resealed. I'd better get on to the brigadier.'

'Don't you mean Pound?' Lockridge inquired.

'Yes, sir. Of course. Pound. He'll know what to do about it.'

'Right,' Joanna said. 'And tell him I want to see him.'

'My dear woman,' Lockridge said. 'Pound doesn't see his agents. That is my job as Pound One.'

'He's seen me before, and he'll see me now.'

Lockridge looked at Rachel. 'I'll just find out if he's available,' she said, and used the phone, then looked at them above the receiver. 'He's out of town in a conference.'

'Then I am in command,' Lockridge announced.

'Oh, shit,' Joanna commented.

'Madeleine! How well you look.' Franz Hoeppner was waiting on the Bordeaux Central station.

Madeleine allowed herself to be kissed on each cheek. 'Do you really think so?' She wore a flowing cape and a loose dress; she was just starting to show.

'I think a pregnant woman is the most entrancing of sights.'

'Then why have you never married?'

'I never seem to have found either the time, or the right woman. My car is outside.' It waited in the courtyard, watched from a respectable distance by the other disembarking passengers and those who had come to greet them. When Madeleine emerged there was a rustle and a whisper. 'One would almost think they know you,' Franz remarked.

'They do. I grew up in Paulliac, which means Bordeaux.'

'Of course.' He showed her into the open tourer, sat beside her. 'All right, Willi.' The driver engaged gear. A soldier sat beside him, a submachine-gun resting on his knees.

'Is that necessary?' Madeleine asked.

'It could be. We know we are not very popular.'

'Well, it is very good of you to meet me.'

'I could hardly do less. How long will you be staying?'

'I suppose for as long as I am welcome.'

'Your parents are expecting you?'

'I wrote them, but they never replied. I suppose it's the mail. All those censors opening letters.'

'Yes,' Franz said, thoughtfully. They were out of the city now, and driving down a country lane with the river on their right.

'Have you seen them?' Madeleine asked.

'Oh, yes. I met them when they arrived, in May, and I come out every couple of weeks to see how they are getting on.'

'And how are they getting on?'

'Ah . . . being imprisoned is a pretty awful experience, especially for people like your mother and father, who have never, shall I say, come into contact with the seamy side of life. But surely you saw this for yourself.'

'The last time I saw my parents, Franz, was the day I married Freddie.' She made a moue. 'You were standing at his shoulder.'

'My God, but that is a year ago.'

'Almost to the day.'

'And before the bomb outrage and their arrest. Well . . .'

'Tell me.'

Franz looked away from her as the trees parted and they could see the water. 'I have said they underwent a rather grim experience.'

'But they are well?'

'Physically, they have recovered very well.'

'But mentally?'

'They harbour a deep resentment. This is entirely natural.'

'Resentment against whom?'

'Well, the Reich.'

'And?'

He had been looking straight ahead. Now he glanced at her. 'I have told you, the Reich. And anyone connected with the Reich.'

'I see.' The car turned a corner and the high iron gates were before them. Two armed German soldiers stood to attention. 'So you keep them under arrest.'

'These guards are for their protection. They may be resentful of the Reich, but many of the people of this area consider their arrest and subsequent release as evidence of some kind of collaboration.' The gates swung open and the car proceeded down the drive, to stop before the huge porch. Dogs barked and the Alsatians came bounding round the house. 'Will they greet you?' Franz asked.

'Dogs never forget a friend.' Madeleine stepped down. The Alsatians charged up to her, then licked her hands as she took off her gloves. Franz also got down, signalling the soldier to take Madeleine's bag to the steps. 'Will you not come in?' she asked.

'No. It is best you see them alone. But Madeleine –' he held her hands – 'if, well, you feel unwelcome –' he took his wallet from his inside breast pocket and extracted a card – 'call me, and I will come and pick you up.'

Madeleine gazed at him for several moments, then put the card in her handbag.

A man wearing a somewhat shabby frock coat had appeared at the top of the steps. He frowned as he looked at Madeleine, then came down the steps. 'Mademoiselle Madeleine? How good . . .' He changed his mind. 'Welcome home, Frau von Helsingen.'

'It is good to be home, Paul. Are my parents in?'

'Indeed, madame.' He looked past her at the car, which was turning to drive away, then at her suitcase.

'Bring that in, will you.' She went up the steps and into the porch. The front doors were open, revealing the wide hall and the great staircase. Madeleine went forward, stopped as a man appeared from the doorway of the drawing room. He looked far older than his sixty-seven years. Almost completely bald, what was left of his hair was quite white. His head had always seemed too large for his body, had hung forward between his shoulders like an outsize blood-hound; now it seemed almost too heavy for him to sustain. He had been a big man, but his frame had dwindled, and he moved hesitantly behind a tapping stick. 'Papa? Oh, Papa!' She ran forward. Albert de Gruchy accepted her embrace without protest, but did not respond. 'I am so glad to see you,' she said.

'Your mother is in here.' Albert stepped away from her, and indicated the drawing room door.

Behind them, the butler waited with the suitcase. 'Take it up to my room,' Madeleine commanded.

Paul hesitated, looking to his employer for confirmation, but when there was none carried the suitcase up the stairs.

Madeleine went into the drawing room, and faced the woman who had been sitting, reading a book, but who was now rising to her feet. 'Madeleine? My God! What are you doing here?'

Barbara de Gruchy had been an English aristocrat before she had married into the French mercantile aristocracy. She had always looked, and been, an imperiously beautiful woman, who had bequeathed her looks to her four children. Now, like her husband, she seemed to have shrunk, her hair white and her shoulders bowed, although the superb bone structure of her face remained, as did the fire in her eyes.

'I have come to see you, Mama.' Madeleine went forward with outstretched arms.

'You are pregnant!'

Madeleine stopped, a few feet away. 'Yes. Will you not congratulate me?'

'I assume you are expecting a blond, blue-eyed Aryan superman.'

'If he takes after his father, hopefully yes. I had hoped you would congratulate me.'

Barbara sat down again, still without touching her daughter. 'How long do you intend to stay?'

189

'How long would you like me to stay?'

'That is entirely up to you. Lunch is served at one sharp.'

Barbara picked up her book again.

Nine

The Price of Spying

Liane de Gruchy gazed up the hill at the men coming through the trees. She stopped walking to wait for them, bringing her shoulder bag round in front so that she could thrust her hand inside and find the butt of the Luger. But she did not suppose she was going to need it, as she recognized at least one of them. 'Etienne!'

'Liane!' He embraced her. 'It is good to see you. But what are you doing here? Has there been trouble?'

'That is what I would like you to tell me.'

'I do not understand. You think there is trouble here?'

'Who is here?'

'Monsieur Moulin, and your sister, and half a dozen of us, and Mademoiselle Round.'

'Who?'

'Mademoiselle Round. She is an English agent. Oh, the experiences she has had. She has been captured by the Gestapo twice, and escaped each time. She was tortured by them, terribly.'

'I must meet this woman.' Liane resumed the walk up the hill. 'But where are the rest of the men? My brother, and Henri?'

'They are still away, on the mission to St Valery.'

'Ah.' Liane decided to wait until she could speak with Amalie and Jean. She had no idea what had been happening during her slow progress from Paris, moving only by night. She had seen a newspaper which had mentioned a great naval battle in the Channel, and it had occurred to her that

191

it might be something to do with the raid on St Valery, but the reports in the heavily censored French papers had been sketchy, and of course there had been no mention of any Resistance involvement. But Amalie would know because of her radio contacts with James.

'Liane! Oh, Liane!' Amalie hugged and kissed her. 'To have you back, safe and sound.'

'Did you ever doubt it? Jean!'

More hugs and kisses. 'But why?' Moulin asked.

'I was told by Pound to get out.'

'But does that mean the route has collapsed?'

'The route is in good hands. I was instructed to get out and return to base. So here I am. Now tell me why?'

'I cannot think of a reason.'

Liane looked at the dark-haired woman standing behind Amalie. 'You must be Mademoiselle Round.'

'Monica,' Amalie explained. 'She is a British agent, and our friend.'

'And you are the famous Liane,' Christine said. 'I am so pleased to meet you.'

'Am I famous?'

'Oh, indeed. Everyone speaks of you.'

'I am flattered. Perhaps you will explain to me how you got here.'

'When you have eaten, and had something to drink,' Amalie said. 'And a bath.'

'That first,' Liane agreed.

She bathed in the stream, washed her hair to remove as much of the dye as possible; Amalie could renew it when it was time to return to Paris. While she did so, Amalie and Christine washed her clothes, then Amalie lent her something to wear – some sizes too big – and she sat with them and Jean and Etienne to have a meal. She was in fact very hungry, as she had existed on sparse handsout for the past fortnight. But she was more interested in what Amalie and Christine had to tell her. 'Isn't it incredible,' Amalie asked, 'that Papa should have been an English agent all of these years?'

'Yes,' Liane agreed. Incredible, she thought, was the only word to use. She knew that because she had chosen to live her own life – one not approved of by her parents – she had seen far less of them during the few years before the war than she should have, and had really drifted apart from them, the estrangement accentuated by the Joanna affair, and the fact that she had refused to stop seeing her old friend, even if their meetings had hardly been more than once a year. Therefore Papa could well have been an English agent. But according to this woman Monica Round, he had been such an agent before the war. Telling the British what? Only about French affairs; certainly not German. Papa had had many friends in French military circles, she knew. But that would mean that, although Britain and France had been allies even before the war started, Papa had been a traitor to France. She could not believe that, nor did she want to consider it. And then, Joanna . . . 'But how did she find you?'

'She said she knew we were situated in these mountains.'

James must have told her. Liane knew that Joanna had become a courier for the SIS, like them under James's control, in the summer of 1940, because of her furious determination to hit back at the people who had not only raped her but had murdered her brother; she had been a contact of Pierre's in Paris before he had had to flee the city hours before the Gestapo had raided his flat to arrest him. It had always been a comfort to her that she and Joanna were working together, even if in widely separated areas. But why would James have sent Joanna to the base? And then . . . 'You say she was captured by the Gestapo?'

'I think they were the Wehrmacht,' Christine said.

'But why? She's a neutral.'

'There was a wanted poster of her,' Amalie said.

'Yes, there was,' Christine agreed. 'But I think it was

193

really because when they asked her where she was going she told them to see the de Gruchys. The Germans knew about your father, you see.'

'But if that were the case, why did they let him go?'

'I think perhaps because they hoped to use him to entice you or your brother out of the hills to see him.'

'And they got Joanna instead. What happened to her?'

'I don't know. As I told you, it was dark, and they were interested only in her, so I slipped away.'

'And they did not follow you?'

'They shouted, and one of them fired his gun. But there were only four of them, and all they really wanted to do was make sure your friend did not escape. I suppose they felt they could get who I was from her.'

Amalie shivered. 'Can you imagine Joanna in the hands of the Gestapo?'

'I imagine she would tell them where they got off. But we must find out what has happened to her, and I must get in to see Mama and Papa. First thing, we must call James, put him in the picture, and find out what he wants done.'

'Who is this James?' Christine asked.

'Our control. Pound One is his code name. What is yours?'

'Ah . . . I am not ever supposed to divulge that.'

Liane regarded her for some moments, then shrugged. 'You are right. I was careless. But what are your plans?'

'Well,' Christine said, 'Amalie tells me that there is some-times a plane bringing in munitions. I would like to have it take me back to England.'

'It would have to be arranged in advance.'

'I know this. I wanted Amalie to call out for me, but she said she had to maintain radio silence until the men came home.'

Liane rumpled her baby sister's hair. 'She is very disci-plined. But things have changed. We'll call London now.'

'Nothing has changed,' Moulin objected. 'Our instruc-tions were to maintain absolute radio silence until the raid on St Valery was completed and our people returned here. This has not yet happened. You will remember that James was very insistent upon us obeying his orders to the letter.'

'The raid was more than a fortnight ago. And I am sorry to tell you that London believes James is dead.'

Moulin and Amalie stared at her, ashen-faced.

'I know,' Liane said. 'I am as devastated as you. It seems he took part in the raid and has not been heard of since. Now we must move on. Our men must be nearly back by now. We must find out the reason for my recall. I know the Gestapo were on my trail in Paris. But I do not think they would have found me. In any event, as London apparently knew the situation, they told me to get out. But Pound Two specifically told me to return here. There has to be a reason for that, and it may be urgent.'

Moulin stroked his chin. 'Perhaps you are right. Very good. Call them, Amalie.'

They all went to the radio, waited while she turned it on. 'It is dead. Shit!'

'You have allowed the batteries to run down,' Christine suggested.

'Well, put in the spares,' Liane said.

'I have them here.' Amalie opened the box, and stared at the empty space. 'But . . . there were twelve of them.'

'You are sure you haven't used them all?' Moulin asked.

'Yes, I am sure. I have not needed to replace any. They were all here a fortnight ago. You remember, Monica. I showed them to you.'

'That's true,' Christine said. 'But then . . .' She looked from face to face. 'What can have happened to them?'

'They have been stolen,' Liane said.

'Who would have done such a thing?' Moulin asked.

Liane turned to Etienne. 'Two of those men out there are strange to me. Who are they?'

'Monterre's people. He brought in twenty recruits, oh, just over a month ago. Eighteen of them went off with Pierre to St Valery.'

195

'Monterre's people. You mean they are Communists. Who take their orders from Moscow.'

'I suppose they do. But we're all on the same side now.' He grinned. 'Marshal Stalin says so.'

Liane looked at Moulin. 'There is no one else.'

'What can we do?'

'We are not in a position to do anything at the moment. Except shoot them both.'

'We cannot do that. We do not know they are guilty.'

'And to do that would destroy the group,' Etienne said. 'When Monterre returns—'

'Yes,' Liane said, 'when Monterre returns, hopefully he will have Pierre and Henri with him. Then we will be in a position to sort this out. And Henri will have the small radio. So whatever the reason for preventing us from calling out will be useless.'

'But what can the reason be?' Christine asked. 'Surely these people have as much wish to defeat the Nazis as us?'

'That we will find out when our men come back. Until then, we act entirely normal. And wait.'

'Good morning, *sir*.' Major Lockridge stood to attention. 'I mean, Pound. Sir.'

'At ease, Major.' The brigadier entered the office, nodded to Rachel, and then turned his attention to Joanna. 'Causing pandemonium again, I see.'

'Doing my job, sir.'

'I see.' As Lockridge was still standing beside the desk, the brigadier sat behind it. 'Well, your information was unfortunately correct. Even more unfortunately, we received it too late. Where did you get it?'

'From a German agent.'

'One of these people you now claim to be working with?'

'They claim that, sir. Was there anything of value in the letter I delivered?'

'It was a blank sheet of paper.'

'Oh!'

'MI5 say not to panic. They estimate your new employers are testing you out. You are prepared to carry on?'

'Of course, sir.'

'Understanding the dangers? This German agent who informed you that they were on to both the St Valery raid and the route, did he not know you were working for SIS?'

'No, sir. She thought I was a journalist. As I am.'

'She?'

'Yes, sir.'

'And where is she now?'

'I imagine she has returned to Berlin.'

'Hm. Now what about Pound Twelve?'

'I managed to contact her, sir,' Rachel said. 'And instructed her to leave Paris and return to base as rapidly as possible.'

'Why did you wish her to return to base?'

'Because I understood that something had gone wrong there, and we have always considered Pound Twelve as the ultimate commander.'

'I thought Pound Eleven was the commander of the group?'

'He is in nominal command, sir, certainly. But . . .'

'I know. James has more confidence in Pound Twelve. All right, Sergeant. You instructed Pound Twelve to go home. This was a fortnight ago. Presumably she is there by now. Has she called?'

'Well, sir . . .' Rachel looked at Joanna. 'We don't know that she has. She could have been picked up.'

'What?'

'The Gestapo claim to have her in custody,' Joanna explained.

'Do you believe them?'

'I was allowed to speak with her on the telephone.'

'Then that's it. She will have compromised the entire route, and the group.'

'That is not certain, sir.'

'Oh, come now, Jonsson. There is no woman in the world, not even Liane de Gruchy, not even you, that could survive

197

a Gestapo torture chamber without telling them everything they wish to know.'

'I am sure you're right, sir. But we don't know for certain that Pound Twelve *is* in German hands.'

'Jonsson, I cannot abide confused women. You just said she was.'

'I said I was allowed – actually, I was invited – to speak with her. But . . .' She told him of the trap she had laid into which the woman at the other end of the line had fallen. 'Of course, she could have already been tortured into a state where she didn't know what she was saying, but . . .'

'Well, there is a simple way to find out. If she hasn't been captured by the Gestapo, she will have obeyed orders and returned to the Massif Central. Call her up.'

'This is what we wanted to do three days ago, sir.' Both women glanced at Lockridge, who had been looking increasingly agitated at being excluded from the conversation.

'I was following the instructions left by my predecessor, sir, that absolute radio silence was to be maintained until the completion of Windrush.'

'But that's damn near three weeks ago. Sergeant, get JJX on the line. I wish to speak to Pound Eleven personally.'

'Yes, sir.' Rachel seated herself before the radio.

'Don't you mean Pound Twelve, sir?' Joanna ventured.

'No, I do not mean Pound Twelve. If I had meant Pound Twelve I would have said Pound Twelve. We are required to pull Pound Eleven out.'

'Sir?'

'It's this fellow de Gaulle again. He's fighting a running battle with our people to control what we are doing in France. Well, we won't let him get his hands on any of our own people, of course, but when it comes to French nationals it is a tricky situation. Now he wants all what he calls his local commanders brought to London for a conference. Just like that, as if they could go to the nearest airport and catch a commercial flight. Unfortunately, the PM seems to feel that he needs to be humoured, where possible. And

198

one of the people he specifically wishes to see is the erst-while prefect of Chartres, so we have to inform Moulin of this and make arrangements to pick him up. For God's sake, Sergeant, what are you doing?'

'There's no reply, sir.'

'Damnation! What does that mean?'

'That they've been wiped out,' Lockridge suggested, and gulped as everyone looked at him as if he were a stain on the carpet.

'Can that have happened?' the brigadier asked.

'Yes, sir,' Joanna said. 'I believe a raid on the group head-quarters was being planned, but I understood it was not to be until at least the middle of the month.'

'It could just be a functional failure of their radio,' Rachel pointed out.

'But how do we know? How do we find out?'

'Someone will have to go in,' Rachel said.

'You mean that fellow Brune?'

'That would be difficult, sir. If they don't know he's coming, the guerillas will not light the landing strip. There is no way he can land in the dark, or fly over occupied France in daylight. It will have to be a drop.'

'Blind?'

'Well, sir, most of our agents are dropped blind.'

'But if Jerry has got control of the group headquarters it would be a suicide mission.'

'I don't think Jerry, if he has succeeded in eliminating the group, will still be there, sir. That is Vichy territory, and any seek-and-destroy mission would have to be in and out as rapidly as possible. I would be happy to volunteer, sir. I have done parachute training.'

'Have you? Hm.'

'But if you did that,' Lockridge objected, 'even if the group is intact, if they have no radio you will be unable to contact us to arrange a pick-up.'

'I will take a radio with me, sir.' Rachel might have been addressing a small boy.

'Yes,' the brigadier said, 'that does seem to be the best option. I don't like sending you out on a job like this, Sergeant, but . . .'

'With respect, sir,' Joanna said, 'I will make the drop.'

'You?' Rachel demanded. 'Have you ever jumped?'

'I did parachute training at Ashley Hall. The point is that I know these people. I know the de Gruchys and I know Monsieur Moulin. And they know me. They wouldn't have a clue who you are.'

'That's a good point,' the brigadier said. Rachel glared at him. 'But what about this MI5 thing? They'll want you to take this fellow Burton's reply back to Germany.'

'I will be back in forty-eight hours, sir.'

'Hm. Yes, I suppose you will be. Very good, Jonsson. I'll set it up.'

'Thank you, sir,' Joanna said, and smiled at the furious Rachel.

'Henri! Oh, Henri!' Amalie ran through the trees to greet her husband.

Liane and Christine followed more slowly. They had become friends over the past couple of days. Liane was conditioned to being suspicious of all strangers, and thus her initial reaction to encountering the Englishwoman had been hostile. But she had not been able to fault her, certainly in her knowledge of England, and of English manners and mores. She had not, of course, been to a top girls school like the de Gruchys, and admitted to having been born and brought up in Surrey, which explained her totally unaccented English. In addition, the part she was playing in the encampment, her willingness to undertake the most menial of tasks, and her fervent anti-Nazism contributed to her acceptance, while that she knew weapons and their use could not be doubted. As for her refusal to divulge any aspect of her control or her activities, that was entirely reasonable; she had no reason to trust the guerillas more than she needed to.

200

Only her claim that she had been sent to contact Albert de Gruchy, and that he had been a British agent before the war, jarred. But even here, as she had thought from the moment of their first meeting, Liane had to admit that she had not known her parents as well as she should have.

Yet she was very happy to have the men back again, and not only to sort out the business of the stolen batteries. There was also the fact that she had to get in to Paulliac, less to see her mother and father – although she certainly wished to do that – than to confirm the financial arrangements she had instituted before the next audit.

The question was how was it to be done. She was not sure she could manage it on her own, and she had gained a strong impression that Monica regarded her mission as a failure and wanted only to get back to England; it was even possible that her nerves had gone, which was not unlikely if she had been tortured by the Gestapo. Thus the return of Pierre became ever more important.

But these were only some of the men. 'Henri!' she embraced him, and then looked past him at the six scarecrows who were with him. 'Monterre! Where is Pierre? And the others?'

'We do not know. Monica!' He hugged Christine.

'You know her?' Liane was surprised.

'I brought her in.'

'I hadn't realized that. But when you say you don't know where Pierre is . . .'

'There has been a catastrophe.'

'Pierre is dead?' Her voice was high.

'I don't know. He was alive when last I saw him. But he would stay. And he was in a mood of despair . . .'

'Tell me what happened.'

'Up at the camp,' Henri said.

Amalie and Christine prepared food and served wine to the exhausted men, and while they ate Henri and Monterre told them what had happened. 'Oh, my God, God, God!' Christine moaned. 'Who could have done such a thing?'

'Who indeed,' Moulin agreed. 'It can only have been a Nazi agent in England.'

'Or an English traitor,' Monterre said savagely.

'But to betray so many men,' Christine said.

'I do not think the traitor was in England,' Liane said. They all looked at her. 'You say the raid took place on the night of the 7th/8th of August,' she said. 'At six o'clock that morning I was called from London by Pound Two, who told me I had been betrayed and to get out of Paris and return here because there was a crisis here. The point I am making is that the only people in the world, outside of this camp, who knew both that there was going to be a raid *and* that I was going to Paris is Pound Control. I refuse to believe that James would betray his own people, and certainly that he would betray me, much less sign his own death warrant: he was on the St Valery raid.'

'James? James is dead?' Amalie was horrified.

'Pound thinks so.'

'But what about Pound Two?' Henri asked. 'You say she called you. Do you know her as well as you knew James?'

'I have never met her, but I know that James had the highest confidence in her. But again, my point is, why should she betray our plans and then call me to warn me? That doesn't make sense.'

'What are you saying?' Henri asked.

'That the traitor is, or was, right here.' She looked at Monterre.

'You are accusing me?'

'How well do you know your people?'

'Well enough to trust them absolutely.'

'Do you know that someone has stolen all the spare batteries for our radio? We have been waiting for you to come back, Henri, so that we can call out and find out what is going on.'

'My radio is out,' Henri said. 'We were escaping a German patrol and I fell down a culvert. It was smashed.'

'Shit!' Christine said. 'What a fuck-up.'

'It is a serious situation,' Moulin agreed. 'But let us concentrate on discovering this traitor. It has to be someone who knew our plans, and who was able to leave the camp and get in touch with the Germans.' He also looked at Monterre.

'We travelled in groups of four,' Monterre said angrily. 'Always in sight of one another. Are you accusing four of my people? Why don't you accuse Pierre, or Jules? Or both? They stayed behind when we withdrew. They said it was to see if they could help any British survivors. But it could have been to join their German friends.'

Before anyone could move, Liane had opened her shoulder bag, drawn her pistol, and presented it to Monterre's head. 'Retract that statement or die,' she said.

'I retract, I retract,' Monterre gabbled. 'I was just exploring every possibility.'

'Oh, my God!' Christine said. 'That woman!'

'What woman?' Henri asked.

'The woman Joanna?' Christine looked at Amalie.

'Joanna? You can't be serious.'

'She was captured by the Germans . . .'

Liane had lowered the pistol. Now she looked at it, as if considering using it again. 'You are accusing Joanna of betraying us?'

'I am not saying she betrayed us. But she knew about both the raid and what you were doing in Paris.'

'How?'

Christine looked at Amalie. 'I told her,' Amalie said miserably. 'I mean, Joanna . . . I couldn't believe . . .'

'Neither can I,' Liane said grimly.

'I know she is your friend,' Christine said. 'But she was captured by the Gestapo, and she was in possession of the knowledge that was betrayed. Who knows what they did to her.'

Liane's shoulders hunched. She had always supposed Joanna indestructible. But when they had been captured by those German deserters on that terrible day last year, it had been Joanna who had been crushed and almost hysterical, while she had merely closed her mind to what was happening and looked to the future. Of course, Joanna had already been in a hysterical mood, having just watched her brother being shot to pieces. But still, the thought of her being tortured was horrific.

'What are we going to do?' Amalie asked.

'Wait for Pierre to come home,' Liane said. 'There is nothing else we can do.'

'Madeleine! How good to see you.' Franz Hoeppner kissed Madeleine's hand. 'Is all well?' He showed her to the chair before his desk. Outside the office window Bordeaux baked in the late summer heat.

Madeleine, as flawlessly dressed as ever, sat down. 'No.'

Franz also sat, behind the desk. 'Tell me what is the matter.'

'I wish to go back to Berlin. Will you arrange it for me?'

'Of course. But you have only been here three days.'

'That is three days too long.'

'Your parents—'

'Pretend that I do not exist. At meals they speak to each other as if I was not there.'

'My dear, I am so terribly sorry. I had supposed that after all this time, and with you being pregnant . . .'

'They have not forgiven. The fact that I am pregnant with a German baby makes them more bitter yet. As you say, I hoped that they would get over their initial reaction, but it has just grown worse. So . . .'

'I will arrange a seat for you on tomorrow's train. But what about tonight?'

'Oh, I can stand another night.'

'But you'll lunch with me, as you are in town.' He looked past her at the young woman wearing a white shirt and black skirt and stockings standing in the doorway. 'What is it, Martine?'

His secretary, a blunt-featured young woman, looked nervous. 'There is someone to see you, Herr Colonel.'

'Well, I am busy right now. Tell him to wait.'

'Ah . . .' Her shoulders were grasped and she was set aside to allow the visitor to enter.

Franz was on his feet. 'What the . . . ?'

'Heil Hitler! Colonel Hoeppner? We have not met. Oskar Weber.'

For the moment Franz was speechless, while Weber looked at Madeleine. 'Frau von Helsingen! What a pleasant surprise. But what are you doing in Bordeaux?'

'Bordeaux is my home, Herr Colonel. Or it was.'

'Of course. Paulliac. You have been visiting your parents.'

'Yes. But I am leaving tomorrow.'

'Are you? Would you excuse us? I have some urgent business with Colonel Hoeppner.'

'Of course. It looks as if our luncheon date will have to be postponed, Franz. If you could let me have the travel documents this evening—'

'I do not wish you to leave the building at this moment, Frau von Helsingen,' Weber said. 'I would like to speak with you later. Have this young woman make you a cup of coffee and take a seat until we are finished.'

Madeleine looked at Franz, eyebrows arched. 'I think I should remind you that this is my office, and my command, Herr Colonel,' Franz said.

'As of this moment, Colonel Hoeppner, it is my office, and my command. If you wish to have this confirmed, I suggest you telephone General Heydrich in Berlin.'

The two men glared at each other, and Madeleine said, 'I'll wait outside.'

'And kindly close the door,' Weber said. Madeleine did so, and Weber took the chair she had vacated. 'Now, Colonel, tell me what that woman is doing here.'

Franz also sat down. 'That woman is the wife of my closest friend. As she told you, she is on a visit to her parents, who live in Paulliac, a village situated a few miles down the Gironde.'

'I know where Paulliac is, Colonel, and I know who lives

205

there. What I wish to know is why Frau von Helsingen is visiting them now, when she has not done so during the three months they have been living there since their return from Germany.'

'Is this any business of the SD?'

'Everything is the business of the SD, Colonel. Including your relationship with this woman.'

'If you were not what you are, Weber, I would have you thrown out. My relationship with Frau von Helsingen is that of my best friend's wife. She also happens to be six months pregnant, as you may have noticed. As to why she has chosen this time to visit her parents, I have no idea. But I can tell you that the visit has not been a success. She is returning to Berlin tomorrow morning.'

'I think that will have to be postponed.'

'You are speaking as if you have reason to suspect Frau von Helsingen of some crime.'

'Only one crime. Treason.'

'Are you mad?'

'I cannot prove it, but we have had suspicions of her for some time, and her presence here suggests a possibility that Frau von Helsingen is in possession of information of vital importance to the outlaws who are skulking just across the Vichy border and who, as I am sure you know, are commanded by her sister.'

'What information? And how is she supposed to have obtained it?'

'How she obtained it remains to be discovered. The point is that her reason for coming here is to tell her so-called estranged parents so that they can send a messenger to warn the guerillas. I do not know whether she has achieved this. How long has she been here?'

'Three days.'

'And she is leaving again already? That proves it. She came here to deliver a message, and is now hurrying away.'

Franz sighed. 'She came here to see her parents, who have rejected her. That is why she is leaving.'

206

'If you believe that, Colonel Hoeppner, you will believe anything. I wish her returned to Paulliac, and I wish the de Gruchy house placed under the strictest guard. No one is to leave or enter without my permission. It is possible that although Frau von Helsingen may have delivered her message, it has not yet been forwarded to the Resistance. In any event, we will take steps to negate its value.'

'Frau von Helsingen will object to being treated as a prisoner.'

'She can object as much as she likes. It will only be for a few days.'

'She may take her objections to a higher authority.'

'General Heydrich will deal with that. Now, Colonel, what I have to say to you is to be treated as top secret. Here is what I have come here to do.'

Franz listened in growing perturbation. 'It will cause an international incident.'

'An international incident with Vichy is something we can stand. In any event, as I have just told you, Laval accepts the situation. He cannot do so publicly, and will have to condemn our action, but he has promised there will be no repercussions.'

'I am thinking of world opinion when it becomes known that German soldiers have crossed the borders of a friendly power.'

'German soldiers are not going to cross the border. Your people will merely occupy positions along the border to prevent any of the guerillas from escaping across them. My SS people will be in plain clothes. Any more questions?'

'Yes. You say the date is the 30th of September. That is more than a month off. Does this mean that I am to keep Frau von Helsingen in custody for another month?'

'No. If she is in possession of our plans, she is in possession of the proposed date of the operation. Therefore we will negate the value of that knowledge by attacking the moment my people are ready. That should not be more than a week.' Weber grinned. 'Cheer up, Colonel. This will earn you a commendation.'

'Liane! Come quickly!' Etienne was panting from the haste with which he had climbed the hill.

Liane, sitting beside Moulin, jumped to her feet and hurried down the hill, checking at the sight of her brother. 'Pierre! Oh, thank God!' She ran forward to hug the haggard, bearded figure. 'We have been so worried. Jules!' Another hug. 'And . . .' Slowly she released the big man to stare at the third man they had been half carrying, wearing the tattered remnants of British combat dress, who was sinking to his knees. 'James? Oh, my God! James!' She dropped to her knees and held his shoulders to look into his eyes.

He managed a smile. 'The sight of you makes it all worthwhile,' he whispered.

Now she could see the bloodstains on his uniform. 'What happened?'

'I stopped a bullet. But Pierre not only dragged me from the water, but he patched me up.'

'But he has lost too much blood on the walk back,' Pierre said. 'A village doctor took the bullet out and cleaned and dressed the wound, and gave us some bandages and painkillers, but he was in no condition to walk so far. He needs rest.'

'And you shall have rest,' Liane promised. She put her arm round his shoulders and Jules took the other side, and they got him to his feet.

'But I don't understand,' he said. 'What are you doing here?'

'I am here because Pound ordered me to come here. What I would like to know is what *you* are doing here.'

'It's a long and unhappy story.'

'Well, let's get you cleaned up and fed, and we'll talk.'

James looked around the faces as they ate. He was in constant pain, and had been for three weeks, so much so

208

that it now almost seemed a natural state of affairs. That he had got ashore at all was a miracle. He had only been half conscious in the water, had been kept afloat by his life jacket as Lewis had promised . . . Whatever had happened to Lewis? he wondered.

The tide had carried him down from the little seaport, and when he had gained the beach it had been at the foot of some quite steep cliffs. By then he had been too exhausted to move, so he had lain on the sand, half in and half out of the water, feeling deathly cold, waiting for daylight, when he assumed he would be found by the Germans and packed off to a prison camp. Instead he had been found by Pierre and Jules. That the guerillas had had the sense to avoid the trap was the only good thing that had come out of the operation. That Pierre and Jules had risked their lives to see if they could help any survivors was gallantry of the highest order. That they should have found him he regarded as another miracle. They had actually found four of the raiding party, but two were already dead, and the third had only lived a few hours. That they should have determined to half carry him right across France had been the height of foolhardiness.

He had asked them to leave him, pointing out that they were endangering their own lives, but they had refused. And they had, indeed, brought him right across France to this sanctuary, where he was surrounded by friends, and to the presence of Liane. Even if there was a great deal he did not understand.

'If Rachel called you on the morning of the 8th of August, whatever caused her to make that call must have happened the night before, after we had left. Some message must have been received. But from whom?'

'We are all wondering about that. From what Rachel said, she knew you were betrayed as well,' Liane said.

'But she did not recall us.'

'Perhaps she tried, but couldn't.'

James drank some wine while he tried to think. 'There

was no one outside of the brigadier, Rachel and I who knew about *both* the raid and the route. Apart from you people here, of course.'

Liane and Amalie exchanged glances, and they both looked at Christine. 'And Joanna Jonsson,' Christine said quietly.

James frowned at her. He had not really taken her in up till now. That she was a stranded British agent seemed remarkable. That she seemed very friendly with Amalie was equally *un*remarkable: Amalie made friends very easily. That she was stranded because of the radio failure was entirely reasonable; she certainly seemed anxious to get back to England. And that she was accepted by Liane meant that she was acceptable to him. But now she was not making sense. 'Joanna was here,' Liane explained.

'Here? How on earth did that happen? She doesn't know where you are.'

'She found us. And, well . . . it all seems rather miserable.'

'I told her what was happening,' Amalie said. 'And then she stole the batteries for the radio.'

'Joanna?'

'It could have been no one else. And then she went off. She told us she was going to see Mama and Papa, but she went to the Germans instead. Monica was with her.'

James turned to Christine. 'I trusted her,' Christine said, 'because she was a friend of Amalie's, and said she was a friend of Liane's as well. And when she was arrested, I thought it was genuine, so I escaped and came back here. But now it is obvious that she was working for the Nazis all the time.'

That was so unbelievable it required a lot of thought. James looked at Liane, and she looked back; her face was a mask of misery. He needed to concentrate. 'But why did you go with her? If you were already on the run from the Gestapo?'

'I wanted to complete my mission.'

'What is your mission?'

'Monica came to reopen contact with Mama and Papa,' Amalie said.

'You'll have to explain that.'

'You must know that Papa was a British agent before the war.'

'No, I didn't know that.'

'But . . .' Amalie stared at Liane.

'I think you should know,' Liane said to Christine, 'that James is an officer in the SIS, with control over all of our family. Including, if it were necessary, our mother and father.'

Christine looked at her, and then at James, and then seemed to uncoil herself, reaching her feet and drawing the pistol in her belt at the same moment. James, unarmed, could only throw himself to one side. But even as he did so, he realized that the woman was not intending to kill him, but Liane. But Liane had also reacted with lightning speed. Her Luger was drawn and presented to Christine's head before the German woman could level her weapon. 'Drop it, or die.'

Christine hesitated, fatally. What had happened had been so sudden, so unexpected, that even her highly trained brain, while immediately understanding that if James *was* an intelligence controller she was finished, needed a moment to decide her best course, and in that moment Amalie had thrown both arms round her and hurled her to the ground, while Pierre tore the gun from her grasp. Christine gasped and tried to free herself, but Amalie retained her grip, and now Pierre pinioned her arms. 'My God!' Moulin said. 'You think she is a German agent?'

'I think she is going to tell us that,' Liane said.

'You are going to die,' Christine snarled. 'All of you. Our people know where you are, and they are going to stamp on you like cockroaches.'

'That's one question answered,' Liane said. 'Now tell us what happened to Joanna.'

'I handed her over to the Gestapo. Hopefully she will have been shot by now.'

Liane looked at James.

211

'But I think she is still alive,' James said. 'And that it was she that tried to warn us that our plans had been betrayed, by you.'

'Dream, Britisher, dream.'

'Do you want to know anything else?' Liane asked.

'We need to know who she works for, and how she is so sure that we are going to be wiped out.'

'You heard the major,' Liane said.

'The major can fuck off.'

'You need to understand your situation,' Liane said. 'None of these people are going to help you. And if you are responsible for any harm befalling Joanna, I will person- ally enjoy torturing you to death. However, I give you my word that if you tell us what we wish to know, you will die painlessly.'

'But you are going to kill me.'

'Well, of course. You must know that.'

Christine looked around the grim faces, and knew that Liane had been right when she had said she would find no sympathy there. Even Amalie's face was cold, although there were tears in her eyes. She sighed. 'How will you do it?'

'You have a choice. Either a bullet in the back of the head, or a cyanide capsule.'

Christine licked her lips. 'I do not wish my head blown off.'

'Very well, then. The capsule. But first, the answers.'

'My name is Christine von Ulstein, and I am a member of the Sicherheitsdienst.'

Liane looked at James. 'The SD,' he said. 'The German secret service.'

'I thought that was the Abwehr.'

'Very roughly, the Abwehr relates to our MI5. The SD is their equivalent of our MI6, but with considerably more powers. Who is your commander?'

'The overall commander is General Reinhard Heydrich. My immediate commander is Colonel Oskar Weber.'

'And you were sent here to locate this group. How did you get that information out?'

'When I went into Bordeaux with the woman Jonsson, I did not escape as I claimed. I denounced her to the garrison commander, who is a friend of mine, gave him all the information I had obtained, including the details of the proposed raid on St Valery and Mademoiselle de Gruchy's presence in Paris, and then returned here with my story.'

'And you also gave him this location.'

'Yes.'

'What other instructions did you have?'

'Above all else, I was to kill Mademoiselle de Gruchy.' Christine's mouth twisted. 'Only in that have I failed.'

Liane looked at James, who hesitated, and then nodded. Henri gave her the cyanide capsule, and she handed it to Christine. 'I am told it is very quick, and will cause no pain.'

For a last time Christine looked around the faces; then she took the capsule and stood up. Liane stood also, her pistol in her hand. But Christine merely placed the capsule in her mouth. Then she stood to attention and thrust out her right arm. 'Heil Hitler.' Then she bit. But she remained standing. 'What is happening?' Her voice was high.

Liane looked at James. 'It is possible that was a dud?'

'Now he tells me,' Henri remarked.

'Well, then . . .' Liane held out her hand, and Pierre gave her his.

'Can it not be considered an act of God?' Christine asked.

'No.'

Christine stared at her for several seconds, then took the second capsule. 'Give me some wine.'

Amalie gave her a cup; her hand was shaking. Christine bit, and then swallowed the wine. For another dreadful second she stood there, then her knees gave way and she fell to the ground.

Ten

The Coup

They stood around the crumpled figure. However often they had been in the presence of death, or, in Liane's case, actually killed, this was the first fatality within the group.

'I liked her,' Amalie said, openly weeping.

'She was a handsome woman,' Monterre remarked, and flushed as Liane looked at him.

'Do you believe what she said?' Moulin asked. 'That the Boches know where we are?'

'It's possible,' Pierre said. 'But they have known roughly where we are for a year now, and they have done nothing about it. Because they *can* do nothing about it. We are in neutral territory.'

'What is your opinion, James?'

'I agree with you both. I imagine the Germans do know where we are, but I agree with Pierre that they aren't in a position to do much about it, unless they really want to stir up Vichy. On the other hand, if we are pinpointed by the Germans, we are vulnerable to infiltration, as by this woman. I think some thought should be given to relocation.'

'Where?' Pierre asked.

'Well, perhaps somewhere south of Bordeaux. In the Pau area perhaps. I know we have agents in Pau.'

'That removes us even further from Paris.'

'I said it is something to be considered.'

'Meanwhile, Ulstein has to be buried,' Liane said.

'I will see to it,' Monterre volunteered, and summoned some of his men.

214

'There must be no desecration of the body,' Liane warned.

'I will go with them,' Amalie said. 'I would like there to be a marker.'

Liane looked at James, who shrugged. 'Why not?'

'She is riddled with guilt,' Liane said as she lay in James's arms that night, in the privacy of the wood as they liked best. 'She is guilty because she befriended Ulstein, because she told Joanna about me and about the raid, and now because we have executed her friend. She is a mess.'

'She'll get over it. She's tougher than she looks. And she has Henri.'

'And I have you. Oh, James, when I think how you could have drowned . . .'

'When I think of you in Paris with the Gestapo snapping at your heels. How close were they?'

'Close enough for me and my partner to have to shoot our way out.'

'My God! Did you say "partner"?'

'It would not have been possible for me to exist without a partner. Who is now controlling the route, with a little help from a bunch of whores.'

'You are going to have to write your memoirs one day.'

'But you forgive me for what I had to do.'

'I will forgive you anything. But I'm not keen on you having to do it again. When we manage to reopen contact with London—'

'When. There is still a lot to be done.'

'You say the route is running smoothly.'

'It is. But it requires a constant flow of money. I am using Gruchy funds.'

'We can't have that. I will arrange money from England.'

'As you say, when contact is reopened. But we don't know when that will be. Meanwhile we are running low, because Papa and his new manager do not know what is happening. I must get to them and put them in the picture.'

'You mean go to Paulliac? That is too risky.'

'It is not at all risky for me. I know Paulliac far better than any German.'

'I will come with you.'

'My darling!' She hugged him, and put her hand down inside the blanket. 'You have not got your strength back yet. You cannot even erect. Now you must sleep. We'll make plans in the morning.'

'Listen!'

'I said tomorrow.'

'I mean, listen.'

Liane frowned, and then sat up. 'That is an aircraft.'

'That is a Lysander. Flying low.'

'Brune?' She threw off the blanket and stood up, a sliver of white in the darkness. 'There are no lights. He'll crash.'

James also got to his feet. 'He's got more sense than to try to land in the dark.' They ran through the trees to stand in the clear of the plateau and stare upwards.

The sentry joined them. 'I heard it too. He's going away again.' The noise was certainly diminishing.

'Shit!' Liane said. 'Do you think he was trying to contact us?'

'Had to be,' James said. 'In which case he'll try again tomorrow. We must have the lights ready.'

'Look there,' the sentry said. They peered into the starlit sky, made out the glimmer of white floating downwards.

'It's a drop,' James said. 'We'd better get down to it.'

'Ahem,' the sentry remarked.

They looked down at themselves. 'He has a point,' Liane said.

They dressed themselves, alerted the rest of the camp, and Liane and Pierre hurried down the hill. James knew he could not match them at the moment, so remained with Amalie and Henri and Moulin, until they came back up the hill an hour later. Then he blinked in amazement. 'So what do you know,' Joanna said. 'I'm the Fifth Cavalry.'

They hugged and kissed her and told her about Christine.

'That bitch,' Joanna said. 'Seems to me she got off lightly.'

'So what's the word from England?'

'First thing, I've brought you a spare transmitter.' She tapped her knapsack. 'Supposing it survived my bump. And I have a lot of orders.' She outlined them.

'They want me in England?' Moulin asked. 'But my business is here.'

'Pound thinks it might be a good idea to stay on the same wavelength as de Gaulle. At least get to know him.'

'I met him once, before the war. He was only a colonel then. I didn't like him. He was a bumptious fellow.'

'I gather he's even more bumptious now. But he has the ear of the PM. So we're to call Pound and arrange a date. He'll want you out as well, James. Rachel certainly does. She's stuck with a shit.'

'And you'll be going back as well,' Liane said softly.

Joanna squeezed her hand. 'I'm afraid this is a flying visit. I'd like to take you all, but there's only room for five, besides the pilot.'

'Five,' Liane said thoughtfully.

'But the rest of you have got to get out of here, even if it means scattering for a while,' Joanna said. 'The Krauts are about to come after you.'

'This is Vichy territory,' Pierre objected.

'They've done a deal. I even know when, roughly. It'll be around the end of September, probably a little before. You have time.'

'This from your Berlin source?' James asked.

'Another one. This is absolutely reliable.'

The guerillas looked at each other. 'Sounds like Ulstein's threats were genuine,' Henri observed.

'Still, virtually a month does give us a little time for manoeuvre,' Pierre said.

'Dawn,' Amalie said. 'Time for breakfast.'

After the meal Joanna and Liane wandered off. James let them go. He felt no jealousy, and knew they would have a lot to talk about. Besides, Moulin also wanted to talk, while Pierre was busy setting up the radio, and fitting fresh batteries to Amalie's.

'How can I leave at such a time?' Moulin said. 'That amounts to desertion in the face of the enemy.'

'Well, de Gaulle doesn't know the Germans are about to attack you,' James said. 'And I'm sure he'll be happy for you to be flown back in as soon as you've had your meeting.'

'After my people have been destroyed, you mean.'

'They won't be, now that we've been warned. As Joanna said, if necessary, they'll scatter and regroup.'

'If they scatter, they will never regroup. Morale is very low following that fruitless tramp across France. And seven of them have not returned at all.'

'You think they were captured?'

'It is possible. Or they were killed. Or most likely of all, they have just gone home.'

'The group will survive,' James said, with more confidence than he felt.

'We are in business,' Pierre said.

James selected the correct wavelength, took the mike. 'Pound Two, Pound Two. Pound One calling. Come in, please.'

There was a moment's silence, then Rachel shouted, 'Pound One! James! You're alive! My God! You're alive! He's alive,' she told someone else.

A man's voice came on the mike. 'Pound One? This is your replacement. Where are you?'

'I am with Pound Eleven.'

'But . . .how did you get there?'

'I don't think this is the time for chat. We require a pick-up. This should be on . . .'

'Next Sunday,' Liane said from behind him.

'Next . . .' He turned his head to look at her.

'Sunday,' she repeated. 'There is a lot to be done.'

James looked at Moulin, who shrugged. 'Next Sunday,' he said.

'You mean the day after tomorrow.'

Liane was shaking her head. 'I mean Sunday week.'

'Sunday week,' James said.

'Understood. The 7th of September. Do we understand that Pound Three has made contact?'

'You may presume that, yes.'

'Very good. Pound One out.'

But before he could close down Rachel came back on the line. 'Oh, James,' she said. 'I am so happy you're alive.'

'So am I,' James said. 'Pound One out.'

Pierre closed down. 'That is devotion above and beyond the call of duty.'

'Yes,' James agreed, and turned to face Liane, who had Joanna at her shoulder. 'Just what are you playing at? Nine days?'

'There is a lot to be done,' Liane said again.

'Nine days brings us awfully close to the date Joanna says the Germans are going to move in.'

'Three weeks? That is time enough. They will stick to their schedule. They always do.'

'You are angry with me,' Liane said that afternoon when she and James were alone.

'Of course I am not angry with you,' he lied. 'I just wish you'd tell me why you put back the date so far.'

'Don't you think I might wish to keep you here a few days longer?'

'Or is it that you want to keep Joanna here that much longer?'

'James! Now you are both jealous *and* angry.'

'I am neither,' he said, angrily. 'I just wish you'd tell me the truth.'

'You are my two favourite people in all the world. But if I had to choose between you, I would choose you.'

'Oh, you darling! Listen, if you'd come with us, you could have us both. At least for a while.'

'And you know I cannot do that. Certainly with Jean

219

going. I must remain here. But listen, I have a favour to ask of you.'

'All right. You have it.'

She kissed him. 'I would like to sleep with Joanna tonight.' She laid her finger on his lips. 'Just for tonight; then I will be yours for the other eight days. But it has been so long since we have seen each other, and she lives such a dangerous life. She has told me she has to go back into Germany.' She gave a girlish giggle. 'We will probably do nothing more than talk.'

He could not refuse her. To refuse Liane anything was an impossible thought, and not only because of his love for her. The idea of making an enemy of such a woman was impossible.

'One night,' she promised him. He slept in the cave with the other senior men, but when he went outside the next morning, both Liane and Joanna had disappeared.

'They left just after midnight,' the sentry said.

'You did not stop them?' Pierre asked.

The sentry rolled his eyes. 'How was I to stop Mademoiselle de Gruchy?'

'Were they armed?' Moulin asked.

'They each had a pistol and a tommy-gun. And a haversack.'

'They have deserted us,' Monterre growled. 'You can never trust a woman.' He looked at Amalie speculatively.

'Of course they have not deserted us,' Amalie snapped. 'They have gone to Paulliac.'

'Eh?' All the men spoke together.

'Don't you see? It is three days from here to Paulliac, providing you are fit enough to keep going all day. Two days to the border, and then another to circle Bordeaux and get to the river. That is why they wanted the pick-up put back a week, so they can get there and back in time.'

'Great God Almighty!' James said. 'She said something about going to Paulliac, and I told her it was madness.'

'She wants to see Mama and Papa,' Amalie said. 'And she

220

has to have someone to go with her. Until Joanna came she thought she had no one. I would have gone . . .' Tears welled up in her eyes. 'She didn't think I would be up to it.'

She also wants to arrange the financing for the route, James thought. The silly, stupendous, heroic woman. Thus the pretence of needing some time with Joanna had been merely a ploy to allow them to escape. 'What must we do?' Pierre asked. 'They have an eight-hour start, and they *are* fit enough to keep going all day. And all night, too.'

'There is nothing we can do,' Moulin said. 'Except pray that they come back.'

'They do not seem to be following us,' Joanna remarked.

'They know they cannot catch us,' Liane said.

The two women lay on a shallow hill overlooking the border. The road and the checkpoints were a mile to their right, so that when they crossed the line they would already be well south of the city. 'You still reckon James will be happy?'

'Of course he's not going to be happy. He's going to be hopping mad. But he'll forgive me.'

'And he'll take them out?'

'You said the plane could take five, apart from the pilot.'

'James and Jean and me, and your folks. You know, you could sit on James's knee. Or mine.'

'Forget it.'

'You really have a death wish.'

'Don't you, going back to Germany?'

'I'm in no danger.'

'Because you're an American? Don't you think that when they're ready they'll arrange an entirely plausible accident?'

'I'm in no danger,' Joanna repeated. 'Because they think I'm working for them.'

'That's the most dangerous thing of all.' Liane squinted at the setting sun. 'We'll be able to move in a couple of hours. Let's get some sleep.'

* * *

They crossed the border as soon as it was dark, then made their way towards the river. Liane knew almost every inch of the country from her childhood explorations, but as she chose to avoid the main road and stick to paths and fields, it was three in the morning before they saw the gates . . . and the sentry walking to and fro. 'There'll be at least one more,' Joanna whispered.

'No problem. The property runs down to the water.'

'You mean we're going for a swim?'

Liane smiled. 'Don't you reckon we both need a bath?' They crept through the trees, well away from the gates, and reached the river bank. 'We should be able to wade the whole way,' Liane said. 'But it runs pretty hard. Don't lose your footing.'

'And you reckon to bring your folks out this way?'

'No,' Liane said. 'They wouldn't make it.'

'Then how do we do it?'

'Just let's get in, first.' The water was surprisingly cold, and deeper by the bank than Liane had anticipated. Soon she was up to her shoulders and struggling to keep her footing. Joanna, taller and more powerfully built, found the going easier, but they were both exhausted by the time they clambered up the bank and lay on the grass beneath the trees, looking across the lawn at the house.

'You used to have dogs,' Joanna said.

'I imagine we still do. But they're locked up at night.' She looked at her watch. 'Four.'

'You mean that thing still works?'

'It's waterproof. Let's move. It'll be daybreak in an hour.'

They crept across the lawn and round the back of the house. They passed the kennels and the dogs barked, but the sound was muted. The door to the kitchen was locked, but Liane got to work with her knife and a few moments later they were inside. 'When this is over you should set up as a burglar,' Joanna whispered.

'If that's all I'll have on my plate I'll be laughing.' They crossed the darkened downstairs hall and up the stairs. Liane went along the corridor to her parents' room, and checked as she heard a door open. She swung round, instinctively unslinging her tommy-gun, and stared at Madeleine.

Even in the gloom the sisters recognized each other instantly. But before either could react Joanna had darted forward to grasp Madeleine's throat, at the same time pressing her knife into her breast. 'Make a sound and you're dead.' As she spoke, she pushed Madeleine back into the bedroom. Liane followed and closed the door.

Joanna released Madeleine and she sat on the bed. 'Ugh! You're all wet.'

'What are you doing here?' Liane asked.

'I am visiting Mama and Papa.' She glanced at Joanna. 'She sent me.'

'To get a message to you, warning you of the German plans,' Joanna explained.

'We received no message.'

'Well, I never sent one. I meant to see what I could do, but they have treated me like dirt.'

'And for that reason you could have condemned your brother and sisters to death?' Joanna inquired.

'Well, in this war it is every man, and every woman, for herself.'

'I swore that the next time I saw you I would kill you,' Liane said. 'I have a good mind to do it now.'

'I'm your sister!'

'Not anymore.'

'Hold it,' Joanna said. 'She's actually one of us. Reluctantly, I guess. But effectively.'

'Tell me about it.'

'She's one of my principal sources in Berlin.'

Liane stared at her sister. 'Is that true?'

'Well, we're all going to be hanged. I know it.'

'Nobody is going to be hanged,' Joanna said, 'if we all keep our heads.' She glanced at Liane. 'I've been considering our problem.' She turned back to Madeleine. 'You are going to get us out of here.'

'Me? I'm a prisoner already.'

'Who says so? Not Franz Hoeppner?'

'No, no. He's as upset as I am. But he, the Bordeaux command, has been taken over for the time being by that dreadful man Weber of the SD. This is so he can make his attack on your people. The whole thing is terribly hush-hush, and they're afraid if I am allowed to leave before the attack I may spill it.'

'If it's all hush-hush, then no one apart from Franz and Weber and you know what's going on, right?'

'Well, I suppose some of Weber's people know of it.'

'But none of Hoeppner's. Now listen very carefully, and I'll tell you what you have to do.' She smiled at Liane. 'Both of you.'

'I can't believe it,' Barbara de Gruchy kept saying. 'Oh, my darling, darling girl. To have you here, and looking so well . . .'

'It's the open air life,' Liane said.

Albert just sat and stared at her. Liane realized that he had taken the past year far worse than his wife, and looked a crushed and very old man.

'And can you really take us out of here?'

'Yes. It will be very hard. Very tiring. Very dangerous. Are you prepared to risk it?'

'To get back to England? I would risk anything.'

'There is something that has to be done first. Papa! Is Bouterre trustworthy?'

Albert blinked at her. 'He has proved so up to now,' Barbara said. 'Why?'

'I wish you to give him instructions not to carry out his usual audit of the Paris books this October, and I also wish him to inform Brissard that he will not be doing so again before next spring at the very earliest.'

Barbara frowned. 'He will find that very irregular.'

'But will he do it?'

'Well, I suppose so. He will ask for a reason.'

224

'You say he can be trusted. Tell him it is for France.'

'You are saying that Brissard is in the Resistance.'

'In my business, one says nothing. One merely gets things done.'

'Very well, my dear. You have become a very positive person. But then, I suppose you always were . . . only we never saw enough of you to notice. I will—' She checked abruptly as Madeleine appeared in the doorway. 'My God!'

'Franz has replied,' Madeleine said. 'He will come to dinner.'

'I do not understand,' Barbara said. 'She is—'

'One of us, Mama. And she is going to help us to escape.'

'Madeleine! Oh, Madeleine!' Barbara stood up to embrace her younger daughter. 'To think how I have hated you. And you say that Pierre and Amalie are also alive and well. This must be the happiest day of my life.'

'They are waiting for you, Mama,' Liane promised her. 'All we need now is for all of us to play our parts.'

'Come back for me at eleven, Willi,' Franz Hoeppner told his driver. 'I do not wish to be out late.'

'Eleven, Herr Colonel. Have a nice dinner.'

'I intend to.' He went up the steps and nodded to Paul, who opened the doors for him. He was so pleased that Madeleine had so far decided to forgive him as to invite him to dinner. And he was so pleased to be able to accept. No doubt Weber would criticize, but even if that dreadful man had been able to take over his command, there was no way he was going to take over his private life. 'In here, Herr Colonel,' Paul said, accompanying him down the corridor.

Franz glanced at him in surprise; the poor fellow's voice was trembling, but then, he was actually trembling all over. No doubt he was not used to having German officers in the house. The door was opened for him, and he stepped into the brilliantly lighted drawing room, gazed at Madeleine. She too was looking extremely agitated, and he felt sure

225

that she had recently been weeping. 'Madeleine?' Behind him the door closed, softly.

'Franz!' Madeleine stepped forward.

'Stop right there.'

Franz turned towards the new voice, which was not one he had ever heard before, although he found it extremely attractive; as he did the owner of the voice with the classically beautiful features and the waving shoulder-length yellow hair. But he did not care for the expression on her face, or the Luger pointed at his head, while her resemblance to Madeleine told him instantly who she was. 'My God!'

'They made me do it,' Madeleine said. 'She said she would shoot me.'

'Your own sister?'

'She is a traitor to France,' Liane said. 'She deserves to die.'

Franz looked at the older de Gruchys, who stood together against the far wall. 'You would permit this?'

'She is no longer our daughter,' Barbara spat. 'She is a Nazi.'

Again Franz looked from face to face. 'Why did you bring me here? Do you not realize that now I shall be forced to hang you all? Or am I to be murdered too?'

'That is up to you,' Liane said. 'Is your car still here?'

'No.'

'But it will come back for you. When? Please do not lie to me, Herr Colonel, or you *will* die.'

He looked into her eyes, and thought what a pleasure it would be to meet this woman in a ballroom. But she was a cold-blooded killer. Even if he had not seen the file on her, he could see it in her eyes. 'Eleven.'

'That is ideal. We shall have dinner. Mama?'

Barbara rang the bell, and Paul appeared. 'You may serve, Paul.'

'Are all your servants suborned?' Franz asked.

'All of our servants have been dismissed,' Barbara said.

'Save for Paul. As he has had to cook the dinner as well as serve it, I'm afraid it will not be up to our usual standard. But we will be serving Gruchy Grand Cru. Some of the last bottles left in our cellars. I am sure you will enjoy it.'

It was the strangest meal Franz Hoeppner had ever experienced. The food was actually excellent, the wine quite superb – he had only ever drunk Gruchy Fourteen Grand Cru once before in his life. The conversation flowed, at least between Barbara and Liane, as they reminisced about old times and looked forward to their return after the war. Albert said little; he was clearly in a fog. And Madeleine spoke only when directly addressed; she was clearly terrified. Of her own family! But of one thing he was certain: she had to be protected from them, whatever the cost. While he had to do the best he could. It could only be with words, as Liane, seated opposite him, had her Luger under her right hand and pointing at him all the time.

'You are hoping to escape into Vichy,' he suggested. 'But you do understand that however long it takes, you will be hunted down, eventually.'

'It all depends on whether your "eventually" happens before the end of the war, don't you think?' she asked.

'The end of the war will make no difference to our determination to bring to justice those who have committed crimes against us.'

'Ah, but it will, Herr Colonel. Because when the war ends you will be in no position to hunt down anyone. You will be too busy trying to avoid being hunted down yourselves.'

'Do you really believe we can lose this war, mademoiselle? Have you looked at a map recently?'

'Herr Colonel, you lost this war the moment your first soldier crossed the Polish frontier in September 1939.'

They stared at each other, and he managed a smile. 'I see we must agree to differ. But I will say with all sincerity that I have enjoyed meeting you, and that I shall be genuinely sorry when they put the rope around your neck.'

'Do you know, I think I will say snap to that.' She looked at her watch. 'But you have not seen the last of me yet. We are to take a midnight drive together.'

'Do you really think you can get away with this?'

'I am going to be beside you every minute of the way, Herr Colonel. If I do not get away with it, you will be dead long before they get around to putting that rope round my neck. It is a quarter to eleven. We must move. Mama, will you take Madeleine upstairs. You know what to do. But try to be gentle. Remember she is pregnant.'

'With a German baby!'

'With your grandchild, Mama. Go along, Madeleine. Behave yourself.'

Madeleine got up. 'You are not going to let them get away with this, Franz. Tell me that.'

'What is going to happen to her?' Franz asked.

'We are merely going to tie her up so that she cannot get free until we are well away. Now, will you finish your wine?'

'Well, Roess, what do you think of my dispositions?' Weber asked as the two men breakfasted together.

Roess had just arrived by the overnight train from Paris, and needed a shave. 'I have not actually seen them yet, Herr Colonel. But I am sure they are admirable. May I ask when is the day?'

'The official day is the 30th of September.'

'That is three weeks away. May I ask why you have brought me here at this time?'

'We are going to capture, or kill, the de Gruchy clan, Roess. These are people you have been hunting for over a year. I supposed you would like to be in at the kill.'

'Indeed I would, sir. But three weeks is a long time to be away from Paris.'

Weber smiled. 'It is not going to be three weeks. We are surrounded by spies and treachery. Thus I have told all my commanders, including Hoeppner, that the date is the 30th of September, and instructed them to be ready for that. In fact, I intend to go in the day after tomorrow.'

'But will your men be ready?'

'They are ready now. I just needed to make sure all, or at least most, of the guerillas would have returned from the abortive attack on St Valery. Heydrich said to give them five weeks. I have allowed them just over four. I assume you have had no success in tracing Liane de Gruchy?'

'The woman seems to be able to vanish into thin air.'

'That may be. But if she has left Paris I would say it is a certainty that she has returned to Vichy. So we have every reason to suppose that she will be there as well. It will be a great coup.' He looked at the doorway to where Hoeppner's secretary, Martine, who he had appropriated along with this office, was hovering. 'What is it?'

'Excuse me, Herr Colonel, but there is a woman here.'

'What sort of woman?'

'Well, sir, she claims to be an American.'

Weber was on his feet. 'Jonsson! Send her in.'

Roess was also on his feet. 'Jonsson? But . . .'

'She has been turned. I turned her.' Both men faced the door as Joanna came in, and both men's jaws dropped at the sight of the bedraggled figure. 'My God!' Weber said. 'What has happened to you?'

Joanna sank into the chair Roess had vacated. 'Do you have anything to drink?'

'Cognac, Martine!' Martine hurried off. 'You are supposed to be in England,' Weber pointed out. Roess had retreated against the wall; he had never expected to find himself in the same room as this woman.

Martine returned with the glass of brandy and Joanna drank deeply, then raised her head. 'You lied to me! You made me think you had Liane de Gruchy in your cells.'

'Well, as they say, all is fair in love and war. You mean she is in Vichy? What did I tell you, Roess? I can read these people like a book.'

229

Joanna turned her head, sharply. 'Roess? You are Roess?'

'I am Colonel Roess, yes.'

'You see, Roess, you are famous,' Weber said. 'But what were you doing with the guerillas, Joanna?'

'I wished to see them. To . . .'

'I see. You wished to see if what I had told you was the truth. And you found it to be a lie. Tell me, did you mail my letter?'

· 'Of course.'

'And did you receive a reply?'

'Yes.'

'Where is it?'

'I mailed it to your office in Berlin.'

'Mailed it? From where?'

'Zurich. I went from England to Switzerland, as I intended to come down here. Have I done wrong?'

'I imagine Switzerland is safe enough, although it was your business to deliver the letter personally in Berlin. But I am confused. You say you carried out your mission in England. Were there any problems?'

Joanna finished her brandy and held out the glass. Martine looked at Weber, received a quick nod, and went off to refill it. 'There were no problems,' Joanna said. 'I have never had any problems in England.'

'Very good. Then you returned, not to Germany, but to Switzerland, and from there made your way into Vichy to visit your friends. There you discovered your lover alive and well, I assume. At any rate, she was not in a Gestapo cell, as I had said. Yet you are here. You have to explain this.'

'Well . . .' Joanna accepted the second glass of brandy, sipped. 'They knew you are planning to attack them.'

'You told them this?'

'Of course I did not. They already knew.'

'How?'

'I don't know. But they are preparing to move out before the 30th of September.'

'And you came here to tell me this?'

'I came to tell Colonel Hoeppner. I did not know you were here.'

'Why did you do this, when you knew I had tricked you? When you must have felt I had no further hold on you? And when you must realize that your information may well mean the deaths of your friends. And your lover.'

Joanna's shoulders hunched. 'They are not my friends.' She glanced at him, then looked away again. 'She has taken a lover. A *man*! She told me she did not wish to see me again.'

'Well, well. What did some English playwright once say, Roess? Hell hath no fury, et cetera. But such emotional upsets are always useful. Thank you, Fräulein. Martine, has Colonel Hoeppner come in yet?'

'Not as yet, Herr Colonel.'

'He has taken up sleeping late because he is annoyed that I have taken command. However, will you please get hold of him and tell him I wish to see him immediately.' The girl hurried off, and Weber returned behind his desk. 'We shall act on your information, Fräulein.'

'They are moving in three days,' Joanna said. 'They have already started. You cannot get there in time.'

'On the contrary. I will be in their midst tomorrow morning.'

'Tomorrow?' Roess asked. 'It is sixty kilometres from the border to the guerilla camp.'

'Two days' journey for a motorized column, eh? But only fifteen minutes by air.'

'My God!' Joanna gasped.

'Exactly. One must be up to date.'

'But that is mountainous country. How will you put a plane down? And you will need more than one.'

'I have three small transports standing by. According to the information given Hoeppner by Ulstein when she was here, these people regularly receive supplies from England by light aircraft. She has marked on the map the exact place

231

where this plane lands. Where a Britisher can land, so can we.'

'But surely that plane comes in at night, to a lit strip.'

'A facility we will lack. But we can land at dawn, overwhelm the opposition, and be off again by midday. How is Ulstein, by the way? You must have met her.'

'Ulstein is dead,' Joanna said, trying desperately to think. The use of airborne troops had simply not occurred to her. 'They found out who she was and executed her.'

'Now, that is a shame. She was a brave and dedicated woman. Was she ill-treated before execution?'

'I do not believe so.'

'Well, that is something. I am sure she will have died well. Yes, Martine?'

'Colonel Hoeppner is not in his quarters, Herr Colonel. His servant says he did not return at all last night.'

'Return? Return from where?'

'Colonel Hoeppner went out to dinner, sir. At the de Gruchy house.'

'What? And he has not returned? You are saying he is still there?'

'I do not know, sir.'

'Well, send somebody out there to find out what has happened. Tell him to break into the house if necessary.' Martine scurried from the room. 'Those fucking people . . .'

'They would hardly have harmed a German colonel when everyone knew exactly where he was,' Joanna protested. 'And the de Gruchys are not murderers.'

'Their daughter certainly is.'

'But Liane is in Vichy.'

'You think you know these people. You do not. Not since the start of the war. They have become a pack of mad dogs. Well?' he glared at Martine as she reappeared.

She was now looking positively terrified. 'There has been a telephone call from Sergeant Boden, Herr Colonel. From frontier crossing six.'

Weber was on his feet again. 'Guerilla activity?'

232

'Well, no, sir. It is very strange.'

'What are you saying?'

'Sergeant Boden reports that at one o'clock this morning Colonel Hoeppner's car crossed the frontier.'

Slowly Weber sank back into his chair. 'It was not stopped?'

'Well, yes, sir, it was. But it was definitely Colonel Hoeppner, and he commanded the barrier to be lifted.'

'He was alone?'

'No, sir. He was accompanied by his driver, and three other people. One, an elderly gentleman, sat in the front beside the driver. The other two were women. One is described as elderly, the other as young.'

Weber stared at her for several seconds. Then he said, in a quiet voice, 'At one o'clock this morning. It is now nine o'clock. That is eight hours. Why is he reporting it now?'

'Well, sir, although he thought it strange, and entered it in his log book, as it *was* Colonel Hoeppner, and he was giving instructions in a clear, calm voice, he assumed the colonel was on some undercover mission into Vichy. But when, as you say, sir, several hours had passed and the colonel did not return, he became worried. He wants instructions as to what to do next.'

'Very good.' Weber continued to speak quietly. 'You may call him back, Fräulein, and tell him that my instructions are to cut his stripes from his sleeve and burn them, because he will not get them back again. Also, instruct the guard at the de Gruchy estate to enter the house, by force if need be, and place everyone found there under arrest.' Martine gulped, and left the room. 'That bitch,' Weber growled. 'That unutterable bitch.'

'Who?' Joanna asked. 'The old people must have been Monsieur and Madame de Gruchy. But who could the woman have been?'

'That bitch Madeleine von Helsingen.'

'Madeleine? But she is in Berlin!'

'She is right here in Bordeaux, pretending just to be

233

visiting her parents. She has to be the one who got that warning to the guerillas. I knew it. And now she has seduced Hoeppner. I knew that too. I could see it in his eyes every time he looked at her.'

'Oh, come now, Weber. Madeleine is six months pregnant. And she is the wife of his best friend.'

'Ha! Well, we will have to sort that out after we have cleaned this business up.' He picked up his phone. 'Get me Captain Rinteler.' He tapped his fingers on his desk while he waited, and Roess and Joanna regarded each other with smouldering hostility. 'Rinteler? Operation Hillock will commence at dawn tomorrow. What? They are ready enough. Of course there will be casualties: we are fighting a war. I will join you at midnight for final preparations. Yes, I will be coming with you. Very good.' He hung up. 'Now . . .'

Martine was back. 'The de Gruchy guard sergeant is on the line, sir. He confirms that Colonel Hoeppner left the residence just after eleven last night, accompanied by the two senior de Gruchys and another woman.'

'Stale news.'

'Yes, sir. But he says the other woman was not Frau von Helsingen, who he has seen several times during her stay at the chateau. What is more, sir, obeying your orders, he broke into the house and found it absolutely deserted, not even a servant, with one exception.'

'Yes?'

'He found Frau von Helsingen, bound and gagged and tied to her bed.'

Weber stared at her in stupefaction.

'Is she all right?' Joanna asked.

'I believe so, Fräulein. But she is very angry. She says she has been betrayed by her family.'

'I must go to her,' Joanna said.

Weber had recovered. 'Then who was the other woman? Was the guard able to describe her?'

'Well, it was dark, Herr Colonel. And she was wearing a headscarf. But he got the impression that she was fair.

234

And he says that she was very handsome. He used the word "beautiful".'

Weber turned to Joanna.

'Liane de Gruchy.'

'*What* did you say?'

'That is a perfect description of Liane.'

'You said she was in Vichy!'

'She was. She must have left the moment my flight was discovered. It took me four days to reach here on foot. She must have had transport.'

'And you mean she calmly went to her parents' house, inveigled Hoeppner into going there for dinner, kidnapped him, and drove across the border?'

'That sounds like Liane,' Joanna agreed. 'And now she has got away again. I would like permission to accompany you, Herr Colonel.'

'You?'

'I would like to see the end of this bitch, personally.'

'Yet again, hell hath no fury, eh? Very well, Joanna, you will have your pound of flesh. Roess, I will leave Frau von Helsingen to you. She will have to be interrogated first, to find out exactly what happened. But as she appears to be innocent of acting against the Reich, you will treat her with the greatest respect, and return her safely to Berlin. Is that understood? Roess? What are you doing?'

Roess was taking off his spectacles and placing them on the floor. Now he stepped on them with great deliberation.

Liane looked at her watch. 'Nine o'clock,' she said. 'Stop the car.' The driver braked, switched off the engine. Liane got out, keeping her tommy-gun, hitherto concealed beneath her cloak, levelled. 'Now, gentlemen, step down, if you will.'

The driver got out of the front door, Franz the back. 'Now,' Liane said, 'if I were truly the cold-blooded killer your propaganda machine describes me as, I would shoot you both, now. It would certainly be the simplest thing to do. And it is what you would probably do were the situation to be reversed. But I really only believe in killing when it is necessary.' She gestured at the hills which surrounded them on every side. 'You are in the foothills of the Massif Central. The border is about forty kilometres behind you. You should be able to walk that in a day or so. I am sorry I have no food to offer you, but there are streams which will provide you with water. There is a village about ten kilometres down that slip road, but I do not recommend you go that way. I do not think they will take very kindly to a couple of German soldiers appearing in their midst. So I will say goodbye. Oh, one thing more, Herr Colonel. Please remember that my sister had nothing to do with this.'

She got behind the wheel, and Franz clicked his heels. 'I will make sure she is not implicated, Fräulein. And may I say that I look forward to our next meeting.'

'I really wouldn't do that,' Liane advised. 'I could be in a bad mood.' She engaged gear and drove away.

'Do you see what I see?' Jules asked.

Monterre, seated beside him on the brow of a hill overlooking the distant road, squinted into the morning heat haze. 'Holy Mary Mother of God! That is a German command car.' He unslung his tommy-gun.

'Hold it,' Jules commanded. 'Let us see what they want.'

'They must be mad.'

'Maybe. Maybe not. Fetch Pierre.'

Monterre looked as if he would have liked to stay, then changed his mind and climbed the hill. Jules watched the car approaching the foot of the hill, and then turn on to the rough path leading up. Pierre arrived. 'What is it?' Jules handed him the glasses, and Pierre levelled them. 'My God!' Pierre handed them back and ran down the hill as the car came to a halt. 'Mama? Papa? Liane? But how?'

'We will tell you up at the camp.'

The entire group gathered to hear, in a mixture of awe and apprehension. 'But Madeleine!' Amalie cried. 'You mean she is on our side after all?'

'Oh, yes,' Barbara said. 'She is a heroine.'

'What will happen to her?' James asked.

'Hopefully nothing, if she acts as well as I know she can.'

'And Joanna?'

'The whole thing was her plan.'

'And you say she's gone back to Germany?'

'Well, she's gone back to the Bordeaux headquarters.'

'You don't think she's putting her head into a noose?'

'She seems entirely confident.' Liane squeezed his arm. 'Don't you think I worry about her too?'

'I know you do. And I love you for it.'

'So when does the plane arrive?'

'Two o'clock tomorrow morning.'

'And you'll take Mama and Papa out?'

'If that's what you wish. But leaving you to face the music . . .'

'Leaving me to organize our relocation. We'll leave the moment you take off. So if we're rising so early . . .'

'Time,' Liane said. The camp was stirring.

James put both arms round her waist. 'Did I ever tell you that I adore you?'

'So many times that I've lost count.' She kissed him. 'But I still love to hear it. Let's go.'

They hurried down the hill, waited until they heard the engine, then lit the flares. Within ten minutes the Lysander was on the ground. Still unable to move very freely, James remained in the tree fringe while Pierre and Henri hurried forward with Jules and Etienne, followed by Monterre and his men, but then he heard Pierre say, as the door was opened, 'Good God! I remember you. But what are you doing here?'

'I have come to collect my boss,' Rachel said.

James stumbled forward, Liane at his side. 'What the hell . . . ?'

Brune had also got down. 'She had permission, Major. Don't ask me how.'

'I pulled strings.'

'Pound Two!' Liane said. 'I recognize your voice.'

'Snap,' Rachel said. 'Pound Twelve.' The two women gazed at each other.

'Ah,' James said, realizing that he could be in a critical situation: while Rachel knew about Liane, Liane did not know about Rachel. 'You'd better meet. Rachel Cartwright, Liane de Gruchy.'

Rachel shook hands. 'I've heard so much about you, mademoiselle.'

'I am honoured.'

'But,' James said, 'what *are* you doing here?'

'I told you. I have come for you. The brigadier gave me permission. We didn't know how bad you were.' She squinted into the gloom. 'You look quite good.'

'I am perfectly well.'

'He isn't really,' Liane said. 'When you get him home, Miss Cartwright, put him to bed.'

'I shall do that, mademoiselle. And do please call me Rachel.'

'So who's minding the shop?' James asked. The meeting had gone off far better than he could have expected. So far.

'Don't ask. I'm hoping we're going to be getting rid of him.'

'Well, let's get up to the camp and you can bring me up to date. Brune, you'd better come up as well.'

'Will do, Major. Just as soon as we have the old girl properly covered up.'

He joined them an hour later, just as the sky in the east was beginning to lighten. The group were seated around the fire, drinking wine, and Rachel had met Amalie and Moulin and Henri and the senior de Gruchys, and had an explore. 'Reminds me of when I was a girl scout. And you live like this all the time?'

'We have been very comfortable here,' Liane said.

'James never struck me as the sort of man who would enjoy camping out.'

'That depends who I'm camping out with.'

'And now you'll have to find a new home,' Rachel said, a trifle acidly. 'I hope I'll be able to visit you again.'

'We'd like that very much, once we're relocated. You must give her permission, James.'

'Ah . . .' The sky was lightening.

'I hear aircraft,' Amalie said.

What am I doing? Joanna wondered as the aircraft bumped to a halt. What am I going to do? They had to be warned. But how. She jumped out of the doorway at Weber's shoulder, looked left and right. To either side of her there were men, armed with tommy-guns, squads carrying the two mortars. Then she looked at the trees which surrounded the field. She wondered if Brune was down yet. There was no sign of his machine. Perhaps he had come and gone again . . . with James and Moulin, and the elder de Gruchys? But situated as they were, at the foot of the hill, it was going to take the SS a good half an hour to assemble and begin their assault: Weber was relying on the fact that no one knew they were coming this early. Half an hour. And half a mile.

She moved apart from the men as they lined up, checked her weapons: she was armed with both tommy-gun and Luger pistol, but neither was loud enough to alarm someone at half a mile. Most of the men in front of her had strings of grenades in addition to their firearms. No one was paying much attention to her; none of them had any clear idea of why she was along. But now a sergeant came towards her. 'Come along, Fräulein. We must hurry.'

The rest of the men had already moved off up the hill. 'I am ready, Sergeant,' Joanna said, stepping against him. He turned in surprise, and she plucked a grenade from his belt, drew the pin and hurled it into the backs of the advancing troops. The sergeant gave a shout and reached for her, but she had already drawn her pistol, and shot him through the heart at close range. As he fell, she plucked

239

another grenade from his belt, let it fall, then she threw herself to the ground beside him.

In front of her pandemonium raged. At least one man had been killed in the explosion, and several injured. Officers and NCOs barked commands. And Weber, who had been at the head of his men, hurried back, demanding explanations. 'Back there, Herr Colonel,' someone shouted.

Joanna was slowly sitting up, rubbing her head. 'What happened here?' Weber demanded.

'This man suddenly went berserk,' Joanna panted. 'He threw a grenade at his comrades, then drew another. I tried to stop him, and he threw me to the ground. Then I saw he was about to throw the second grenade, so I shot him. I couldn't think of anything else to do.'

Weber gazed at her for several seconds. 'Have I fucked it up?' she asked.

A captain stood beside them. 'Shall we abort, Herr Colonel?'

'Abort?'

'The guerillas will have been alerted,' he replied.

'We cannot abort,' Weber said. 'So they have been alerted. We outnumber them by more than three to one. The assault will commence now. Get your men moving.'

'Heil Hitler!' The captain hurried off.

Weber pulled Joanna to her feet. 'You stay close to me.'

'Can you forgive me?'

'There is nothing to forgive. It was not your shot that will have alerted the enemy. And you acted correctly in executing this traitor.' He kicked the dead body. 'Now we must finish the job.'

'That was a grenade,' James snapped. 'They've come in early. Monterre, get everybody up and here.'

Monterre hurried off. 'Where can we go?' Liane asked.

'We can't. Once we're in the open we're done.'

'But if we stay here . . .' Moulin said.

'They have to come to us, in our chosen position. One

240

determined and well-placed defender is worth ten attackers. And we have one immense advantage: as they are acting illegally, they cannot take the time to starve us out. If they want to destroy us, they have to carry the cave by assault. Right. Monterre, get your men inside. Each side of the entrance.' He surveyed them. 'Now remember, do not show yourselves unnecessarily, and do not waste ammunition. Fire when you see a clear target. Ladies, to the back.'

'I can fight,' Liane said.

'And I,' Rachel said.

'And you will. But let the men handle the first assault.'

'What am I to do?' Brune inquired.

'Keep out of the line of fire. We need you to fly the old girl.'

'It's the old girl I'm worrying about.'

'Well, don't. They can't possibly know she's there.' A shot rang out, and then another. James turned to see the shadowy figures coming through the trees. 'Take cover,' he called, and took his position just inside the doorway.

'Isn't he terribly exposed?' Rachel whispered.

'He can take care of himself,' Liane said.

'I suppose you and he have done this before, often.'

'I have, several times. Only once with James, though. But we're still here. Haven't you?'

'I have never been shot at in my life.'

Liane squeezed her hand. 'It can grow on you.' She winked at Amalie, also clutching a tommy-gun. 'She's never seen action either. But I'll bet she's looking forward to it.'

'Oh, yes,' Amalie said.

'Cease that shooting,' Weber told Captain Korlovy. The captain gave the order, while Weber studied the cave and the hillside through his binoculars. 'You have been in there,' he said to Joanna. 'Tell me about it.'

'It is a rabbit warren. There are several inner compartments. And there is a well,' she lied. 'They can stay in there for a considerable time.'

241

'I did not come here to besiege them,' Weber said. 'Is there another entrance?'

'No.'

'Very good. Korlovy' – the captain had rejoined them – 'it will have to be a frontal assault.'

Korlovy had also been studying the position. 'It will be costly, Herr Colonel. If those men are well armed, and resolute . . .'

'I doubt their resolution; they are bandits, not soldiers.'

'Some of them, perhaps all, will have served in the French army.'

'Then they are used to losing. What arms do they have?' Weber asked Joanna.

'Tommy-guns, pistols and grenades.'

'Heavy machine-guns?'

She hesitated. But she had to tell the truth, just in case the Germans did manage to get inside. 'I did not see any.'

'Very good. Captain, bring up your mortars. There will be a five-minute bombardment to soften them up. Then you will fire a barrage of smoke and tear gas grenades. Under that cover we will go in. Give the orders.'

'Yes, Herr Colonel. Do we take prisoners?'

'No male prisoners. But there are two de Gruchy sisters in there. I wish them alive. Liane de Gruchy certainly. The Führer wishes her to be publicly executed.'

'Will we know her, sir?'

Weber looked at Joanna. 'She is a very good-looking blonde,' Joanna said. 'But I will be with you to point her out.' She could do nothing more, and if they did manage to capture Liane arrive, that was her best chance of saving her. As for the others . . . She felt sick.

'Carry on, Captain,' Weber said. 'Put on your gas mask,' he told Joanna.

'When will they come?' Pierre asked, crouching beside James.

'When they are ready.'

'Do you know, after Dunkirk, I never supposed you and I would ever fight shoulder to shoulder again.

'Not so soon, anyway,' James said. 'Here we go.'

He had seen the flash, and a moment later a shell smashed into the cliff face, above the entrance, bringing down a cascade of stones and small rocks. The guerillas moved, restlessly. 'Artillery!' one gasped, and James remembered that none of these men had ever fought a winning battle against the Germans. In fact, being mostly Communists, they would have been the first to run away, under orders from Moscow.

There was another explosion, and another rock fall. 'They mean to seal us in!' Monterre said, his voice high.

'I think they will come in,' James said, feeling increasingly uneasy as to the capabilities of his fighting force. He looked over his shoulder, gazed at the pale faces of the women. They at least did not looked scared, although they were certainly tense.

'Grenades,' Henri said. As he spoke there were a series of explosions, and the cave became filled with searing, choking fumes.

'Shit!' Pierre exclaimed. 'Tear gas. Back up.'

'Stay put,' James snapped. 'Put something over your eyes and nose.'

But several of the Communists were already retreating, and now the morning became filled with the rattle of automatic weapons. Blinking tears from his eyes as he tried to peer through the smoke, James loosed a burst of fire. Then he was sent sprawling as bodies crashed through the entrance, hitting his head on the rock wall to be left senseless.

Liane buried her face in the crook of her arm as the gas surged through the cave, and threw herself to one side as the men started fleeing. From her prone position she saw James go down, and struggled to her knees. The front of the cave had been entirely deserted, save for half a dozen

243

dead bodies, and Rachel, who was also lying on the ground, but was stirring.

The defenders had fled into the interior, and the assault force had followed; in the confused space the noise of the firing was ear-shattering. Then she looked up as the entrance darkened again, and two more people came in. They both wore gas masks, but she recognized Joanna immediately. And now the man pulled his off. 'My God!' she muttered.

The man was staring at her. 'You,' he said. 'But you . . .'

'Liane de Gruchy,' Joanna said. 'Meet Colonel Oskar Weber of the SD.'

'You,' Weber said again. 'You were the whore . . . My God!' He looked left and right for his men, but he and Joanna were isolated as the battle had moved away from them into the recesses of the cave. He reached into his belt for his whistle, and Joanna struck him on the back of the head with the butt of her pistol. Weber gasped, fell to his knees, and then on to his face. Joanna reversed the pistol, levelled it, and shot the unconscious man through the shoulder.

Rachel sat up. 'You missed!'

'I never miss.' Joanna knelt beside him.

'He's losing a lot of blood. '

'He can stand some of that. But you are dead. You too, Liane. And you, James,' she said as he tried to get up. 'Just lie there and don't move.'

'Joanna . . .'

'I'll be all right: I'm this guy's mistress. I'll see you in London. Sometime. Now do it.' She watched them subside, and blew several blasts on the whistle she took from Weber's breast pocket. Men came running back, led by Korlovy. 'Is it over?' she asked.

'I believe there are still some holed up. But the colonel . . .'

'One of these bastards shot him. Don't worry; I killed the bitch. They are all dead.'

'But the woman de Gruchy . . .'

'She's dead too. We have to get the colonel down the hill for first aid, and then get him back to Bordeaux.'

'But shouldn't we finish the job here, Fräulein? There are still several people hiding in these caves.'

'The job is finished. We came here to destroy the de Gruchys. There is only one important de Gruchy. This carrion.' She nudged Liane's body with the toe of her boot. 'Without her, they will simply disintegrate. I know these people. Our business now is to save Colonel Weber's life, and get ourselves out of here. Our time is all but up.'

Korlovy hesitated, but he had observed how intimate, both physically and mentally, the colonel and this woman had been. 'As you say, Fräulein.' He blew his whistle. 'Out,' he shouted. 'Out. Everybody out.'

The noise of the retreating Germans faded, and Liane raised her head. As did Rachel. 'I never really liked that woman,' Rachel said. 'Now . . .'

'She is a heroine.'

'Does she know the risk she is taking?'

'Yes,' James said.

Liane knelt beside him. 'Are you all right?'

'I'll manage.' He squeezed her arm. 'You?'

'When I get some fresh air.'

'Did you really . . . well . . .'

'Just once. I was hiding from him and his friends, and, well . . . I had no idea who he was.'

'Well,' Rachel said, 'you seem to have made an impression. But do you mean you were hiding from the Gestapo in a *brothel*?'

'It is the safest place to be when one is on the run.'

Rachel looked at James.

'Let's find out who else survived,' he suggested.

There were a surprising number. 'Amalie!' Liane embraced her sister, 'Henri! Pierre! Where are Mama and Papa?'

'We are here.' Barbara helped her husband out of the darkness; like everyone else, their eyes were still streaming. She hugged her daughter. 'My darling! Do you live like this all the time?'

'Only now and then. But you are never going to live like this ever again.'

'It was a miracle,' Moulin said. 'They had us cornered, and just suddenly pulled out.'

'It was Joanna's miracle,' James told him. 'Brune? You've been hit!'

'I can still fly. If the old girl's still there.'

They went outside together, watched the German planes rising into the air. 'I suggest we find out,' James said. 'Once we've dressed your wound, and buried the dead.'

'Our dead,' Liane said. 'If we are abandoning this place anyway, I think we can leave the Germans just where they are.'

When the work was done, they sat together on the hillside as the evening drew in. 'Do you know, I have been happy here,' Liane said.

He knew better, now, than to remind her that she could be much happier somewhere else. 'Where will you go?'

'As you suggested, we shall go south to the Pau area. Will you alert your people there?'

'As soon as we get back.'

'And you will keep us supplied and continue to control us?'

'You mean to continue the Resistance?'

'Of course we do. We shall start recruiting as soon as we have found a base. Pierre will command until Jean returns, and until I return from Paris.'

'There is no reason for you to take that risk again.'

'The route is my creation. I must make sure it is running smoothly. And there is no risk. I am dead, remember?'

'Liane . . .'

'Besides,' she said. 'I wish to go on working for you,

246

being your woman. Do you not wish that?' He leaned towards her, and she looked past him. 'Here is Rachel.'

She stood above them. 'Believe it or not, the plane is absolutely intact and undamaged.'

'Oh,' James said. 'Well . . .'

'Don't get up. We can't take off for another two hours.' Her mouth twisted. 'You have a couple of hours to say goodbye.'

'Where am I?' Weber asked, blinking at Joanna's face, and then at Franz Hoeppner and Roess. 'What happened?'

'You were shot,' Franz explained. 'And hit your head falling. You had concussion. You would have died had Fräulein Jonsson not killed your assailant and saved your life.'

Weber clutched Joanna's hand. 'You did that?'

'You're my boss, right?'

'But the attack!'

'That was a complete success. We had to leave a few of the guerillas holed up in the back of their cave, but the de Gruchys are all dead, as is Moulin. The rest are nothing without their leaders.'

'That is good news. Good news. Eh, Roess?' Roess looked as if he was sucking a lemon. 'And Frau von Helsingen?'

'As you instructed, Herr Colonel, I sent her back to Berlin.'

'That is good. Very good. There will be congratulations all round.' He squeezed Joanna's hand. 'You are a treasure.'

'Well, then I'll say cheerio,' Lockridge said.

'Do you know where you're going?' James asked, seating himself behind his desk.

'I hope somewhere a little less exciting. I don't think I'm cut out for this sort of work.'

'I shall be sorry not to continue working with you, sir,' Rachel said with a straight face.

'I'll miss you too, Sergeant. Give my regards to Jonsson when next you see her.'

The door closed, and she shouted, 'Wheee!' and hugged James.

'Easy,' he said. 'There are certain places where I hurt.'

'Sorry.' She released him. 'I did enjoy meeting those people. Even if the circumstances weren't quite right. And when I think of poor Brune . . .'

'Yes. But without you sitting beside him we wouldn't have made it. I never knew you could fly a plane.'

'Well . . .' She made a moue. 'You came over a bit strong to the brigadier.'

'I simply told the truth.'

'But I don't want to be promoted. I want to stay here, working with you.'

'You made that perfectly clear. Tell me, what did you think of Liane?'

'That she is everything I thought she would be.'

'But?'

'I'm not sure I'd ever want to get *too* close to her. She'd scare the pants off me. But I suppose you scare the pants off her.'

He grinned. 'It's a mutual thing.'

'But seeing she's not here . . .' She sat on his lap and kissed him. 'Will we see Joanna again?'

'Joanna is indestructible.'

'Because she's Joanna?'

'Partly. But more importantly because she is an American citizen. And a prominent one. Even if she's found out, they won't dare do more than deport her. She knows this, which is why she's so confident.'

'And if America enters the war on our side?'

'Chance would be a fine thing. Do you realize that it's September 1941? We have been at war for two years, virtually begging America to give us a hand. And they've hardly lifted a finger. They're only going to come in if Hitler, or someone, is crazy enough to attack *them*.'

'But if that were to happen?'

'We'd have to get her out, fast. And pray that we'd be in time.' He kissed her. 'It'll never happen.'